BOOK FIVE IN THE RECKLESS SERIES

Reckless LOVE

NYSSA KATHRYN

An NW Partners Book
Cover by Deranged Doctor Design
Developmentally and Copy Edited by Kelli Collins
Line Edited by Jessica Snyder
Proofread by Amanda Cuff and Jen Katemi
Cover Photography by Madison Maltby Photography

❀ Created with Vellum

Two years ago, one decision changed everything...

Callie Ward knows what love feels like. She's lived it. Breathed it. It was the kind of love she'd thought would last forever...until it didn't. And the resulting heartache almost destroyed her. So she ran. Left the small town of Misty Peak, not sure if she'd ever return. But thanks to fate and family ties, she's back—and so is the man who broke her heart. Ignoring him is her only option, until that proves impossible.

One split-second decision lost Lock Walker the only woman he's ever loved, a mistake from which, two years later, he still hasn't recovered. A mistake that cost him everything. Now, finally, Lock and Callie are both home, and he's determined to make amends. Except, she won't give him the time he needs to earn his redemption. But that soon changes when Lock learns he's not the only one happy about her homecoming.

Someone's watching Callie. Someone who wants her all to themselves. Lock needs to earn her trust back fast in order to protect her—because losing her a second time isn't an option.

ACKNOWLEDGMENTS

Thank you to my amazing team who helps me tear my stories apart and put them back together—Kelli, Jessica, Amanda and Jen —they're always so much better after you've touched them.

Thank you to my ARC team and readers. You enable and inspire me to write the next book.

And to my family—Will, Sophia and Alexia—I love you more than you know, and it is only with your support, that I am able to work a job that I love.

PROLOGUE

 *wo Years Ago*

LOCK WALKER SCANNED the front yard through the living room window.

Callie was late.

The yoga class she was teaching should have finished fifteen minutes ago. She'd offered to cancel and pick him up from the airport, but he'd said he'd make his own way to her house. It had been the wrong damn decision.

He checked his watch and cursed as another minute passed.

Usually, he wouldn't care that she was late. Hell, to most people the delay would be nothing. But he wasn't most people. He was on a dangerous Ghost Ops team, and two nights ago a team member's girlfriend had been killed. Fucking murdered right in her house by one of *their* enemies.

Lock's hands fisted, the same familiar anger slipping through his veins.

The asshole shouldn't have been able to find their identities. No one should have. But Malone was an IT expert in a deadly terrorist organization. An organization Lock and his team had been tasked with eliminating. And they'd succeeded in that mission, eliminating all but one. One man who they'd had an ongoing search for when the murder had occurred.

Fuck, this was bad.

You thought you could eliminate my team with no consequences?

That's what the fucking note had said. Was she the only one? Did Malone intend to target more of their loved ones?

He was here to organize security for Callie. Make sure she was kept safe and warn her about what was going on. Then he'd be back with his team, and they'd find and eliminate Malone.

He paced the room.

He couldn't let anything happen to Callie—he loved her too damn much. They'd only been dating a year, and fuck, most of it had been long distance, but she was in his blood, his bones. She occupied his mind.

Dammit, where was she?

He pulled his phone from his pocket to call her, but it rang before he could hit her number.

Jesse. Why was his teammate calling? They'd all seen each other yesterday.

"Jess—"

"He's dead, Lock. Winnie's dead."

Lock stilled, the air in his lungs becoming so stuck it felt like he'd suffocate right there and then. "No..."

"*Yes.* Remi too. Kill shots to the chest in their apartment. Antwan found them."

Lock's vision hazed, a darkness slipping around him so distinct that it faded every vibrant color in the room.

Winnie was more than a teammate. He was a brother. The pain was so visceral it felt like a blade against his skin.

He shook his head, still not believing what his friend was telling him, because it didn't make fucking sense. "We saw him yesterday. He was there. Right fucking there."

And Winnie was deadly. They all were. No one should have been able to get the jump on him.

"They broke in through a back window while the alarm was deactivated." Jesse's voice was raw with pain. "He's gone, Lock. And the asshole who killed them left another note."

"What did it say?"

"'Who's next?'"

Suddenly, Lock wanted to drop to his knees. Let the weight of his devastation crush him to the floor. It curled and weaved inside him. Poisoning him.

Dead. His teammate was *dead*. And another team member's girlfriend. The second partner murdered in two days.

His gaze moved back to the window. Callie would be here any second. Did this asshole know about her?

"Lock," Jesse said in a whispered growl. "We're going to find the fucker...and we're going to end him."

And just like that, Lock's pain shifted, changing into something else. Something darker and uglier. Something so powerful it consumed him.

Rage. It tangled its claws around his limbs. Squeezing and clenching.

"I know we will."

Suddenly, a car pulled up outside. He turned from the window. He wasn't sure what words came out of his mouth before he ended the call. Everything was a blur.

When the click of the door opening sounded, he turned, and the pounding of his heart halted.

Callie.

Her long, dark hair was down and flowing over her shoulders, and her green eyes beamed straight into him.

The sight of her had the anger inside him shifting again, but this time to something far worse than disbelief or rage...

Fear. Fear that he'd lose her. Fear that this asshole who was targeting his team and the people they loved, would target *her*. Because he did love her. So damn much he'd die for her. And despite how much he loved her, he'd give her up to keep her safe.

* * *

CALLIE WARD TOOK three deep breaths before looking through the car window at her house.

She was nervous. Huge, gigantic-butterflies-in-the-belly kind of nervous. She was never nervous seeing Lock, but today she was.

At the slight tremble in her fingers, she fisted her hands.

Stop it, Callie. It's going to be fine.

This was Lock, the man she loved, and the man who loved her. Over the last year, they'd tackled long-distance dating and only seeing each other for brief moments between missions. Most new couples wouldn't have survived it, but they'd not only survived, they'd thrived, counting down the days until the next time they saw each other. Making the most of every second together.

It felt longer than a year. Somehow, it felt like she'd loved this man her entire life.

It was crazy. Out-of-this-world, stuff-fairy-tales-were-made-of kind of crazy. But it was true.

What she needed to tell him today would change everything, though.

Oh Jesus.

What if he couldn't handle it? What if it destroyed any plans they had of him getting out of the military and moving back to Misty Peak?

She pressed a hand to her stomach. No. Lock loved her. They'd make it work.

She climbed from her car and walked to the door.

For over a month, she'd been sitting on this information. Every phone conversation, every Skype call and text message, she'd wanted to break down and tell him. Release the life-changing news into the world. The words had been there on the tip of her tongue each time they spoke.

But she'd held them in because he deserved to hear this in person. And maybe there was also a tiny selfish part of her that wanted to see his expression when she told him. A part of her that wanted to feel his energy and know whether he was as excited about this as she was.

She lifted her key to the door, then stopped, fear trickling through her veins, making the beats of her heart stumble over one another.

Come on, Callie, this is Lock. He's never given you any reason to doubt him.

She opened the door and stepped into the living room to see him facing away from her.

He didn't turn toward her right away, and those seconds that passed felt like a lifetime. A thousand seconds to play over a million scenarios of how this could go in her head.

Finally, he turned, his gaze clashing with hers, and she was hit by the same thing she always was when she saw him.

Love. Calm. Peace.

"Hey." She took a step toward him, only to stop when he stepped back.

Why had he done that?

She studied his face, noticing for the first time how pale he was. And his eyes…they were angry, but there was also something else there. Fear? No, that couldn't be it. Lock was never scared.

She frowned. "Lock, what's wrong?"

A long second ticked by, and no one spoke. The silence was so thick it sent a chill over her skin.

"Lock—" Another step forward by her. He didn't step back this time, but the thick muscles in his arms visibly tensed.

What was going on? Did he already know?

No. That wasn't possible. She hadn't told anyone. Not her father, not even her best friend, Aspen.

"Hey…talk to me." Her words were quiet. She felt almost as if, by speaking too loud, she'd scare him away.

His gaze shifted to the window before flicking back to her. "We can't do this."

Her lips parted, confusion muddling her thoughts. "Do what?"

He ran his fingers through his hair, a look she'd never seen before crossing his face. A look she couldn't even begin to describe.

"We need to take a break."

Three times. She had to repeat those words in her head three times before she was able to make sense of them. And the second they did, she wanted to be sick. Bile churned in her gut, crawling up her throat.

"A break?"

"There's stuff going on with the team, and I…we can't date right now. And we can't be seen together." Again, his focus flicked to the window.

"You're breaking up with me because something's going on with your team?"

She wanted him to tell her no. To give her something, anything, that made this comprehensible. But he just stood there staring at her like he was in a house he didn't want to be in. With a woman he didn't want to be with.

No. She was not just going to accept this. "I need more information from you. I need to know why you're doing this, and then maybe we can fix the problem. We spoke last week, and everything was great." Heck, they'd talked about buying a freaking house together!

Finally, a crack of emotion passed over his face. Pain.

He looked out the window for a third time like he was searching for someone. "I…"

Whatever he was about to say was cut off by the ringing of his phone. He looked down, agony darkening his eyes.

"Antwan." His teammate's name was almost a whisper. When he glanced up, his features were harder, his expression closed off. God, he looked like a stranger. "I need to go, Callie. Don't contact me."

His words felt like a slap in the face. She might have actually flinched, she wasn't sure. Everything was a haze. A nightmare she couldn't escape.

He stepped around her.

She turned to watch him walk into the bedroom. She wanted to follow. To yell at him. Scream that she loved him and he couldn't do this. But her feet wouldn't move. All she could do was stand there, disbelief making her limbs heavy.

He stepped out of the bedroom, bag in hand.

Oh God. He was really doing it. He was really leaving.

"You can't just end things without telling me why," she whispered, using every scrap of strength she had to hold off the tears. "That's not fair to me."

"I know, but—"

"No. No buts." Finally, her feet worked, and she crossed the distance between them. "You said you loved me. You said we were going to buy a house together. Build a future together. And today, I came home to tell you—"

"We can't do this right now!" Lock shouted. "I'll stay at Nylah's place until I can get a flight out. I don't want you to contact me. No calls, no emails, and no texts. We *need* to be separate."

Separate. The word was heavy and ugly and hurt so much that she almost grabbed her chest.

There was the smallest flicker of sadness in Lock's eyes, then he whispered two words. "I'm sorry."

The door closed behind him…and suddenly there was silence. It rang in her ears, settling deep in her bones.

Gone. He was gone. And she was alone.

CHAPTER 1

resent Day

"Why do you insist on torturing me?"

Callie's lips twitched as she glanced up at her friend from behind the desk. "Some call it torture. Others call it Pilates."

Aspen scoffed, pushing a lock of blond hair off her face as she sprawled across the yoga mat. Anyone would think the woman was dying. "I call it a special kind of misery."

"I don't mean to state the obvious, but you do realize you *chose* to take this class. Signed up and everything, and I don't think anyone held a gun to your head."

"I know that, but how else am I supposed to bond with my fitness-loving long-lost best friend?"

"First of all, we live together, so there's plenty of bonding being done. Secondly, I was only away from Misty Peak for two years, and we spoke and texted every day. I'd hardly classify that as long or lost. Besides, you're a romance author. Don't you believe that absence makes the heart grow fonder?"

"Absolutely not. My readers would kill me if the characters were absent from each other's lives for years. Not that I have many readers these days."

Callie tilted her head. "You have readers. You just need to release your next book."

"I know, but I'm uninspired."

She was tempted to tell Aspen that her boyfriend might have something to do with that, but she bit her tongue. Callie had never liked Dylan. She wasn't entirely sure why; there was just something about him that was…off-putting.

Her friend climbed to her feet. "Even though your classes resemble a bit of a torture chamber, I do kind of like the six-pack I'm getting."

"So this place isn't all bad?" Callie signed out of her laptop and closed the lid before glancing back over at her friend, who was now cringing as she stretched her quads.

"No, not all bad. And you know I'm ridiculously proud of you for coming home and opening your own studio."

Callie's heart gave a little kick. She was ridiculously proud of herself too. For the last two years, she'd been living in Bali, running yoga retreats, and she'd loved it. Lived and breathed it. She hadn't planned to return to Misty Peak and open a studio, but she knew better than anyone that plans changed. Sometimes for the better, but not always.

"Thank you."

Aspen's smile softened. "Did you see Hamish looking at you today?"

"Hamish wasn't looking at me."

"He was. And I'm pretty sure he does your classes just to see you. He's cute. Weird, but cute."

Cute? She supposed he was kind of cute. He was tall and broad-shouldered, but there was also an awkwardness about him. "He doesn't do the classes just to see me."

"Whatever you say." Aspen tilted her head. "How's your dad?"

The usual tightness wrapped around her chest. "He says he's fine."

"But…"

Of course there was a but. Callie rounded the desk. "But I wish he'd let me take care of him more, like he did for me when I was in a hard situation. I want to help him."

Her father was a stubborn man, but he was also kind and protective and the entire reason she'd come home.

Aspen dropped her leg to the floor and stepped forward, setting a hand on Callie's arm. "You being here *is* helping him. You're his whole world, Callie."

Guilt swamped her. Because it was true. She was his whole family, and he was hers, and she'd left him for two years. And during those two years, her father had started having symptoms and had to deal with them himself. It was only after he'd finally gotten his diagnosis that he'd told her.

"Thanks," Callie said.

"Of course." Aspen nibbled her bottom lip. "Now, there was also something else I wanted to talk to you about before I head out on my search for story inspiration."

Callie's belly dropped…because she knew exactly what her friend was going to ask. "I haven't seen him yet."

Aspen nodded slowly. "I did."

Oh God, she didn't want to talk about this. She'd heard he was home. In the small town of Misty Peak, it was impossible for anything to go unnoticed.

Lock was back. And every day since learning that, she'd almost been afraid to step out of her house. Eventually she'd run into him, and she was nervous as hell for that day.

"Where did you see him?" she finally asked.

"I was walking down the street near Meridian, and he was coming the other way with one of his brothers."

She almost asked which one. Lock had four brothers and a sister. The sister no longer lived in Misty Peak, but all his brothers did.

"I think he was with Jace," Aspen said, as if reading her mind. "The two of them seemed to be deep in conversation, and I almost thought they wouldn't notice me. Then Lock looked up."

His ocean-blue eyes flashed in her mind. The image cut off her breath. "Did you talk to him?"

"No. He stopped talking to his brother and almost looked like he wanted to say something to me, but I looked away and walked faster. It was for his own safety. If I'd stopped, I probably would have kicked him in the shin."

She shouldn't ask. She knew she shouldn't, but… "How did he look?"

"The same. Tall. Broad. Serious. But also different."

"Different how?" *God, Callie, stop.*

She lifted a shoulder. "I'm used to seeing him with you."

What did that—

"And he was always happy with you."

Her heart thumped. Yep, she really needed this conversation to be over. "You should go. You've got a book to write." She went to step away, but Aspen grabbed her arm.

"Hey. I'm sorry."

"For what?"

"I'm sorry he's back. I'm sorry that it's going to be hard for you before it gets easy."

It wasn't hard. Hard was waking up at six a.m. while it was still dark outside. It was learning to play the piano when you'd never played an instrument before.

Being back in the same town as the man she'd loved more than anything in the world, only to have her heart broken, wasn't hard. It was excruciating.

She lifted a shoulder. "Life can't always be easy."

"Let me know if next time I see him, you want me to kick him where the sun don't shine, okay? Because I will, and I can do some serious damage."

Despite everything, Callie laughed. "Really? You'd kick a former Ghost Ops team member?"

"Hell yeah, I would. Then I'd run like hell."

Callie laughed again, because not only was Lock tall and strong, he was also fast. There'd be no getting away and Aspen knew that. "You're a good friend."

"I know. That's why the next time I sign up for another hour of suffering, you're going to let me sit out those side-lying crunch things."

"Again…voluntary. The class is voluntary."

"Yeah, yeah. I'll see you tomorrow." Aspen tugged Callie into a tight hug before heading out of the studio.

Callie was still smiling as she watched her friend move toward her car through the window. It felt good to be back with her best friend. Leaving this town two years ago had meant leaving both Aspen and her father. It had been hard, but at the time, she hadn't felt like she'd had a choice.

She was back now though. The only thing she hadn't counted on was Lock being back too.

Her heart gave a little twist. Aspen was right. She couldn't avoid him forever. Misty Peak was too small for that. But the idea of seeing him made every put-together piece of her tear apart. She hadn't seen him since that day. But she'd thought about him. God, had she thought about him. Even when her heart had screamed to forget.

She swallowed and turned, grabbing some spray and wipes before moving around the studio and cleaning the machines. Everyone wiped down their reformer at the end of each class, but she always gave them another once-over before leaving her studio for the day.

Her studio. It sounded crazy. She'd actually opened her own studio, something she'd wanted to do for as long as she could remember.

There were five reformer machines on one side of the room

for her Pilates classes and five mats on the other side for yoga. The classes were small and intimate. The perfect size for her.

When the machines were clean, she grabbed her laptop and a pile of mail she hadn't opened yet and headed into the back room. There was a small kitchenette on one side and a table with a couple of chairs on the other. There was also a small bathroom across from this room.

She dumped the mail onto the table before throwing out the wipes. Her plan for the rest of the day was a trip to the grocery store to get supplies for prime rib—her father's favorite.

She turned back to the mail and was rifling through the pile when one letter had her pausing. The fine hairs on her arms stood on end, and a chill swept over her skin.

No…it couldn't be. She hadn't received one of these letters in years—since the last time she'd lived in Misty Peak.

She traced the familiar handwriting with her eyes. The indentation of the ink was deep, like the person writing it used so much pressure they almost pushed their pen through the envelope.

For six months, she'd received letters from this person while still living in Misty Peak and dating Lock. Letters about her looks. About the brown locks of her hair shining in the sun. The green of her eyes reminding him of a forest. They were never signed with a name.

Even though she'd been dating Lock, she hadn't told him. He'd been special operations in the military, working a super dangerous job. He didn't need to worry about her too.

After a few months, she'd gone to the sheriff at the time, but there'd been nothing he could do. There'd been no prints on the notes and no return address, and the person had never escalated past sending letters. They'd only stopped when she left, and she'd almost forgotten about them…until now.

Quickly, she tore open the envelope to see two words.

Welcome home.

Her heart punched her ribs. There was nothing threatening about those two words. There'd never been anything threatening about any of the letters. But whoever it was, they knew she was back…and they wanted her to know that.

Her skin crawled.

Who was it? Two years had passed…surely they should have lost interest in her in that time?

She'd just shoved the letter back into the envelope and dropped it to the table when the creak of a floorboard sounded in the other room.

She took a deep breath. A potential client was in the other room. She needed to forget about the letter, at least for a few minutes.

She turned and stepped into the studio, only to grind to a halt as she looked up, way up, into the familiar blue eyes of the man she'd loved. The man who'd changed her. Hurt her. Left her.

Lock Walker.

CHAPTER 2

"So, what exactly are you going to say to Callie?"

The sound of her name made Lock's skin feel too fucking tight. *That's* what she did to him. What she'd always done to him.

He looked at his brother as they walked down the street. "I'm going to be honest and tell her why I broke up with her."

Kayden nodded slowly. "And tell me again why it's taken you two years to tell her."

Two years...a long damn time. And it had felt longer. "I panicked. I was scared. Hell, I thought he was watching the fucking street. And I thought if I told her the truth, she'd still try to contact me, so breaking all ties and putting security on her until we killed Malone felt safer. In my head, it was only supposed to be for a few weeks, until we eliminated him. But by the time I came back, she was gone, and no one would tell me where she was."

She'd left Misty Peak, disconnected her old phone, and deleted all social media accounts. Her father and best friend had refused to tell him where she was.

The familiar frustration slid up his throat like acid.

A frown cut into Kayden's brow. He was one of four brothers, all former military, and all back home now in Misty Peak, Tennessee. Their only sister lived with her partner in Cradle Mountain, a small town in Idaho, so they didn't see her nearly enough.

"What do you think she'll say?" Kayden finally asked.

A muscle ticked in Lock's jaw. "I don't know. I don't even know if she'll hear me out."

The memory of her face when he'd ended their relationship flashed in his head. The disbelief. The hurt. Walking out of that house had taken every ounce of strength he'd had.

His brother clenched his arm. "So make her listen. You love her too much to lose her."

He *did* love her. And time had done nothing to change that.

Lock looked at his brother. "You and Tilly seem to be doing pretty well." Which was surprising as hell, considering who Tilly's father was and Kayden's trust issues.

Kayden's eyes warmed. "I love her, man. She's become the best part of me."

They stopped in front of the studio. "I'm happy for you."

"Thanks. I want the same for you."

There'd been a time Lock would have sworn that he and Callie were unbreakable...until he broke them. "I'll see you Monday night. Dinner at your place, right?"

"Don't be late." Kayden thumped his shoulder before continuing down the street. Spending time with his brothers was one of the best parts about being home and out of the military. Would Callie be the next best part?

He looked through the glass to see the place empty. Was she even here? Damn, had he missed her?

Wrapping his fingers around the door handle, he pushed.

Unlocked.

So she was here. Good. It had already taken him too long to find her.

He was done waiting.

Quiet slipped over him as he stepped inside. His gaze moved over the reformer machines. The big mirrors and bold writing on the wall that read Callie's Yoga and Pilates Studio.

She'd finally done it. How many times had she spoken about wanting to open her own studio? It had always been a dream of hers.

Fuck, he was proud of her.

He crossed the studio and was about to enter the back room when she stepped out.

Every muscle in his body locked at the sight of her. At her red lips. Her moss green eyes. Even that small scar on the base of her chin had him thrown back two years.

Damn, she was beautiful. And he'd been starved of that beauty for too long.

Her chest rose and fell, her gaze shifting between his eyes before she whispered one word. "Lock."

The way his name fell from her lips was like a punch to the gut. He'd always loved the way she said it, but today, he felt it harder. "Hey, Callie."

Her throat bobbed, and he could hear every whisper of air moving in and out of her lungs.

Two years. Two long damn years without her. It shouldn't have happened, but it had. His hand twitched to reach out and touch her. Run his fingers down the pink of her cheek.

He clenched his fists to stop himself, forcing words from his lips instead. "How are you?"

Her brows pinched in a familiar scowl, and for a moment her mouth just opened and closed. "Really? It's been two years, and you just show up unannounced and ask how I am?"

He had a million things to say to her and a million questions, but yeah, the first thing he wanted to know was how she was doing.

He opened his mouth to respond, but before he could get a word out, she got in first.

"You need to leave."

Leave? He'd only just gotten here. "Don't you want to know what I'm doing here?"

"Nope. I don't want to know what you're doing here, I don't want to know why you left the military, and I *certainly* don't want to know why you broke my heart."

She shoved passed him, and fuck, even that small touch of her shoulder against his was enough for awareness to rush through every limb.

"Callie—"

"I'm not doing this, Lock. I have too much going on. I can't deal with you too."

"What do you have going on?"

She scoffed. "You really think I'm going to bare my life story to you?"

Once upon a time, she would have. "You could."

"No, I can't." She spun back toward him, and he just stopped himself from walking into her. "You broke up with me, remember? With barely a reason. *Then* you stopped answering my calls. You didn't respond to my texts. You cut me off completely."

That was true. It had taken them two weeks to locate and kill Malone and another week for debriefing and all the other shit he'd had to do before he could finally come home.

She'd tried to contact him every day, multiple times a day, and he'd never responded. Fear had dictated his every move, a desperate need to keep her separate from him and safe.

"So don't walk in here expecting anything from me," she continued. "I don't owe you a damn thing."

He knew that. *He* was the one who owed *her*.

She turned again and took a step toward the door, but he couldn't let her go. He reached out and grabbed her arm. It was the first touch of her skin in years, and it slammed him back in time. Back to a time when life was easy. When it made sense. When she belonged to him.

* * *

THE SECOND HE TOUCHED HER, she stopped. Stopped moving. Stopped thinking. She wasn't even sure if she was breathing. It was like his touch froze time.

Her back was still facing him, and it took four long seconds to look down at his strong fingers wrapped around her arm. Immediately, she wished she hadn't. Because it set off a battle in her chest. A need to both run and tug him closer. A fight between her head and her heart.

The thud of his shoes sounded, then his heat spread into her back. He was everywhere. His body too close to hers, his deep sandalwood scent filling the air.

Everything about him was so achingly familiar; it was like he'd been imprinted into her soul.

"Please..." he whispered. "Let me explain what happened. Let me fix this."

Fix it...

She closed her eyes, a part of her, such a big part, *wanting* him to fix it. But then a memory played in her head. Of a night that still haunted her. A night when she'd called him, *needed him*, and he hadn't come. Hadn't even answered her call.

She yanked her arm away, and the second his hand fell, her skin felt cold. A cold that slipped deep inside her.

"You can't fix it, Lock." Her words sounded as hollow as she felt. She opened the door but didn't look at him, because she was scared that if she did, she'd cave and fall back into his arms. That she'd let him convince her the past hadn't happened. But it had, and it would forever be a part of her. "Please go."

He didn't move, and the beats of her heart grew frantic and uncontrolled. Her breathing became shallow.

She couldn't do this. Not here. Not now.

"I need you to go," she pushed, desperate.

"Okay." His tone was soft, like he understood how close she was to breaking. And maybe he did. He'd always read her better than anyone else. "But I'll be back. We're not finished, Callie. We'll never be finished."

He stepped outside, and it was only when he was out of sight that she finally closed the door. Her fingers shook as she clicked the lock. Then she dropped her chin to her chest and let the air rush out of her.

She'd missed him. God, she'd missed him so much.

But that night when he hadn't answered her call, she'd promised herself never again. That she would never make herself vulnerable to a man who couldn't be there for her at her worst moment ever again. No matter how much her heart told her she still loved him.

CHAPTER 3

*P*ain punched through Callie's belly, tugging her from dead asleep to wide awake. She groaned as she rolled to her side and grabbed her stomach, eyes scrunching as she panted through the ache.

What was happening? It felt like cramping but worse. So much worse.

Something between her thighs had her body freezing. A wetness.

Oh God.

Fear crawled up her throat, shaking her limbs and making it hard to breathe.

With trembling hands, she reached over and switched on the bedside lamp. A part of her didn't want to pull back the covers, because she knew what she'd see, and she knew exactly what it would mean.

But she had to. She had to see.

She tugged the sheets back.

Crimson blood. It soaked her thighs and bled into the bed, so stark against the crisp white of the sheets. She touched it, as if needing confirmation that it was there and real.

Red colored her fingertips, sticking to her skin like glue.

Real...this was real.

Another cramp hit her belly, this time more painful, making her groan and lean forward.

She gulped air and blindly reached for her cell on the bedside table. Her fingers shook so violently that she knocked it to the floor.

Shit.

She leaned down and picked it up, barely able to see the screen through the tears. Everything hurt, not just her belly. A deep, emotional pain that made the world around her a blur.

The screen smudged with red prints from her fingers as she unlocked the cell, making nausea rattle in her belly.

Lock. She needed Lock. She needed to hear his voice. For him to tell her that she'd be okay. She needed his touch and his comfort. For almost three weeks, she'd been calling and he hadn't answered. This time he had to answer.

She hit his name. The phone rang. Then it rang again. Every ring sounded louder, cutting through the silence of the room.

His voice sounded, and for a single second, hope bloomed in her chest...but it wasn't him. It was his voicemail.

He hadn't answered. Just like he hadn't answered any of her other calls.

She choked back a sob, hanging up and calling again.

She wasn't sure how many times she called him, but at some point, she stopped.

He wasn't coming.

She was alone in this.

The desolation felt like a rock on her chest, pushing and squeezing, making the room around her sway and the color shift to a grayscale.

Almost blindly, she scrolled up until she found the name she was looking for, then she clicked on it. He answered on the second ring.

"Callie, baby, what's wrong?"

"Daddy...I need you."

* * *

CALLIE SHOT INTO A SITTING POSITION, eyes whipping open, heart pounding in her chest. Immediately she tugged the covers back, needing to see the crisp white of her sheets.

No blood. It was just a dream. A nightmare. A memory.

She dropped her head into her hands, sweat coating her palms. She hadn't woken like this in a long time. Had it been naive of her to think the nightmares were behind her?

Of course it had. Lock was back, and with him came all the memories.

Closing her eyes, she focused on her breathing. On letting her pulse return to normal and the panic slip away. That memory, that day, would forever be ingrained inside her. Like a permanent fracture to the person she once was.

Scrubbing a hand over her face, she was about to get up when the ringing of her phone had her flinching.

Jesus Christ. Calm down, Callie. It's just a call.

She reached over, smiling when she saw who it was.

"Hey, Dad."

"Hey, baby. Just checking in because I haven't heard from you in a while."

Her grin widened. "We spoke yesterday when you did one of my classes."

"Exactly."

Man, she loved him. She climbed out of bed. "Well, lucky for you, I'm coming over for dinner tonight." She tried to get to her dad's as often as possible. It had only been a few days since she'd made him the prime rib, and tonight she was making him meatloaf.

"Okay, but I'm cooking."

She stepped into the bathroom. "No, Dad, I'm already—"

"You've made me dinner the last three visits."

"Because I want to take care of you."

"I'm your father. *I* take care of *you*."

She rolled her eyes. "You've taken care of me my entire life.

It's my turn." Although, she *could* use some looking after. She checked her reflection, noting the deep circles under her eyes. Gah. She looked like she hadn't slept in a week. "Are you doing okay?"

"I'm doing great because I get to see my daughter as often as I like and that makes me happy."

But was he really happy, or was he just saying that for her sake? The man had been diagnosed with Parkinson's disease. There was no cure, and it broke Callie's heart.

"How are you doing with Lock being back, baby?"

She straightened, the question catching her off guard. "I-I'm fine."

Jeez, really believable with the stutter, Callie.

There was a brief pause, and in that hesitation, she cringed. Because of course her father would hear right through her lie.

"You don't need to pretend with me. If you need me to go and kick that boy's ass, you let me know."

She bit back a laugh. Lock was a million feet tall, with the broadest shoulders she'd ever seen. He was also a highly trained soldier and probably knew a million ways to kill a person, while her father was a former accountant who didn't even hit six feet.

"I don't need you to do that, but I appreciate the offer."

"Offer stands if you change your mind."

"Thank you, Dad. Now, tonight—"

"Come hungry because I'm making tuna casserole."

Guess her meatloaf would have to wait, because there was no saying no to tuna casserole. "My favorite. I'll bring the chocolate chip cookies."

"I'm looking forward to it. I love you, sweetheart."

"Love you too, Dad."

The second she hung up, there was a yearning in her chest to have him back on the phone. He'd always been her greatest source of comfort. Her mother had died when she was a kid after a skiing trip accident, so he was all she'd had. And while some fathers became consumed by their own grief after losing a wife, hers hadn't. He'd put her first, always.

She set the phone onto the bathroom counter before stripping and stepping into the shower. As the warm water beat down on her skin, her dream trickled back into her mind. The blood. The panic.

She squeezed her eyes shut, trying to push it away, only to have another image take its place. An image of beautiful blue eyes. Of broad shoulders and a strong jaw.

How she'd survived losing so much in such a short period of time, she'd never know. One thing was certain—she hadn't come out of it unscathed.

She stayed in the shower for so long her skin wrinkled and the air fogged with steam, but even when she got out, she didn't feel better. But then, after a nightmare, it always took a while to feel okay again.

On her way out of the bathroom, she checked the time. Crap. Seven thirty. Her first class was at eight. Quickly, she threw on her yoga pants and a sports crop. Before going to the kitchen, she opened the second door off the hall.

"Wake up. You have a book to write."

Aspen groaned and pulled the blanket over her head. "I choose sleep."

Callie turned on the light and threw a fallen pillow at her head. "Get up, or I'm taking all the coffee pods to work with me."

The sheet lowered. "You wouldn't."

"Oh, I would. Get up." She turned and headed down the hall toward the kitchen. She'd give Aspen ten minutes. If she didn't hear the shower running, she was going back in there to jump on the bed.

The house was actually owned by her father. He had a couple of rentals, and it just so happened that his tenants had moved out right when she'd moved back to town. Aspen's lease had also been up, so they'd moved in together.

Callie had been surprised Aspen had asked. She'd thought her friend would have moved in with Dylan. Aspen had said it was more about money, because her dad gave them a super-cheap rate, and even though the books she self-published usually brought in a steady income, she hadn't released one in a while.

But there was a part of Callie that wondered if Aspen had other reasons to not want to move in with her boyfriend.

Callie put a pod into the coffee machine.

Once upon a time, she'd talked about buying a house with Lock. She'd even found a place. It was old and run-down, but Lock had always been good with his hands, so she'd known he'd be able to fix it up.

Argh. Stop thinking about him.

She'd just switched on the pod machine when a breeze ran over the back of her neck. Frowning, she turned to see the back door slightly ajar.

Shit. That freaking door. She'd known it would only be a matter of time before that happened. They'd had trouble latching it since moving in, and Aspen often went out there to work and forgot to lock it when she came back in.

Callie crossed the room and shoved it closed, making sure it latched before flicking the lock.

She needed to fix it, but there was no way she wanted to dump this on her dad. He had enough to deal with. Surely it wouldn't be too hard to do herself.

CHAPTER 4

*L*ock swept the paintbrush over the living room wall.

Snowy Mountains Half. That's what the shade of white was called. It was warm and homey, and for some damn reason, it reminded him of Callie.

His gaze shifted to the kitchen. To the curved wooden island. The floating wooden shelves. It was almost finished; just needed the concrete countertops and brushed copper sink and tapware.

The house was coming together slowly, but then, he'd known it wouldn't be a quick job. He'd bought this house over two years ago, and even then, it had needed a complete remodel. But the vision of what it *could* be had been there. It had always been there.

The only people he'd told about it were his team. His mind flicked back to that conversation.

Lock leaned forward on the log, his gaze on the flames of the fire in front of him. He was having one of those moments. Where everything felt pretty damn perfect. Maybe it was because he was with his team—men who felt like family. Maybe it was because they were between missions.

Or maybe it was because Callie was with him. She'd made the trip from Misty Peak to visit for the weekend.

His gaze shifted to the women on the other side of the fire. Callie's eyes weren't on him at the moment. She was laughing at something Amber was saying, her head flung back, little wisps of hair swinging in the evening wind.

Fucking gorgeous. She had the kind of beauty you could stare at for hours and never get tired of.

"Shit, you got it bad, man."

He turned to look at Jesse, sitting beside him on the log. "I bought a house for her." The words slipped from his lips. Shit, he hadn't meant to say that.

His friend's brows shot up. "A house? You couldn't have just gone with a sweater? That's huge! But you've only been dating for—"

"Less than a year. And the house is for the next sixty we're going to spend together."

"Damn. Guess when you know, you know. She must be happy."

"I haven't told her."

He laughed. "Ballsy. I like it. I've gotta ask, though. What if she hates the place?"

It was a dump. Most women would hate it. But Callie? "She found it. She just doesn't know I bought it. It has everything we need." Or it would, once he was done with it. He'd work night and day to make sure it was exactly what she deserved.

"You're happy."

He turned to look at his friend and said with not a shred of humor in his voice, "Happier than I've ever been."

Because of her.

Lock pulled himself out of the memory, forcing his attention back to the painting.

Some days, those memories kept him going. Gave him the hope he needed to get out of bed and do another day without her.

Other days, they drowned him. Reminded him of what he'd had and lost.

Life had been good back then. And he'd been a naive asshole to think everything could stay that way.

He was just finishing the last coat on the wall when his phone rang. His lips twitched at the name on the screen before he set the phone to his ear.

Had his teammate known he'd been thinking about him?

"Jesse. How are you doing, man?" His teammate was back in his hometown of Amber Ridge, Montana.

"I'm good, brother. How are *you*?"

A part of him wanted to be honest and tell him what seeing Callie had done to him the other day. But then he'd have to relive that moment. Remember the caution in her eyes. Feel the way she'd pulled away from him and asked him to leave.

"I'm okay." A simple lie.

"That doesn't sound reassuring. Have you seen Callie yet?"

His muscles locked at her name. Of *course* Jesse would ask. He knew exactly what she meant to him. All the guys did. "Yeah, I've seen her. She wants nothing to do with me."

There was a brief pause, and when his buddy spoke again, his voice was lower. "You're home though. It's a start."

He ran frustrated fingers through his hair. "I couldn't find her for two years, and now we're here, in the same town, but it's… different. *She's* different."

"Two years is a long time. I'm guessing you didn't tell her why you did what you did back then?"

"I barely got a chance to say hi."

"Try again. Eventually, she'll listen and understand."

"And if she doesn't?"

Jesse's exhale was loud. "She will. She loved you once. That love doesn't just go away."

That's what he'd thought too…until she'd disappeared on him.

He walked into the master bedroom, scanned the bare walls. He hadn't painted this room yet. He hadn't done much at all.

Because it was supposed to be *their* room. And he didn't want to mess that up.

"You a deputy now?" he asked.

"I am. Got a badge and everything."

"Good. And how are your brother and sister?"

"Riding my ass, as per usual."

Lock laughed, and damn it felt good. "Well, you need people to put you in your place."

"They certainly do that."

His gaze returned to the walls. "I've got to get to the hardware store and get some supplies."

"The house. Shit, I almost forgot. How's it going?"

"Getting there."

"I need to come visit. Check it out and help where I can."

"Anytime."

Jesse sighed. "Well, it was good to chat. Don't be a stranger."

"You too." He hung up, still staring at the plain wall.

It hit him—moss green. It would be the perfect shade for the bedroom. Also, the color of Callie's eyes.

* * *

"Tell me again why we're not hiring a qualified contractor to fix the door?"

Callie climbed out of the car and watched Aspen rise from the passenger side. "Because then I risk the information getting back to my father, which it would, because everyone knows everyone in this miniature town, and then I'll be in trouble for not letting him take care of it. And I don't want to add anything to his plate right now."

Aspen's brows flickered, sympathy darkening her hazel eyes. "Got it. Okay. So, we're going to fix a door. With our hands. Someone here should be able to give us very detailed instructions on how to do that, right?"

A cool breeze ran over her skin as they headed toward the entrance of the hardware store. "Actually, I've already done some research online and the problem might be that the latch bolt doesn't align with the strike plate opening when the door closes."

Aspen pulled a face. "English, please."

"Basically, we need to adjust the door up or down so that it latches."

"Okay, and did Master Google tell you *how* to do that?"

They stepped inside the store. God, this place was huge. "First, we need to try tightening the door hinges with a Phillips-head screwdriver and check that nothing's loose."

"I see. So, we're here to get a screwdriver." Aspen crossed her arms, her gaze moving around the store as if she'd been here a hundred times, when she'd probably never stepped foot inside the building. "And if the good old *tighten the hinges* doesn't work?"

"I can't remember plan B, but I'm counting on plan A working."

"Optimistic. I like it." Aspen's eyes landed on a man in a uniform. "Oh, he's hot—let's ask him."

"You've got a boyfriend."

She rolled her eyes. "Not for me."

Before Callie could protest, Aspen grabbed her and tugged her toward the guy.

Aspen stopped in front of him, giving her widest smile. "Hi there. I'm Aspen, and this is my *single friend* Callie."

Oh Jesus.

"We were wondering if you know where we might find a Phillips-head screwdriver, and whether you're single."

"No," Callie jumped in. "Just the screwdriver location will be fine."

The guy grinned at her. "Aisle eight. And yeah, I'm single."

Aspen opened her mouth, but Callie pinched her side.

"Ouch!"

Callie gave the guy a tight smile and pulled her friend away. "Eight. Thank you."

The guy cleared his throat. "Let me know if you need help."

"Don't go far. We just might do that," Aspen called behind her before sending an angry glare at Callie. "That was rude."

"No, that was necessary."

"He was cute."

"I'm not interested."

"You know what I'm going to do? I'm going to send my happy fairies your way because you're a grouch today."

"I'm not a grouch. I just don't want to be set up with a random guy from the hardware store."

Eight. Found it. She turned into the aisle—only to halt at the sight of a very broad, very familiar set of shoulders.

Without explanation, Callie whipped Aspen out of the aisle, and tugged her straight into the previous one, ignoring her friend's yelp.

Aspen's jaw dropped, an are-you-crazy crease drawing her brows together. And yeah, she probably was.

"What the heck was—"

Callie slammed a hand over her friend's mouth. "Shh. Not so loud! He'll hear you."

If possible, Aspen's frown deepened. She grabbed Callie's hand and pulled it off. "*Who* will hear me? And if you say my happy fairies, I'll have you committed. I made them up. I don't even know what a happy fairy is."

"Lock."

"Lock is a happy fairy?"

Callie rolled her eyes. "He's in aisle eight."

Aspen's mouth dropped open. "Lock Walker? He's here?"

"Yes."

"Oh my gosh. Wait...is this the first time you've seen him since he got home?"

"No, he came into my studio last week."

"And you didn't tell me?"

Callie shoved her hand back over Aspen's mouth. "Shh!"

Her friend rolled her eyes and tugged the hand away a second time. "Okay, we'll come back to the omittance of key information later. What happened when you saw him?"

"Nothing. He just came in, said he wanted to talk, and I said no."

Kind of…

Aspen scoffed. "I might believe that if he wasn't Lock and you weren't Callie and two years ago, you hadn't been ready to buy a house together."

"It's true. He wanted to talk but I didn't. I'm not ready to talk to him. God, I can barely *look* at him, let alone talk to him without remembering what happened."

Aspen's features softened. "Oh, Cal. I'm sorry."

She swallowed, emotion welling in her throat. It was exactly why she hadn't told her best friend about Lock coming to her studio. She'd have cried, and she didn't want to do that. "We have to get out of here without him seeing me."

"What about the screwdriver?"

"I'll get it later."

She turned to walk *out* of the aisle just as a large figure walked *into* the aisle.

She shrieked and stumbled back, tripping over her friend's foot.

Long, strong fingers moved at lightning speed to wrap around her upper arm and keep her upright. And just like the last time he'd touched her, awareness spiraled from her arm through her entire body.

She pulled her arm back and swallowed, shoving her emotions down.

Stay unaffected, Callie.

"Callie." Lock's deep voice weaved inside her.

She opened her mouth, but no words came out. None. It was like she'd forgotten how to freaking speak.

Seconds passed. Long seconds.

Goddammit, say something, Callie. Anything!

Aspen cleared her throat. "Hi, Lock."

His gaze moved to her, and finally Callie could breathe, because his eyes weren't on her.

"Hi, Aspen." When he looked back at her, the same tightness wrapped around her chest. "What are you two doing here?"

The words "none of your damn business" were on the tip of her tongue, but Aspen spoke first.

"We're getting tools to tighten some door hinges. Because we can do stuff like that...tighten hinges."

Oh, Aspen...

His gaze didn't stray from hers. "You've got a door that needs repairs?"

"No." The lie was out before she could stop it, but she couldn't tell him the truth because she knew exactly what he'd do. Offer to help. To fix her problems like he'd done in the past.

No. No way in hell. Just picturing him in her space made her skin feel all hot and clammy.

He lifted a brow, suspicion looming in his eyes before he turned back to Aspen. "Whose door needs fixing, Aspen?"

Shit. He knew her best friend couldn't lie, or at least not well. Literally everyone in Misty Peak knew that. The woman was an open book.

Callie turned to look at her, sending a don't-you-dare glare her way.

Aspen's mouth opened and closed. "Whose door? Um...well... I think—"

"It's Callie's, isn't it?" Lock interrupted.

Aspen scratched her nose and her eyes scrunched. "I guess... Well, technically, it's her dad's."

She pinched Aspen's side a second time, and her friend yelped.

"Ow! Why do you keep doing that? We live together, so I can't tell him it's *my* door hinge."

Where was a hole to hide inside?

Lock looked back at her. "I'll take a look at your door."

She shook her head so vigorously, she probably looked like a psychopath. "No thanks. Excuse us."

She grabbed Aspen's arm a bit too tightly and went to step around Lock, but he cut her off, blocking her way and causing her forehead to hit his chest. His very firm, very muscled chest.

That would probably leave a bruise.

His eyes softened in such an achingly familiar way that her heart squeezed. "Callie, come on. Let me help you."

"I don't need help."

Aspen nodded. "It's true. Google already helped her."

This time he frowned. "Google?"

"Well, we call him Master Google. You know, holder of all knowledge."

Would there be a point where her friend realized she wasn't helping?

"Callie." Lock stepped closer, even though there'd already been no room between them. "Let me help you. Maybe we could talk after."

Talk...but it wouldn't just be about why he'd ended things between them. It would lead to why she'd then left Misty Peak, and all the pain that had trailed behind her for the last two years.

"I can't."

"Cal—"

"I'll see you around." She quickly sidled around him.

"We live in the same town," Lock called. "We're gonna have to talk eventually."

Yeah, eventually. And hopefully when the time came, she'd feel braver.

She didn't stop moving until they were in the car.

For a moment, neither she nor Aspen spoke. They just sat in heavy silence, Callie's chest moving a heck of a lot faster than it should.

"He's right, you know," Aspen finally said quietly. "You'll need to talk to him eventually and tell him why you left."

She swallowed, but it did nothing to wet her dry throat. "I know. But it hurts to think about." It would *always* hurt to think about. "I don't know if I can say it out loud and relive it without completely breaking down. Not right now, with everything going on with Dad, anyway."

Aspen gently touched her thigh. "Okay. Well, it's your choice when you tell him. And if you need me there with you, you know I will be."

She looked across at her best friend. Just like her father, Aspen had always been there when she'd needed her. "Thank you."

CHAPTER 5

*L*ock pushed up from the deck, climbing to his feet. Not his deck. Hamish's. A Misty Peak local who'd needed someone to replace sections of rotting wood for him.

Lock had been getting a lot of calls like this lately. Word had gotten around town that he was home, and everyone knew he was good at this kind of work. Growing up, he'd spent summers with an uncle who was a contractor, and he'd taught him a lot. His uncle had passed away when Lock was eighteen, but he remembered everything the man had taught him.

The work was good. He needed to keep busy. To find things to do other than think about Callie. About the way she was avoiding him. The way she wouldn't give him five damn minutes of her time.

He shoved the hammer into his tool belt with a bit too much force.

Two more times, he'd seen her around town in the last week since the hardware store. On both occasions, she'd turned and basically run from him like he was a predator.

"All finished?"

Hamish was coming out of the house. The guy was about the

same age as Lock, similar height and build. He often spoke with a stutter, but Lock barely noticed.

He nodded. "All done."

Hamish pushed his glasses up his nose. "Thank you for c-coming on such short notice. I overheard Macy saying you were b-back and doing jobs for locals, and after Mom tripped on the rotting wood yesterday, I knew I needed someone."

Hamish lived with his mother. A kind, elderly woman who'd come out to offer him sweet tea a dozen times. "Happy to help."

"So, are you here for g-good? Home, I mean. Or are you going back to the military?" Hamish didn't make eye contact for the last bit. In fact, his gaze seemed to continually shift from Lock's right shoulder to the ground.

"I'm home for good."

Hamish nodded. It was a quick, jerky nod. "Guess you'll be picking things back up with C-Callie then."

His chest contracted at her name. He should probably expect locals to ask him about her. "At the moment, I'd settle for a friendship with her."

Hamish's eyes widened and met his, then shifted back to Lock's shoulder as he nodded.

Lock frowned. "You spend much time with her?"

"Me? Well, I, uh, do her c-classes sometimes. They're good. I mean, she's good. Good at what she d-does." He shook his head. "I should get back inside. Text me the i-invoice."

Before he could respond, Hamish turned and moved back inside his house.

Did the guy have a thing for Callie? It wouldn't surprise him. She was kind and smart and had this damn dimple when she smiled that was hard not to adore.

Fuck, he was losing his mind being home but not being with her. He packed up his tools and shoved them into his truck before heading to his place.

Hamish did Callie's classes. It shouldn't make him jealous, but it did, because *he* wanted to spend an hour listening to her voice. Looking at her sweet smile.

They were open to the public. He *could* do one.

Shit, why hadn't he thought of that earlier?

He hit the Bluetooth on his truck and called his youngest brother. Jace answered and wind blew over the line before he spoke.

"Lock. To what do I owe the pleasure?"

"You've done one of Callie's Pilates classes, haven't you?"

"Uh, yeah, I did. Hurt like hell too. I had to pretend my ass wasn't killing me for the next week. Why?"

"You free right now?"

"Just getting back from a run. Why?"

"Tell me how to book a class."

A beat of silence passed. "One of Callie's classes?"

"No, Alcoholics Anonymous. *Yes,* one of Callie's classes."

"I don't know—"

"She won't talk to me. She won't give me five damn minutes of her time. I *need* to see her." And it was definitely a need.

"Fine. Give me a sec. I'll go online and see if there are any open spots in her next class."

Lock pulled into his driveway and waited. Every second that ticked by felt like ten.

"All right, booked us in."

Lock frowned. "Us?"

"Yeah, us. There were two spots left, and I'm not missing the look on her face when you stroll in."

"Jace—"

"Class starts in thirty. Don't be late." He hung up.

Thirty minutes? *Shit.*

He jogged inside and had the quickest shower of his life before changing into shorts and a T-shirt. When he was back in his truck, he checked the time. Fifteen minutes.

He headed toward the studio, his blood running that bit faster at the prospect of seeing her.

If he tried to speak to her after the class, would she listen to him today? Hell, it wasn't just that he had stuff to tell her; he also had a million questions for her. Where had she been all this time? What had she been doing? Had she dated anyone?

The last question felt like a hand fisting in his gut. Technically, he didn't have the right to care. He'd ended things with her. But he did care.

When he pulled his truck to the side of the road near the studio, he saw Jace climbing out of his car across the street, a half grin on his face.

What the hell was he smiling about?

"I've got a cap in my car if you want to pop it on and pull it over your face, then shout surprise after we step inside," Jace said when he reached Lock.

Lock shoved his brother in the shoulder. "Glad you find my pain so entertaining."

The smile dropped from Jace's face as they moved toward the studio. "Seriously though, she really won't hear you out?"

"No. Will barely let me speak."

Jace's brows slashed together. "That's strange, isn't it? I would have thought she'd been waiting two years to hear the full story of why you ended things, and at least get an apology."

"Apparently not."

They stepped inside to see three women on reformer machines and Callie with her back to them, talking to the woman on the end. She wore tight yoga pants and a sports bra. Her hair was pulled up, and fuck, he couldn't take his eyes off her.

Then she turned, and Lock had to remind himself to breathe. Because that smile…damn, it was beautiful.

But the second her gaze landed on him, the smile turned into a frown and she marched toward him.

She stopped less than a foot away, her sweet strawberry scent filling the air. "I have a class, Lock."

"I know. I'm in the class."

If possible, her frown deepened. "No, you're not."

"Yes, I am."

"*No.* You're not. Jace and a woman named Lola are the last two people. I have a list."

Jace cleared his throat. "Callie, meet Lola."

The fuck? Lola?

"Sorry, it must have been a typo, although I think the name kind of suits him." Jace nudged Lock's shoulder and muttered, "You're welcome." Then moved to a reformer.

Jesus.

Callie glared at him. "Lock—"

"It's just a class, Callie."

Her teeth visibly ground together before she blew out a breath. "Fine. *Just* the class." Then she swung away from him.

She was letting him stay. And it kind of felt like a small victory.

* * *

THE SNEAKY JERK. He'd *known* she wouldn't be able to kick him out in front of the class right when it was about to start. He'd probably have fought her on it, and there was no way she'd argue in front of clients.

But now, because of *him*, she'd fumbled every sequence, at one point not even remembering the exercise that was supposed to come next.

It was a mess. One big, fat, uncomfortable mess. She hadn't been able to think with his eyes on her. And they *had* been on her. All. Freaking. Class.

She forced a smile. "Thank you so much for coming, everyone. I hope to see you in another class soon."

She didn't look at him. Not while she spoke. Not while she handed out wipes to clean the machines. There was a fraction of a second when he took the wipe that their hands touched, and she looked him in the eye...but that was a mistake. A huge, colossal mistake, because there'd been this catch in her throat that she felt completely incapable of stopping.

Then he'd thanked her in that deep, sexy voice of his—and she'd tripped over the floor. Yep, the floor. There'd been nothing in front of her, she'd just tripped and barely caught herself.

If there was a definition for embarrassing, it was that.

As people started to file out, the nerves crawled up her throat.

He was going to talk to her. Of course he was. Only this time, she couldn't run away.

Jace said something to Lock before turning toward the door.

Oh God, once his brother was gone, it would just be the two of them...again.

"Thanks for the class, Callie," Jace called before stepping outside.

The silence that followed felt thick and heavy, weaving itself inside her veins.

Without looking up, she cleared her throat and said, "You need to leave too."

"You can't even look at me now?"

No. She couldn't. Because then she risked forgetting their past and throwing herself into his arms.

Pathetic. She was pathetic.

Slowly, she forced her gaze up, way up, into his ridiculously beautiful eyes. It felt strange thinking of a guy like Lock, someone so big and strong, as beautiful, but he was. He always had been.

"I'm not ready to talk about it." The words came out fast but quiet.

His brows twitched. "Why not?"

"Because it doesn't matter." The lie fell off her tongue. And it was a big lie. Their past and the reason things had worked out the way they did mattered. It had always mattered.

"You don't want to know why I ended our relationship that day?"

"You loved me one day and broke my heart the next. The reason behind it doesn't matter because it doesn't change anything. It doesn't send us back in time or undo what you did. It doesn't give you back to me when I needed you most."

The familiar panic curled in her belly at the memory of the night she so desperately needed him, but he wasn't there.

She breathed through it, only looking back at Lock after a stretch of silence.

Crap. He was looking at her like she was a puzzle to solve.

"When was that?"

She swallowed. "What?"

"When did you need me most?"

She shook her head. "Lock, you can't come in here demanding things from me. I thought we were forever. You *treated me* like we were forever. But then you did what you did and I had to come to the painful conclusion that you were never someone I got to keep. You were a memory. A lesson. But never my ending."

Anger darkened his features. And maybe something else. Frustration? "That's bullshit and you know it."

She grabbed a random pile of papers from the desk and rounded it, moving toward the back room, needing to be somewhere else. "You really need to leave."

"No. Not until we talk about this."

Goddammit, he was stubborn. She dropped the papers onto the table.

"Did something happen after that day? Is that why you left town?"

She closed her eyes, pain skittering through her belly. And maybe some panic.

He touched her hip, and the warmth of his palm seeped through her clothes and into her skin.

"Callie, please, talk to me." His head lowered, his breath brushing over her skin, making the air hard to move through her chest. "Let me in."

Her mouth opened and closed, and for a moment, she almost wanted to tell him. For a split second, she wanted to let the truth slip into the air and be a weight they could bear together. But then red flashed in her mind. Crimson red coating her thighs. Staining her sheets.

And the calls to Lock...the calls she'd so desperately needed him to answer. The ones he *could* have answered.

She stepped away so quickly, her hip hit the small table and the papers fell to the floor.

"Shit." She crouched and began to pile everything back up. Lock lowered opposite her, and they both reached for the last piece of paper at the same time. Too late, she realized what it was —the note from her stalker. The newest one she'd received yesterday.

Why the hell had she left it out?

He grabbed it first, eyes narrowing as they ran over the writing. "I dream about those green eyes of yours."

Yep. Another creepy-ass letter from her creepy-ass stalker.

His gaze collided with hers. "Who the hell wrote this?"

"None of your business." She tried to snatch it from his fingers, but he pulled it away and rose to his feet.

"It is my business because *you're* my business. Who wrote it?"

She rose, again trying to grab it from him. Damn the guy for being so tall. "No. I'm not your business. Give it back."

"Not until you tell me who it's from."

"Lock—"

"I'm not leaving until you do."

Jesus Christ. She massaged her temple. "I don't know who it's from. Someone started sending me these notes before we…broke up."

"*What?*"

She almost jumped at the shouted word.

"How long before we broke up?" he asked.

"Maybe the last six months of our relationship."

"And you never *told* me?"

She straightened. "No, I didn't. Because you worked a dangerous job, and I didn't want you to worry about me while you were on a mission. Plus, I knew you would have overreacted."

His jaw clicked. "It wouldn't have been an overreaction. You've had a fucking stalker for two and a half years."

"No, they stopped when I left town, and they just started again."

A vein popped out on his temple. "So, like I said, you've had a stalker for two and a half years."

"They're just notes."

Going by the narrowing of his eyes, that was the wrong thing to say. "Have you told Eastern?"

"No. I told the old sheriff, and not only could he not do anything, he didn't care."

"My brother's different. He'll care."

"Just give it back."

"Not until you promise you're going to tell Eastern."

Now *she* felt angry. "You don't get to tell me what to do. You broke up with me, remember? Now give it back."

"This asshole's been obsessed with you for over two goddamn years, and you want me to, what? Pretend I didn't see this? Pretend I don't care?"

"What I *want* is for you to let me live my life. This person is creepy, but they've never hurt me. I'll watch my back. Now give it to me, Lock."

"Callie—"

"*Now.*"

The muscles in his arms flexed, and finally he handed it back. But as he did, he leaned down, his mouth almost touching her ear as he whispered, "Fine. But this isn't over. If you thought I wouldn't leave you alone before, that's *nothing* compared to what's going to happen now."

Her throat dried, and before she could utter a word, he turned and was gone, the door of the studio slamming behind him.

CHAPTER 6

"You look frustrated, brother."

Lock glanced up at Cody, who was working behind the bar. The music was loud and the place was packed, but he barely noticed. "Frustrated is an understatement."

"Wanna talk about it?"

"I wouldn't know where to start."

Cody swung a bar towel over his shoulder. "How about at the beginning?"

He could have laughed. "The beginning and the end are the same damn place. Callie."

"Still not getting through to her?"

"She said it doesn't matter." His fingers tightened around his beer. It still hurt to think about. Because how the hell could their past not matter?

Cody frowned. "What doesn't matter?"

"The reason I broke up with her. The reason we *lost* each other. The reason we lost two damn years together." It *did* matter. Out of everything in their past, *that* mattered the most. "She called me a memory and a lesson."

Cody cringed. "Ouch. That must have hurt."

It didn't hurt. Hurting was when he slammed his finger in a door or walked into the corner of a coffee table. Callie calling him a memory felt like a hand punching through his chest and pulling out his heart.

"There's just so much I don't get," Lock said almost to himself. "Like why she won't hear me out, and why she left town and wouldn't let anyone tell me where she was. And I don't know why she seems to think we can coexist in this town without even talking." Because *he* couldn't. Seeing her every week, hearing her name, all while she barely looked at him, was torture.

"I didn't know you guys got so deep."

Of course he didn't. Because just like his other brothers, Cody had been away serving their country. Lock had only gotten to spend time with her when he'd made it back to town or when she visited him. But those moments together...shit, they'd been everything. The fresh air he'd so desperately needed to breathe between missions. The calm in the storm that was his job as a Ghost Ops operative.

"I need her back." Lock wasn't sure if those words were meant for himself or his brother. Maybe both.

Someone called Cody from the other side of the bar, but he didn't move right away. Instead, he looked Lock dead in the eye. "Then fight for her. If you love her like I think you do, fight hard."

Then Cody's gaze moved across the bar, likely to Harper. He was probably thinking that if situations were reversed, fighting was exactly what he'd do for her.

His brother gripped his shoulder before walking down the bar.

Lock looked at his barely touched beer as someone sat on the stool beside him. "Where the hell have you been?"

Eastern lifted his brows. "Hello to you too."

"I've been calling you for days."

"And I've been calling you back."

It was true. They kept missing each other. "I need your help with something."

"Anything."

He turned away from his beer to face his brother. "Callie has a stalker."

The easygoing expression disappeared from Eastern's face. All his brothers were the same. Protectors first. Their father had raised them that way. "What do you mean, a stalker?"

"She got a note from some asshole complimenting her on her eyes." Fuck, even saying the words out loud made him angry. "And apparently it wasn't the first. She was getting them before she left Misty Peak, and they started up again when she got back to town."

"Did she tell anyone?"

"Yeah, she said she went to the sheriff, but he didn't do shit."

"I'm guessing there wasn't much to track the guy. So they stopped when she left."

"Yeah." Two goddamn years and the asshole was still interested in her.

"So he's likely a local if he knows she's back." Eastern frowned. "Why are *you* telling me, and not her?"

"Because I don't think she will." Which was stupid. Just because the last sheriff hadn't done anything didn't mean Eastern wouldn't.

"Lock...if she doesn't want to report it, there's nothing I can do."

He knew that. But he also knew he couldn't sit around and do nothing. "Talk to her."

"Lock—"

"Please. For me. She may not want anything to do with me right now"—every part of him rebelled against the statement —"but I need her safe."

Eastern was silent for a moment, hard gaze boring into Lock, before finally sighing. "If I see her, I'll talk to her."

"Thank you."

Lock's phone vibrated in front of him, and for some reason, he almost thought it would be her. Which was ridiculous. She'd made it clear she wanted nothing to do with him. Hell, he didn't even know if she'd kept his number after she'd disconnected hers.

But since getting back to town, he'd developed this reckless hope that she'd come to him. Want him. Need him as much as he needed her.

It wasn't Callie. It was a local, texting to book a job.

Lock had just texted back when Cody returned, setting a beer in front of Eastern. "You guys still coming to my party next Monday night?"

Lock lifted a brow. "What are we celebrating again?"

Cody's eyes searched for Harper, then his voice lowered. "Well, if you ask Harper, it's a housewarming."

"A little late for that—you've been there for ages." Eastern lifted the beer to his mouth.

Cody nodded. "Correct. Which is why I'm surprised she went for the idea. But it's actually a chance to ask her to marry me in front of our family and friends."

Eastern choked on his beer, and Lock leaned forward. "You're proposing?"

"Got a ring and everything."

Lock's mouth spread into a smile. The first good fucking thing to happen since getting back to this town. "Hell yeah, you did. Congratulations, brother!"

"If Harper wasn't in the bar, I'd be all over you, man," Eastern said, the same smile on his face.

Cody dipped his head. "Thanks. Now I just need her to say yes."

Lock scoffed. "The way she looks at you? She'll say yes."

"I'm counting on it. Don't be late." Cody tapped the bar before moving over to serve a customer.

"Shit, I'm happy for him," Eastern said.

"Me too." And maybe there was also a tiny part of Lock that was envious that the woman Cody loved adored him back. But then, he hadn't royally fucked up like Lock had.

"You gonna tell me where you're living now?" Eastern asked.

"Nope."

He still hadn't told his brothers about the house. He wasn't sure why. Maybe because he wanted Callie to be the first to know. Maybe because a part of him was afraid that every carefully laid plan for his future with her wouldn't eventuate.

His phone rang, Antwan, a former teammate's name, appearing on the screen. "I've got to take this."

Eastern nodded as Lock rose and moved to a quieter corner of the bar.

"Antwan. How're you doing?"

"Hey, Lock, sorry I missed your call a few days ago. Life's been busy."

All his former teammates were like brothers to him, Antwan included. And he'd been affected the most by what had happened two years ago. First, his girlfriend had been murdered in the apartment they'd shared. Then, soon after, he'd been the one to find Winnie and Remi's bodies. He'd never been the same.

"How are *you* doing?" Lock asked.

"I don't know what to do with all my spare time. I thought taking time off before I started working would be a good thing, but now I'm not so sure."

"What can I do to help?"

"Tell me you're doing great?"

Could he lie?

No. He never lied to his team. "Not sure I can do that. Coming back here's been harder than I thought."

He knew part of that was because he was used to living on the edge of danger on a daily basis, with his team at his back to support him. Slotting into civilian life was harder than he'd anticipated.

The larger part was because he wasn't living the life he'd thought he would, with the woman he loved.

"But I'm gonna get there." Lock paused. "Wanna talk options of what you can do to fill your time?" Antwan had no family, and by also not working, he'd of course have way too much time on his hands to overthink everything.

"Not really."

Just like him, Antwan had never been good at opening up. "I was talking to Jesse the other day. He mentioned he might come down to Misty Peak and visit. You should come too."

"To your hometown?"

"Yeah, why not?"

A deep chuckle sounded over the line. "I guess you've missed my sorry ass."

"Damn straight."

There was a small pause. "You sort things out with Callie yet?"

The same question Jesse had asked. "Things are…complicated."

Not that it seemed that way to Callie. She seemed perfectly okay with them remaining broken.

"So you want us down there to help you get back on her good side?" Antwan asked.

"You think I need your help?"

"I know you do."

Lock chuckled. "You're right. I could use all the help I can get."

Whatever Antwan said next was missed, because the door to the bar opened and Aspen walked in, closely followed by a woman wearing the sexiest skintight jeans and low-cut top he'd ever seen. Her hair was down and flowing over her shoulders like a waterfall. And those green eyes…fuck, they gutted him.

Callie.

* * *

"Tell me again why you're making me come out tonight?" Callie tugged at the top of her shirt. It was too low and too tight, but maybe it only felt that way because she wanted to be at home, in a baggy, oversized tee and sweats, watching *Bridgerton*.

"Because…" Aspen said slowly as they neared the bar. "You need to get out of the house. You've been hiding since Lock returned to town."

"I have not."

"Really?" They stopped in front of the door. "So you didn't decline my dinner invitation last week because it was one of your favorite places to go with Lock? And you didn't make me and your dad eat at home on Sunday instead of your favorite Chinese restaurant because you and Lock used to get takeout there and you didn't want him to pop in while you were there?"

Jeez, she was pathetic. "I'm being cautious."

Except for tonight…because letting her best friend drag her to Lock's brother's bar was as far from cautious as she could get. But when Aspen decided something, it was impossible to say no.

"You need to *live*." Aspen frowned. "You're not going to run if he's in there, are you?"

"Run? No. I'll be way more composed than that. I'll turn and walk out with my head held high."

"Callie! You guys live in the same town. You need to learn to coexist."

She was right. Dammit. Served her right for having such a smart best friend. "Fine. I won't leave the bar. I'll stay for one drink."

One. *Then* she might run.

Aspen let out an exaggerated sigh before stepping into the bar and leading her toward a tall table.

"I'm going to get us a cocktail and a shot," Aspen said.

Callie lifted a brow. "A cocktail *and* a shot?"

"We're celebrating."

"What are we celebrating?"

"You not living like a hermit tonight." Aspen winked before heading toward the bar.

She wasn't living like a hermit. And even if she was, it was only because he was *everywhere*. On the street when she'd gone out to get a coffee. In the grocery store when she'd run in to grab some eggs. And maybe there'd been one time that she'd seen him on the street and turned, basically running the other way. At the time, the reaction had felt completely out of her control.

God, she was a lunatic. She just needed to be brave. She could do that. She was brave in most other aspects of her life.

"Hey."

Her head shot up at the sight of Harper, Cody's partner. She sometimes did classes at the studio. Callie liked her. "Hey. You're busy tonight."

"We are. And there have been no bar fights yet, so it's been a good kind of busy."

Callie laughed, not sure if the lack of bar fights was out of the norm. Who would be stupid enough to start a fight owned by a former special forces operative like Cody?

Harper cocked her head. "How are you?"

"I'm good. The studio's been busy, and I've been settling back into Misty Peak."

Good was probably an overstatement. Fine might have been more accurate, and by Harper's knowing smile, it almost seemed she knew. Or knew part of it, at least.

"Well, Cody and I are having a housewarming party next Monday, and we'd love for you to come. Bring your friend as well."

Callie opened her mouth to politely decline, when Aspen returned to the table and set the shots and cocktails down. "Bring me where? I assume I'm the friend."

Harper laughed. "Hi, I'm Harper."

"Aspen."

"I was just inviting you both to mine and Cody's house-warming party."

"We'll be there."

Callie's jaw dropped at Aspen's quick response. What the heck? Lock would definitely be there, and she knew it.

Harper's smile widened. "Great. I'll text the time and address."

The second Harper left the table, Callie glared at her friend. "Aspen! You know I would have declined."

"Exactly why I said yes. No hiding, remember?"

"But—"

"No buts. You are strong and brave, and I don't want to see you hiding those qualities from the world." Aspen gripped her shoulders. "You deserve all the happiness, but you won't find that sitting at home eating leftover Chinese takeout."

"It's been pizza more than Chinese lately."

"Same difference." Aspen cocked her head. "Speaking of being strong and brave…you know how you said you wouldn't run if you saw a certain someone?"

Callie's pulse picked up, her back straightening. "He's not."

"He's at the bar."

Her head swung around so fast she almost gave herself whiplash. At first, her view was blocked by other people. Then the crowd cleared—and there he was, standing beside the bar, looking straight at her.

CHAPTER 7

Callie threw back her shot, the cool liquid burning her throat. Her feet itched to move. Leave. Go somewhere safe and quiet and away from the man she'd loved for so long.

But another part of her, the part she kept buried deep inside, whispered to go to him, even if it was just to hear his voice.

She did neither. She just stood there, unable to move for fear she'd make the wrong decision.

"Every time I see him," she said quietly, "I wish I could go back to before that week. I wish we could be what we were."

So full of hope, with no painful past. She'd been pregnant. They'd talked about buying a house together. She'd had their entire future mapped out in her head.

But she couldn't go back. That was something she'd learned the hard way. That in a split second, everything could change, and she'd be powerless to stop it.

Aspen tilted her head. "He was your first love."

"Yep. He taught me what love feels like. Then he taught me what heartbreak feels like." This time, she lifted her cocktail and took a huge gulp. The sweet liquid sat heavy in her belly.

"You're the strongest person I've ever met, Callie. You know that?"

She turned to her friend, a deep sadness inside her. "I don't feel strong."

"Ah, but that's the thing about strength—it's easier for others to see than for us to feel."

Callie leaned her head on Aspen's shoulder. "I don't know what I did to deserve you."

"Most don't."

Despite everything, Callie laughed. "I still have to leave, you know."

"Dance first."

"Aspen—"

"Come on. One dance, then you can go home to your sweats and *Bridgerton*."

"How did you know that's what I wanted to do?"

Aspen rolled her eyes. "Hello, we live together and share the same Netflix account."

"You're a romance writer. Shouldn't *Bridgerton* be your thing?"

"Nope. Not into the historical stuff."

Callie was tempted to tell her that she didn't watch *Bridgeton* for its historical accuracy, but Aspen grabbed her hand and pulled her toward where a small group of people were already dancing. And even though Lock was right there in the bar, walking distance away, her friend was right—the second she started dancing, she *did* feel better. But then, movement had always been her salvation. It was why she'd become a yoga and Pilates instructor.

The entire time she was on the dance floor, she felt him staring at her, like a hot beam searing into her. It just reminded her that time was running out. That sooner rather than later, she'd need to tell him what had happened and why the timing of him breaking up with her made everything so much worse.

She wasn't sure how long she'd been dancing, but she was

finally closing her eyes and getting lost in the music when large warm hands touched her hips.

She froze. For a moment, she thought it was Lock. But then a body pressed against her, and it wasn't his familiar scent around her or the hard ridges of his chest touching her back.

"Mm, you look hot when you move. Wanna dance?"

She turned to look up into a set of black eyes. "No thanks." She tried to step away, but his arm snaked around her waist and pulled her against him.

"Not so fast."

She pressed her hands to his chest. "Get your hands off me."

He wasn't put off by her words at all. In fact, he smiled, a lopsided grin that he probably thought was charming. It wasn't. It was creepy and a bit slimy. "Come on. One dance. I promise I'll let you go after that."

He'd *let* her go?

She was about to push harder—but suddenly he was whipped off her, and before she could anticipate what was about to happen, Lock swung, nailing the guy in the face.

She gasped, jumping back, jaw dropping.

"Don't you fucking touch her!" Lock yelled. The bar quieted around them as Lock stood over the guy, rage darkening his features. "She's not *yours* to touch."

"Lock?" Her voice was almost breathless with disbelief. "What are you doing?"

The guy on the floor groaned, rolling to his side and grabbing his cheek.

Lock looked at her, but she was already shaking her head, anger replacing the shock before she took off toward the exit.

"Callie!"

It was Aspen who called, but she didn't stop or slow. She almost sprinted out of the bar and onto the sidewalk, toward her car. She was almost there when strong fingers gripped her arm, tugging her to a stop.

"Callie—"

She whipped around, ripping her arm out of Lock's grasp. "What was that?"

"I was defending you."

"I didn't *need* defending. And I certainly didn't need you to hit the guy! I'm capable of looking after myself."

"The asshole pulled you against his chest. It didn't take a genius to see you didn't want to be there."

"I had it handled. And even if I didn't, I'm not yours to protect anymore."

That familiar anger shaded his eyes again. "You'll *always* be mine to protect."

"Stop. Stop saying things like that. Stop looking at me like I'm yours. Just...*stop!*"

"You know I can't do that."

She shook her head, tears of anger and frustration and regret misting her eyes. "I left because of *you*, you know."

He frowned. "I wasn't even here."

"You'll *always* be here. Your presence. Your memory. You're everywhere. But I also felt this crippling sadness, because you're right—you *weren't* here."

He inched closer. "I am now."

She touched his chest, stopping him from closing the last bit of distance. "It's too late."

"It's not."

A tear slipped down her cheek, and she dashed it away. "I have to go."

She turned and took a step.

"We were being targeted."

She stopped, confusion swirling inside her as she turned back to him. "What?"

"We left one target alive after a mission. He was dangerous, and he learned who we were. He uncovered our identities." Lock inched forward again. "He killed Antwan's girlfriend and left a note, telling us her death was revenge for ending his organization."

Her breath caught. "Hollie was killed?"

Callie didn't know. When she'd disconnected her number, she'd cut contact with Lock's entire team and their partners, despite considering all of them friends after a few trips to his base.

She'd always liked Hollie. She'd liked all of them.

"Winnie and Remi were next."

She gasped, a chill sweeping over her skin. Lock's *teammate* was murdered? And *his* girlfriend as well? "I didn't know."

"I didn't tell you that day, because I was scared. You arrived seconds after I received the news about Winnie. I was a mess and I panicked. All I could think was, what if he's watching right now? What if he has fucking cameras or someone watching down the street, and he could see you and me together? What if you're next? I needed you as far away from me as possible. But it was never supposed to be permanent."

Regret squeezed her heart. At the timing of everything. The way he'd needed her far away when she'd needed him close.

Lock touched her hips, his heat seeping through the material of her jeans. "We found the asshole responsible, and we eliminated him. We made sure he died for what he did to Winnie and the women. That was two weeks later, and it took me another week to get home. But when I called you, I couldn't get through. And when I returned to town, you were gone, and no one would tell me where. I had no way to get in contact with you."

Another tear fell, and she dropped her head, so many emotions fighting inside her. Need for this man. Love for him.

But at the forefront of everything was grief over everything they'd lost.

* * *

Come on, Callie. Forgive me. Choose me.

The whispered plea played over in his head. A desperate need to get the woman he loved to love him back. To have her as his once again.

"I wish you'd found a way to tell me." Her voice was so quiet it barely crossed the inches of space between them. "Or that the timing could have been different. It would have changed everything."

"I know." Fuck, he'd made so many mistakes in his life, but this one...this was the worst. "I wish I'd handled things differently. I wish I'd been less emotional in the moment and more rational and come up with a better plan."

She touched his wrists, and for a split second, he thought he'd gotten through to her. That maybe she forgave him.

But then she stepped back, and that distance...*fuck*, it hurt. It felt like an entire damn ocean of space. "I need time, Lock."

Time. The word felt so heavy it almost caved his knees. "Time for what? To think about us?"

"To think about everything."

Finally, she looked up. There was so much sadness in her eyes, and that sadness punched right into him.

She tilted her head, a tear slipping from her green eyes. "I'm sorry you lost Winnie. I'm so incredibly sorry. I know what he meant to you. What your entire team meant to you. And I can understand why you did what you did. But..."

But? But what? But he'd done irreversible damage in letting her think he didn't love her? But too much time had passed?

"Three weeks after you broke up with me...I—"

"Callie."

She stopped as Aspen hurried toward them from the bar.

Dammit. She'd been about to tell him something important. He could feel it.

Aspen stopped beside them. "I'm sorry, I wanted to give you

guys some time but I was worried." She touched Callie's shoulder. "Are you okay?"

Callie put more space between them, and it hurt. Jesus, it hurt. "I'm okay. But I think we should go home."

"Callie—"

"We'll talk soon, Lock."

Then she turned and left, and he wondered what the hell she *hadn't* said. What had happened that she wasn't telling him? What could have possibly turned his ignoring her for three weeks into her disappearing for *two years*?

A hand touched his shoulder, and he turned to see Eastern standing there, a grim expression on his face.

"You angry I hit him?" Lock asked before his brother could get a word in.

"No. I probably would have hit him too, if he'd touched Sadie like that. I talked him out of pressing charges."

Lock nodded, not caring if the guy wanted to press charges or not. He wanted him away from Callie, so he'd done what he had to do.

"Are you okay?" Eastern asked slowly.

"I told her. I told her why I broke up with her. I told her about Winnie and Remi and Hollie."

"And?"

Lock's jaw clicked. "She said she needed *time*."

That single word burrowed inside him, hollowing him out. Why did that word sound so ominous?

Maybe because so much time had already passed, and that time had done too much damage.

"Okay, so give her time." Eastern said it like it was the easiest thing in the world.

"How much?"

"As much as she needs."

That's what he'd been afraid of. The problem was, he wasn't sure how much longer he could survive without her.

CHAPTER 8

*L*ock ran through the mountains, the air whipping over his face while his feet sank into the earth.

Time...the word had been repeating in his head over and over again, and it *still* felt wrong.

Two years ago, he'd had to shoulder losing Callie and his teammate in the span of an hour. It had been so much. But the one thing that had gotten him through, the thing that had kept him alive and breathing, was the unwavering faith in his reckless love for her.

But now, being here, seeing the shadows under her eyes, experiencing her pushing him away time and again, he was questioning whether his love was enough.

And to make it worse, she was receiving those fucking notes. Had she received more since that day in her studio? Was she safe?

He forced his body to move faster, pumping his arms and pounding his legs.

There were so many moments in his life for which he'd like a do-over. So many seconds he wished he could take back or replay. But the way he'd handled that morning with Callie...that was his biggest regret. It would always be his biggest regret.

Because maybe if he'd done something differently, maybe if he'd given her more of a hint as to why he needed them to take a break, things would be different now.

By the time he neared his house, his chest was heaving, the air soaring in and out of his lungs.

A truck in front of the house had his eyes narrowing. Kayden's truck. What the hell was he doing here, and how had he figured out where Lock lived?

Kayden rose from the steps in front of his door, brows lifting. "Looks like you pushed yourself a bit hard, brother."

Lock stopped in front of him. "How'd you know where to find me?"

"Eastern followed you home from the bar last night."

The fuck? He'd had a tail and he hadn't noticed? He was *trained* to notice that stuff. Sure, he hadn't been in a good head-space, but that was no excuse.

"Don't take it too hard," Kayden said, as if reading his mind. "When Eastern wants information, he gets it."

Lock rounded his brother and moved into his house, leaving the door open after him.

"Aren't you going to ask me why I'm here?" Kayden asked, the click of the door closing sounding after him.

"I know why you're here." He grabbed a bottle of water from the fridge and downed half of it. "You want to know when I bought this house and why. And you probably want to know why I didn't tell anyone. You were sent by the others because they thought you'd have the best chance at getting the information, being the oldest sibling."

Kayden smirked and muttered, "Fucking know-it-all," under his breath.

Lock threw him a second bottle. "No, I just know that my brothers are nosy assholes. Nylah would probably be in on it too if she were here."

"I was just on the phone with Nylah, actually. I promised to call back and update her on your house stuff on the way home."

Of course he did.

Lock's phone vibrated on the counter, and just like every other time, there was a second of wild hope that it would be her. That Callie was calling, ready to work things out.

It wasn't her. It was never her. It was another job request.

"This place is looking good."

Lock leaned against the counter. "You saw it before?"

Kayden shook his head. "Not for a while, but I know old man Peterson lived here for sixty years before he passed, and he never updated or fixed a single thing. It was a dump for a long damn time. You've done good."

"It's getting there."

"It is. But my question is, when did you buy it?"

"A bit over two years ago." There was no point in lying.

Kayden frowned as he pieced it together. "You bought it for Callie."

"I bought it for both of us."

If possible, the frown deepened. "I didn't know you two were that serious back then."

"I loved her." No, not loved…love. Present tense. And that was something that would never change.

Kayden's features softened. "I'm sorry you haven't been able to work things out."

"I don't know what to do. I know I hurt her, but I didn't expect her to disappear. I thought after the few weeks it took my team to eliminate Malone, I could return and explain myself." Why he was telling his brother all this, he wasn't sure. Maybe he just needed to get it out. Needed *someone* to hear.

Kayden cocked his head. "She said she wanted time, right?"

Did Eastern just broadcast every fucking thing from last night, word for word? "Yeah."

"So, do it. And in the meantime, just be her friend."

"Callie and I have never been friends."

Kayden lifted a shoulder. "Just because you've never done something doesn't mean you can't."

He was right. And friends...well, it was better than nothing. He just wasn't sure she wanted that, either.

His phone vibrated again, and he expected to see another unknown number, a local asking him to fix something around their house.

It wasn't.

It was Callie.

She was calling him.

* * *

"Honey, stop looking so worried."

Callie shifted her gaze from the road in front of her to her father. "I'm not worried."

"Your fingers are wrapped so tightly around the wheel, your knuckles are white."

Dammit. She forced her grip to loosen, but there was nothing she could do to unravel the tightness in her chest.

"Okay, maybe I'm a little worried." Worried and sad and frustrated and a million other things. She shot another look at her father, taking in the new lines etched into his brow. The shadows under his eyes.

Slowed speech, balance problems, challenges with swallowing...

They were all symptoms the doctor said could develop. And that was on top of the fatigue and muscle pain he already had. Her heart clenched at the thought of her strong, independent father going through this.

"We're upping your classes at the studio." Yoga and Pilates were great for people with Parkinson's.

"Callie, stop."

"Stop what?"

"You're overthinking everything. Stay in the moment, honey. I'm okay."

He said the last two words softly but firmly. Like he knew she needed to hear them.

She pulled into his driveway and sucked in a breath. It took a few seconds to get the words out, and when she did, they hurt. "I just...I want you to be okay."

His hand covered hers in her lap. So warm and familiar. "I am okay."

"But Parkinson's is..." She couldn't even finish the sentence. How was she supposed to describe the illness when someone she loved had it? So many nights she'd gone down the rabbit hole of research, and every time she did, she never found any hope.

"Look at me, sweetheart."

It took a moment, but finally she turned to look at her father. At his familiar green eyes. Eyes that looked so much like her own. "There is no amount of time or space or illness that could take me away from you. I will always be with you...even if it doesn't seem like it. Do you understand?"

Tears gathered in her eyes, and she leaned over to tug her father into a hug. "I love you, Dad."

"Couldn't possibly be as much as I love you."

"Not true."

He hugged her back, his embrace so tight it was like he was holding her together. But then, he'd always held her together, particularly on her hardest days, when all she wanted to do was fall apart.

They separated, and he swiped a tear from her cheek. "Thank you for coming to my checkup with me."

"You don't need to thank me for that, and I've already got the next one on my calendar."

"Callie—"

"I'm coming to all of them. I told you that."

"Jeez, you're stubborn."

"I wonder where I got that from."

Her dad chuckled and the sound made the first real smile stretch Callie's lips since they'd left the specialist.

He gripped the door handle. "I'll see you tomorrow for yoga, then dinner. I'll make—"

"Nope. I'm cooking. I'll make your favorite lentil curry."

He opened his mouth, looking like he was about to argue, but maybe he realized it was an argument he wouldn't win, because he shook his head and climbed out of the car. "I look forward to it. Call if you need anything."

She nodded, even though she wouldn't. No way would she burden him with any of her problems.

She waited until he was inside his house before pulling back onto the road. Instantly, the heaviness returned to her chest. But there was also something else—anger. That people just kept being taken from her. And the saddest part was, she'd always stupidly assumed her father would always be there.

When she pulled into her own driveway, she took a moment to inhale a calming breath before getting out. She still remembered the day her father had called to tell her about his diagnosis. She'd been hit by disbelief. Anger. Sadness. And guilt. So much guilt. That in the process of running from this town, she'd inadvertently run from her dad and lost two entire years with him.

Never again. She was never leaving him again.

She went inside, not surprised to see Aspen's car wasn't in the drive. She would either be out with Dylan or in a park or a café, writing. Her best friend struggled to write at home. Something about needing people and noise and inspiration.

If it was her, those things would distract her. But then, maybe that's why she wasn't a writer.

She dropped her bag on the hall table and paused at the sticky note on the pile of mail.

Pretty sure these are bills, so I haven't looked at a single one, as I'm manifesting a good day. Oh, and I made chili. It's in the fridge. You're welcome.

A smile curved Callie's lips. Of course bills would affect Aspen's day, because she hadn't finished her book in too long so her income had to be dwindling.

Quickly, she shuffled through the mail. Aspen was right.

Bill. Bill. Bill.

She was about to drop the pile when she reached the last one.

All the fine hairs on her arms stood on end at the sight of that familiar writing.

No. This couldn't be from him. This was her home address. It wasn't public knowledge. He shouldn't have access to it. Had he followed her home?

The idea made a shudder roll down her spine.

With shaking fingers, she tore open the envelope to find a single piece of paper.

Whenever I see your hair, I just want to touch it. I bet it's soft like silk.

Nausea curled in her belly.

Lock was right. She needed to tell Eastern. This was too far.

She also had to tell Aspen. If they had her address, this involved both of them.

Quickly, she crossed her living room into the kitchen to grab the other letters she'd stashed in a drawer—only to stop at the sight of the back door. The back door she thought she'd fixed.

Only right now, it was open. *Wide* open.

Her heartbeat stumbled over itself. She lifted her phone and called the person with whom she'd always felt safest. The man she absolutely *should not* be calling.

He answered on the first ring.

"Callie?"

"Lock…I need you."

Biceps. Thick, glistening biceps that stretched the material of the crisp white shirt. A white shirt that, in her opinion, was far too tight. Surely seeing every curve of muscle on the man's body was overkill. And had he always been that tanned? She didn't remember his skin looking so bronzed.

She should still be thinking about the creepy note and the way her open door had scared the crap out of her. But nope. Lock Walker entered her home and suddenly she was undressing him with her eyes.

"You should have let me fix this earlier."

She jumped at Lock's words. The first words either of them had spoken since he'd gotten to work. In fact, he'd arrived, looked at her door, done that jaw-clicky thing he did when he was mad, and immediately gotten to work fixing it.

She cleared her throat. "I didn't want to ask you for a favor, and I didn't want to hire someone else in case word got back to Dad. Besides, I thought I'd fixed it."

Clearly, she was no Bob the Builder.

He shot her a look over his shoulder. "Why didn't you want it getting back to your dad?"

Of course that was the part he focused on. "I didn't want to worry him."

His brows flickered before he turned back to the door. "Call me next time. It's not a favor—it's me taking care of you."

She was tempted to tell him it wasn't his job to take care of her anymore, but that would just start a fight, and she didn't want to fight with him while he was helping her. "Well, thanks for coming."

"So it was just open when you got home?"

"Yeah. Aspen forgets to lock it sometimes."

The muscles in his back visibly tensed. "Have you received any more of those notes?"

Her gaze shifted to the note on the hall table. The note she'd dropped there when opening the front door for Lock. "I, um, received another one…today."

He paused and turned. "What did it say?"

"Something stupid about my hair."

Lock's jaw tightened.

Shit. She needed to change the subject. "Are you finished?"

He straightened, the muscles in his arms once again contracting with his movement.

Jesus, had his arms gotten bigger in the last two years? It didn't seem possible because they'd always been huge.

He closed the door and the click of the bolt catching was loud, making relief wash through her belly. Good. The door wouldn't be opening again. She should be safe.

She forced herself not to fiddle with her fingers as she looked back at him. It was a nervous habit, something Lock knew, and she *did not* want him to know she was nervous to have him in her space.

"Thank you. If you could send me an invoice—"

His growl cut off the words in her throat. "You are *not* paying me to make sure your home's safe, Callie."

"Lock—"

"No."

Oh Jesus. He was using that deep, growly voice again. "Well, thank you then." She didn't look at him when she said it.

Dammit, Callie, grow a backbone.

When the silence stretched, she finally looked up. He was watching her so closely that she was almost scared he could see every secret inside her. He'd always had a freaky way of reading her far too well.

"What is it?" he asked quietly. "The door's fixed. No one's getting through. Is it the notes that are upsetting you?"

He knew she was upset. But it wasn't just the notes or the door...

"It's my dad."

Lock's brows slashed together, and he stepped closer again. They stood so close now that all she had to do was reach out and she'd be touching him.

"Is something wrong?" he asked.

She opened her mouth to tell him, but closed it, scared that if she did, she might cry. Dammit, why was she feeling so emotional today?

He kept watching her, and it was one of those moments where the sympathy in the other person's eyes made you want to cry anyway.

He closed that last bit of space and cupped her cheek. She sucked in a sharp breath because that touch... God, it was everything. Warm. Familiar. Comforting.

"Callie. You can talk to me. You can tell me anything."

"He's sick," she whispered.

"Sick how?"

She swallowed the lump in her throat, and suddenly there was no stopping the words from tumbling out. She wanted him to know so he could tell her everything would be okay. "Parkinson's."

Lock cursed and tugged her into his hard chest. For a

moment, she was still. She hadn't been hugged by Lock in so long, and it was everything she remembered it to be.

Two heartbeats of stillness, then she gave in and wrapped her arms around his waist, letting his warmth envelop her. He was all strength, and she absorbed that strength.

"I'm sorry, C. So damn sorry."

The first tear fell, then another. Silent tears that sank into his shirt, linking them together.

Lock knew how much her father meant to her. He was her only family. He was and had been her entire world for so long.

She cried about her father's diagnosis. About the unfairness of it. About the time she'd lost with him over the last two years, and about every hard moment she knew was coming.

Lock just held her, not uttering a single word, like he knew she needed his touch more than his words.

When she finally pulled away, his hands remained on her hips.

She touched the wet patch on his shirt, tracing it with her finger. "I'm sorry."

"You don't need to apologize." He stroked her hip with his thumb, and she couldn't step away. It was like she was stuck. "What can I do to help?"

Once upon a time, she would have thought that he was the only thing that *could* help. His touch. His deep, gravelly voice telling her everything would be okay.

"Nothing." The whispered word felt painful to release.

A hurt expression crossed his face, and he didn't even try to hide it.

The hand on her hip slipped up to her waist and his head lowered, his warm breath brushing her sensitive skin. "Let me in, Callie. Lean on me."

She opened her mouth to tell him again that he couldn't help her. That the days of her leaning on him were in the past, but then he turned his head, and his eyes burned into hers.

His warm breath skittered over her lips as he whispered, "I still love you."

Her breath caught, emotion welling in her chest, pressing more tears to her eyes. "But love isn't supposed to hurt, Lock. Ours did."

It hurt her in its absence.

Another flicker of pain on his face, this time deeper, shading his eyes to navy. "I'm sorry. I'm so sorry."

"I wish sorry changed the past."

His head lowered, his forehead touching hers. "I don't deserve you...but I'm too selfish to leave you alone."

His mouth hovered over hers before pausing. It was like he was waiting for her to push him away. Or maybe for her to step back. To run from this.

She did nothing. She remained so perfectly still she wasn't even sure she was capable of moving. Then his lips touched hers. A light kiss. A graze of lips against lips. But she felt it everywhere. It slipped through every limb, beating life into her.

His lips swiped hers again, and that kiss...it thrust her back two years. To a time when life made sense. When she hadn't been touched by loss and pain.

When Lock was hers.

* * *

Lock had to remind himself to breathe. Because her lips were too warm, and her skin too soft, and everything about her too damn consuming.

Every day for two years, he'd thought about this moment. *Dreamed* about it. *Craved* it.

She reached up and cupped his cheek, and that one touch lit a fire inside him.

He lifted her and turned, setting her on the counter and stepping between her thighs. His hands slipped beneath her shirt to touch a waist that was as soft as he remembered.

She gasped, and the second her lips parted, he slipped inside her mouth, tangling his tongue with hers.

God, she tasted good. He'd almost forgotten her sweetness. A combination of berries and candy. A flavor that called to him. A taste that was so infinitely Callie.

He touched his chest to hers, pushing her thighs farther apart. He nipped her bottom lip, wanting to take her whimper that cut through the air and store it deep inside him so he never forgot.

But then, he'd never forgotten anything about this woman. Not the angelic sounds she made. Not her sweet scent or taste or the way her skin was soft like silk. She was a part of him. And right now, kissing her, he was whole again for the first time in ages.

He shifted his mouth from hers, trailing it down her neck while his hand slipped over her ribs. He was about to close that last bit of distance and cup her breast when she tensed, then grabbed his wrist.

"Lock…we can't. I…I can't."

He hung his head, the pain so real and visceral that for a moment, he couldn't move. Could barely breathe.

"I'm not giving up on us, Callie," he whispered.

Finally, he gained the strength to look up. Her lips were red and her eyes conflicted.

Good. There was a part of her that was fighting for him. A part of her that wanted him back. He couldn't just see it in her eyes. He'd *felt it* in her kiss.

He gripped her hips and helped her off the counter but didn't step back right away. "You and me…we're not over. We will *never* be over."

Her eyes widened.

Leaning forward, he gently kissed her temple. It took all of his strength to drop his hands and turn away. His steps were heavy as he made his way toward the front door, her soft footsteps trailing behind him. He'd just wrapped his fingers around the doorknob and was about to tug it open when something on the hall table caught his attention. His eyes narrowed.

The note.

Whenever I see your hair, I just want to touch it. I bet it's soft like silk.

But it wasn't just the handwritten words that caught his attention, it was the envelope beneath it. An envelope addressed to her *house* in the same handwriting.

Callie tried to snatch it away from him, and he let her. What was the point in keeping it? He'd already read the damn thing. "He sent it to your *home* address?"

Her mouth opened and closed. "Lock—"

"Tell me I'm not seeing what I think I'm seeing. Tell me he doesn't know where you live."

She blew out a long breath. "Yes, he sent it to my home address. I opened it just before I called you."

Fuck. "You're reporting this to Eastern *now*." He pulled out his phone, only for her to grab his wrist. "Don't argue with me on this, Callie. This is your safety we're talking about."

"I know. I'm going to contact him, but I can do it myself. I don't need you looking after me."

"You clearly do."

Her eyes narrowed.

Shit, he was going about this the wrong way.

He took a breath, trying to dampen the flame of fury in his gut. "We may not be dating, but we can at least be friends." The word tasted bitter in his mouth, but friends was better than nothing. "And friends help each other."

"We can't be friends."

"We can. We can see each other in the street without running. We can talk. And we can help keep the other safe. Let me call my brother so he can investigate this."

When she remained silent, he stepped closer, cupping her cheek once again. There was less hesitation this time. And for the second time that day, she didn't push him away.

Progress.

"Please," he whispered. "I need you safe."

When the anger slipped from her face and her features softened, he knew he had this one.

"Okay."

The air rushed from his chest. Thank God.

He lifted his phone and called Eastern, who answered on the first ring.

"Lock."

"Callie received another note."

She frowned. She didn't know he'd already told Eastern, but surely she'd expected it.

"She's ready to let you help."

CHAPTER 10

"**W**hat do you mean, there's nothing you can do?" Lock tried not to shout. He was at a damn party for God's sake, but *fuck* he was pissed. Cody's house was full of people. This wasn't the time or place, but five days had passed since Callie had given the note to Eastern. Five fucking days and his brother had found nothing.

Eastern set his beer on the kitchen counter and angled his body toward Lock and his back to the crowd. "There were no prints on the notes or envelopes other than Callie's and yours and no return address."

Music boomed throughout the space and voices sounded around him. He blocked it all out to focus on his brother. "You're a sheriff. Isn't there some way to find where it was sent from?"

"I wish there was, but if this guy didn't leave a trail, there's nothing to lead us to him. I'm sorry. For the moment, she needs to watch her back—"

"That letter was sent to her *house*. The asshole knows where she lives. He probably followed her home."

"I know." Eastern stepped closer and lowered his voice. "Which is why she needs to take extra precautions. Triple check her house is locked up. Don't come and go after dark. And I'll get my guys to do extra drive-bys."

It wasn't enough. And what was worse, she still wouldn't let him protect her. If it was up to him, he'd be camped out on her couch, but she didn't want that.

He downed a third of his beer. "I hate this. I hate that someone's sending her notes. And I hate that she won't let me stick close to her." Especially after that kiss. It was like she'd given him a taste of her, only to pull away again. Retreated from him even though they both knew they were meant for each other.

Eastern clenched his shoulder. "She's gonna be okay. And eventually, she'll let you in."

"You don't know that."

"Maybe not. But my gut tells me it's true, and my gut's rarely wrong."

"This gut?" Jace asked, stepping up to them and hitting Eastern in the stomach. "It's getting a bit tubby if you ask me. You worked out since you left the Navy?"

Eastern grabbed his brother in a headlock. "I can still beat your ass."

Despite his frustration, Lock's lips twitched.

Damn, he loved his family. His Ghost Ops teammates had felt like brothers, but being back here with the family he'd grown up with, the men who'd helped shape who he was…it felt good. It was just a shame Nylah wasn't home.

"What the hell are you guys doing?"

Lock swung around at the familiar voice.

What the hell? Had he literally conjured her up?

"What are you doing here?" Jace asked, the first to step forward and pull their sister into a hug.

Nylah chuckled. "You thought I was going to miss my brother's *housewarming*."

Cody had told her. Of course she'd come.

Lock was the last to pull his sister into a hug. "It's good to see you, sis."

"It's good to see you finally home," she whispered. When she pulled back, she looked at him closely. So closely he almost wanted to step back. "You doing okay?"

Was it as obvious to her as it was to everyone else that he wasn't? "I'm getting there."

Her brows flickered before Cody and Kayden joined the group, welcoming their sister home.

Liam, Nylah's partner, stepped forward, clasping Lock's hand. "It's good to finally meet you in person."

Lock dipped his head. "You too."

He hadn't met Liam yet, but he'd heard enough about him and they'd spoken a dozen times. He was a former special forces soldier who now co-owned a security company called Blue Halo in Cradle Mountain, Idaho.

Everyone was talking loudly as Cody came to stand beside him. "We're all here."

"It feels good," Lock said before lowering his voice. "Although I didn't know you wanted to propose in front of all of Misty Peak."

Cody cringed. "I didn't. Harper invited everyone because for all she knew, it was a housewarming party and she wanted to 'fill the space,' as she said."

"Nervous?"

"Nope. I probably should be, but it feels right. Overdue even, like I should have asked her the second she walked into my bar."

Lock was happy for his brother. But he also felt something else. Something a hell of a lot less comfortable—a deep longing to have the woman he loved love him back.

"Probably good you waited," he said, forcing his words to come out relaxed, when relaxed was the last thing he felt. "She might have freaked out otherwise."

"You're right about that." Cody cleared his throat. "So…did Callie tell you she's coming tonight?"

Lock's gut knotted. "What?"

"Yeah, Harper invited her. She does Pilates at Callie's studio. I assume she'll be here soon."

Cody had barely finished the sentence when the front door opened, and Aspen and Callie walked in.

Dozens of people stood between them, but she was all he saw. Her long, dark locks. Her green eyes. The jeans that pulled tightly against her thighs, paired with the pale green top that matched her eyes.

Jesus Christ, he got lost in her every time he saw her.

Someone bumped his shoulder, and he looked down to see Nylah staring at him, a knowing smile on her face.

"I see Callie's here."

Unlike his brothers, who'd been away in the military while he'd dated Callie, Nylah had been here, in Misty Peak. She'd been right there with him that terrible week he'd broken up with her.

"Yeah." He couldn't manage many more words than that.

"I figured you'd come back for her at some point."

Callie's eyes cut across the room, landing on him, and he felt that gaze like a beam of electricity bolting into him.

There was a small widening of her eyes. A lift of her chest. And the smallest smile before Aspen grabbed her arm and guided her toward the drinks.

Nylah was right. He *had* come back for her. He just had to hope he hadn't waited too long.

* * *

THERE WERE TOO many people here. The house was crowded and hot and stuffy. But then, maybe it only *felt* that way because Lock was here. Because his eyes were on her. Had been on her the entire freaking night. No matter where she was or who she was talking to, anytime she glanced his way, it was his beautiful eyes staring right at her.

"I have the best recipe. I could send it to you."

Crap. Hamish. What was he talking about? A meatball recipe? She was barely listening to him. She was a terrible person.

She glanced at the skewered meatball in his hand. "I would love that. The meatballs are delicious."

A moment of weakness got the best of her, and she looked at Lock again.

Yep, still looking at her.

She turned back to Hamish. He looked…disappointed? Had he not been talking about the meatballs? Shit. She was the worst.

She touched his arm. "I'm sorry. I'm distracted." *Understatement of the century.*

Hamish turned his head to look at Lock, then back to Callie. "Why did you guys break up if you're still into each other?"

"I'm not…still into him." Well, that lie came out about as smoothly as sandpaper. "It's complicated."

His brows flickered, and he seemed to consider that for a moment. "Just so you know, you don't deserve complicated. You deserve someone who makes love feel easy."

Her eyes widened, shock skittering through her veins. Whatever she'd expected him to say, it wasn't that. It felt too intimate and kind of pushed the boundary of friendship. She opened and closed her mouth, but before she could respond, he gave her a small smile and walked away.

"Did you know that this many people could fit into one living room? Because I sure didn't."

Swallowing, she glanced at Aspen as she came to stand beside her, beer in hand. She'd always been a beer girl, and Callie had never understood it. Give her wine any day, but beer? No thanks.

"Where's Dylan?"

Aspen tilted her head toward a small group of men, all holding beers and laughing. "Over there."

Dylan's dark brown eyes moved over to Aspen...and there was just something in his expression that Callie didn't like. That Callie had *never* liked. Was it because he always looked so possessive of Aspen?

She'd tried to bring it up once, but Aspen had brushed it off.

That made her a terrible friend, that she was still thinking negatively about him, right? She should like her best friend's boyfriend, especially when they'd been dating for almost a year.

"Everything good with you two?" Callie finally asked.

"He wants me to move in with him."

Callie's brows shot up. "You're leaving me?"

"Don't be silly. Just because he wants me to do something doesn't mean I'm going to. I'm not ready for that. Besides, my mom would have a fit, and I do not need a Karen meltdown right now."

Aspen's mother could switch between completely reasonable middle-aged woman to completely unhinged in a matter of seconds. Aspen had always thought she had undiagnosed split personality disorder. Either that or bipolar. "Has she had any new...episodes lately?"

"She texted me asking if I poisoned her rabbit yesterday. I said no, then I got hit with a million and one abusive texts. I went over and saw her today and she was acting completely normal, like she hadn't been the mother from hell yesterday. When I asked about Floppy, she said the vet gave him some medication and he's fine."

Callie cringed. She'd heard worse stories. A lot worse. It didn't make any of them okay. "I'm sorry."

"It's okay. I'm used to her." Aspen nodded toward someone across the room, a small smile on her face. "What did Mr. Infatuated want?"

Callie followed her gaze to Hamish, standing by the kitchen island choosing a drink. "Mr. Infatuated?"

Aspen rolled her eyes. "You have to have noticed by now."

"He doesn't—"

"He does. But you don't see because your attention is elsewhere." Aspen stared at the spot where Callie knew Lock was standing.

"Every time I look his way, he's staring at me," Callie whispered, not even sure why she was saying it out loud.

"Of course he is. He's made it clear he wants you back."

"I'm going to tell him this week." Reliving the past would be hard, but he had a right to know. And it was time. Past time.

Aspen's expression softened. "I can be with you if you need me."

"No, I need to do this by myself. I should have told him already. I just…" She sucked in a breath, and she lowered her voice to almost a whisper. "Talking about it is already so hard. And telling him…it will hurt."

Aspen gripped her arm. "You're right, it *will* be hard. But you can do hard things."

Emotion welled in her throat, and she pulled her friend into a hug. "Thank you for always being here for me."

"I wouldn't want to be anywhere else."

The music quieted, and Cody and Harper stepped in front of the room. Their smiles were wide, but there was something about Cody's expression that seemed…different.

Was he nervous? He never looked nervous. In fact, most of the time he was the king of calm, cool, and collected.

"Hi, everyone," Harper said, her voice quieting the crowd. "Cody and I just want to thank you all for coming tonight. This house has become our home, and it means the world to us that everyone we love can celebrate it with us."

Cody wet his lips. "It *is* our home. It's the place where we live…and it's the place we'll one day start a family."

Callie's heart constricted at the word "family," and her gaze wanted to seek out Lock.

No. She needed to stop looking at him.

Cody kept talking, but she was so caught up in her thoughts that she was barely listening…until he got down on one knee.

Callie's breath caught.

"Harper Rain, you walked into my life in the middle of a storm, and nothing's been the same since. You added color to my life. Vibrant rays of color. And a love so fierce that I now don't know how I ever lived without it. I've forgotten how to live without you, and I never want to remember."

Callie's pulse sped a bit faster with every word.

He took out a small box from his back pocket and opened it, causing a collective gasp to slip through the room.

Harper's eyes widened, her lips separating and tears shining in her eyes.

"Marry me," Cody said softly. "I'm already yours but make me yours on paper too. Make me the luckiest man in the world."

She couldn't stop herself. She looked at Lock, and his expression held…pain? Regret? Because they both knew the same thing. That this was a story they'd written for themselves. A story that had been erased and rewritten with a different ending.

"Yes!"

Callie forced her attention back to the couple in front of them as the crowd erupted in cheers. Cody lifted Harper into his arms.

And suddenly, the crowd around her, the noise, the emotion… it was all too much.

She lowered her head to Aspen's ear. "I'm just going outside to get some air."

Her friend looked at her, concern brimming her eyes. "Are you okay?"

"Of course. I just need a few minutes."

Understanding crossed Aspen's features, and she squeezed Callie's arm and nodded.

Callie weaved through the crowd. It wasn't until she stepped onto the deck, the cool wind brushing over her cheeks, that she realized just how much she needed that fresh air.

She walked across the yard, not stopping until she had a clear view of the moon. Then she dropped, lying down to let the cool grass seep through her clothes and chill her skin.

She'd had counseling. She'd done all the work. She should be okay. She shouldn't be triggered by another couple's happiness.

So why was she? Because Lock was back in her life? Because it was bringing back everything she'd lost?

A noise sounded behind her. A light crunching noise, like a leaf beneath someone's shoe.

She sat up and turned her head, frowning when she saw no one. Heard nothing but the whisper of wind in the leaves.

Frowning, she lay back on the grass. She was just closing her eyes, when another noise sounded, this one closer.

She opened her eyes in time to see a large figure looming over her, and she opened her mouth to scream.

CHAPTER 11

"$\mathcal{C}$allie…"

Lock! Oh God. It was just Lock.

The air rushed from her chest, and she swallowed the scream.

"What in the ever-loving hell are you doing?" she gasped, covering her eyes with her hands. "You scared the crap out of me!"

A light thump sounded, and she moved her arm to see Lock lowering to the grass beside her. "Sorry."

She frowned at him when he lay down. "What are you doing?"

"Joining you."

"Why?"

"Because it's dark and you're alone out here." He turned his head, his gaze piercing hers. "And because I want to."

She swallowed and looked back at the sky. She told herself it was because the stars were beautiful, but the truth was, lying on her back, looking at him, felt far too intimate. The sky was safer. "Did you know he was going to propose?"

"I did." His smooth voice slid over her skin like velvet. "I know you don't want to talk to me, but at least tell me you've been good these last couple years."

Good? Had she been good? There had been *moments* of good-ness. Smiles that hadn't felt forced. Laughs that, for a moment, let her forget about the life she'd left in Misty Peak.

"I taught at yoga retreats. They were exactly what I needed." It wasn't really an answer to his question, but at least it was true.

"You always wanted to do that."

"I did." She'd actually planned to earlier, but then she'd met Lock and the dream had been put on hold.

"Did you ever think about us?"

She could have laughed. He had to know the answer to that. "Sometimes I'd picture this other life where we got it right."

There was a brief pause. "What does the life look like?"

Gosh, she could picture it so clearly. "We wake up together, you earlier than me because you always had a habit of doing that. Then we head to our separate jobs. On the way home, I text you that I'm picking up dinner, and we argue about whether to get Chinese or burgers. You want burgers, but usually I win and we get Chinese." She turned, expecting to see a smile, only there wasn't one. He looked pained.

"What else?"

She almost didn't want to say, but the words started flowing of their own accord. "Most days, you insist that I wait for you to pick me up from work when I finish late. This starts an argument, and I tell you I'm not waiting, but I do. I always wait."

He frowned but remained silent.

"Dad and I go to your family Christmases and Thanksgivings. Your brothers start to feel like my family, and my dad starts to feel like yours."

"I like that world."

She dragged her gaze back to the moon. It was so bright against the dark night sky. "It doesn't exist."

"It could."

Could it? After everything? "In another life, maybe we could have gotten it right. But we live in this one. And in this one, love wasn't enough."

"It wasn't that love wasn't enough, Callie. It was that I loved you *too much*. I needed you to *live*."

Her belly contracted. Then it rolled and twisted, making her feel so unsettled that she quickly pushed to her feet. "I should get back inside."

She'd only taken one step before he grabbed her arm.

She didn't want to look up at him; each time it was too hard to look away…but she did.

"You gave up on us and ran," he whispered.

"*I* gave up on us? I felt like I was *drowning*. It hurt to breathe! Then I realized I had to let go or get dragged under. So I let you go, Lock. I let you go because I had to."

Instead of releasing her, he inched closer, his fingers slipping up her arm. "I don't think either of us let go. Not really. Regardless of where we were in the world, we've always been tethered to each other. I'm here now. We're *both* here. And we care about each other. That has to mean something."

The truth of those words felt like a kick to the belly. "I'll always care about you, Lock."

He lowered his head, and for a moment, she thought he was going to kiss her again. He didn't. His cheek grazed hers, the warmth of his skin slipping inside her, before he whispered, "I'm not going anywhere. I'll wait as long as you need."

Tell him now. Tell him what happened.

She opened her mouth, begging the truth to set itself free. Begging those words he deserved to hear to finally come out.

"Yo, is Jake out here?"

Lock cursed and stepped back. He turned and yelled something back to the guy, but Callie was already retreating.

What was she thinking? Had she really been about to break the news to Lock of the worst night of her life at his brother's engagement party? When there was music and drinking and dancing just a few feet away?

Jesus.

She jogged back to the house and stepped inside so quickly she ran straight into Hamish. The cup of beer in his hand spilled all over her chest.

She gasped and stumbled back, the cool liquid seeping through the material of her top, onto her skin.

Hamish's jaw dropped. "Callie! I-I'm sorry. I didn't s-see you."

"It's my fault." She weaved around him and down the hall.

Aspen's eyes widened when she passed her. "Callie?"

She kept moving, needing to be away from the crowd and the noise. She didn't get a chance to close the bathroom door before Aspen slipped in after her.

"What happened?" her friend asked, the second the lock clicked.

"I walked into Hamish and—"

"No, not the beer. What happened outside? I saw Lock follow you out there, and now you've lost all the color in your face." Aspen stepped forward, voice quieting. "Talk to me, Cal."

Her heart thudded. "I still love him." The words were barely a whisper.

"Oh, honey, of course you do. He was your whole world for an entire year."

"I'm scared. I am so freaking scared. That morning when he told me it was over, my entire future just disappeared, and I was lost. *So* lost. And I know why he did it. I understand the reason, but it doesn't change how I felt or how vulnerable I was. And it doesn't change what happened next."

"Callie—"

"I lost our *baby*, Aspen!" Her chest moved so fast, the air barely got in or out. "I was scared and alone and hurting, and he wasn't there, and I don't know how to move past that. I want to, but I can't! I...I need to go."

"Wait—"

She opened the door—and froze.

Lock. He was standing right there, shock clear in his features.

Ice slid through Callie's veins.

She wasn't sure how loud she'd been speaking, but by the look on his face…he'd heard.

Now the cold took hold of her limbs, and she had no idea how to chase it away.

She pushed past him and ran, not caring that she was shoving people aside or that everyone was looking at her. She just needed to get out. Get away. Hide.

* * *

CALLIE HAD BEEN *PREGNANT?*

She shoved past him, and finally he pulled himself out of his shock and forced his feet to move. He could have caught up and grabbed her, but he waited until they were outside and away from the large crowd of people to take hold of her arm and tug her to a stop.

"Callie! Tell me what's going on."

"Let go of me." She looked anywhere but at him, and the tears in her eyes…fuck, they gutted him.

"Please. I need to know! Were you pregnant with our baby?" Even though he said them out loud, the words still didn't sound real.

The look on her face told him they were.

And it hurt. Shit, did it hurt. "Why didn't you tell me?"

For the first time since stepping outside, she looked up at him —*really* looked at him—shock and something else burning through her eyes. Disbelief.

"Why didn't I tell you? Did you really just ask me that?"

"You could have gotten in contact with me."

"I tried! I called you every day for three weeks and you didn't answer a single call. You didn't even reply to a text!"

"You know why. I had to cut contact with you for a short period of time—"

"That was all it took."

"All what took?"

Grief like he'd never seen before darkened her eyes. Then he remembered her words in the bathroom. "You *lost* the baby in those weeks."

"Not *the* baby. *Our* baby." Her gaze held his. "I was fourteen weeks pregnant when I miscarried him."

"Him?"

Tears freely ran down her cheeks. "It was a boy. I tried to call you when I started bleeding. Then when I was sitting in the hospital, wondering how I was possibly going to find the strength to live another day. You didn't answer. You *never* answered."

Pain. It was everywhere. In his skin. His blood.

"I needed you," she whispered. "I have *never* needed another person like I needed you that night. And you weren't there. It hurt to *breathe*...and *you weren't there*. Because you wouldn't answer your phone."

He stumbled back, his knees so weak he almost couldn't hold himself.

Footsteps sounded behind him, but he couldn't take his eyes off Callie. She'd lost their baby, been through the absolute worst devastation, and he'd ignored her. He'd barely read her texts or listened to her voice messages because it had been too painful. *Stupid.*

Aspen moved past him, her arm going around Callie's shoulders. "I'm going to take you home."

Callie's eyes were red-rimmed, another tear spilling over her cheek as she nodded.

"No." He had no idea where the growl came from, but he

didn't want her to leave. He wanted her close. He had to fix this, dammit. "We need to talk about this."

He needed to make this right, even though he had no fucking idea how. He needed her to forgive him. He needed to erase the hurt and the anger and the grief even though a part of him knew that wasn't possible.

Aspen's voice firmed. "I'm taking her home, Lock."

She turned Callie away, but he grabbed her again. "I said no." He was losing his fucking mind, and he had no idea how to regain it.

He stepped closer, but suddenly fingers wrapped around his elbow. Nylah's fingers. Then his sister's soft voice. "Let her go, Lock."

He turned his head to see all four of his brothers and Liam behind him.

Jace stepped forward, giving a solemn nod. "There'll be other days to talk."

Lock didn't want to let her go. He didn't even feel capable. But bit by bit, he forced his muscles to ease. For his fingers to unwrap from her arm. Then he had to watch her walk away from him. The woman he loved. The woman he ached for. The woman he'd left to suffer alone.

CHAPTER 12

*L*ock hammered a nail into the wood, throwing so much force into it that the deck shook.

Pregnant. She'd been *pregnant*. And he hadn't known. He hadn't been here.

Memories of her calls slipped into his mind. Of her name coming up on his phone screen. And of him shoving the phone back into his pocket every time she called.

Fuck, he hated himself. Everything hurt so much damn much. But did he even have the *right* to hurt? He'd made everything worse because he hadn't handled the situation the way he should have two years ago.

Anger flared throughout his limbs, and before he could think better of it, he punched the deck. Pain laced up his arm. It wasn't enough though.

"Fuck."

He dropped the hammer and rose, running his fingers through his hair and looking up at the sky, as if that would give him what he was searching for. But he didn't even *know* what he was searching for. Redemption? Peace? Some way of turning back the clock and changing things?

He sat on the steps and dropped his head into his hands just as a car engine sounded. He looked up to see Cody's car. But it wasn't Cody who climbed out. It was Nylah. Her blue eyes pierced his. She didn't say anything as she walked up the steps and lowered beside him.

For a moment they both just sat there, a heaviness in their silence.

"Remember when we were little, and I broke my arm?"

He frowned. Whatever he'd thought she was about to say, it wasn't that. "Yeah. You broke it at the river."

"Yep. We were using that old rope to jump in. But when it was my turn, my fingers slipped. I put my arm out to catch myself, and when I landed, I knew something was wrong." She shook her head. "I was a mess. Screaming. Crying. You, Cody, and Kayden got me home, but boy was Mom mad."

"She rushed you to the hospital and barely said a word to us."

"And you interpreted that as her blaming you, even though you were just a kid."

"We all blamed ourselves." Lock and his brothers had always been protective of Nylah. As her brothers, they'd seen it as their job.

"Once we got home, do you remember what she said?"

"No."

"She told you that she was scared. And that when people are scared, they don't always say what they should have in the moment. And what she should have said was that sometimes, bad things just happen. And it's no one's fault. It's just...really crappy."

He did remember that. "You sound just like her. But why are you telling me this?"

"Because I suspect that she would say something very similar right now."

"This isn't a broken arm, Ny."

"You're right. It's something really big and really crappy that happened. And still, something that's no one's fault."

He shook his head. "I should have been there for her."

"You'd just found out Winnie and two women had been killed. You were scared."

"I was terrified, but that doesn't make it okay." He swallowed the lump in his throat. "Every day, we live a million little moments. So many of them aren't even worth remembering, yet one moment, one damn decision, changed everything for me."

"So go," Nylah whispered. "Talk to her."

"I tried. Aspen won't let me in. She wouldn't even open the door." He'd gone straight there from the party last night, then again this morning. He didn't even get a glimpse of Callie.

"Well, I may have heard that she's not with Aspen this morning. She's at her dad's."

Lock looked at his sister. "Who'd you hear that from?"

"Her dad's neighbor told Mrs. Burns at the grocery store, who just happened to be in front of Cody at the checkout." She lifted a shoulder. "Naturally, he called and told me to come talk to you. I, of course, was already on my way."

If the situation wasn't what it was, he'd laugh at that sequence of events. Like the universe needed him to know exactly where Callie was.

She nudged his shoulder. "Go to her. All you can do is try." She stood, and he rose with her, but before going to the car, she turned back to him and pulled him into a hug and whispered, "I'm sorry."

He closed his eyes and hugged her back, really hugged her, letting the weight of everything he'd lost two years ago bear down on him.

Emotion welled to the surface, and instead of pushing it down, he let it sit there. He let himself feel all of it. And it was as awful as he thought it would be.

When she pulled away, it was too soon. But the second she was gone, he climbed into his truck and drove as fast as it would take him to her father's house. He'd only been there a couple of times while they'd dated, but he remembered the way like he'd stopped by yesterday.

It wasn't until he was standing in front of the door, the wood staring at him, mocking him, that he remembered exactly when the last time was...the day he'd gotten back from that crucial Ghost Ops mission. Malone had been eliminated, and he was finally ready to tell Callie everything and get her back...only she hadn't been here.

He pounded the door with his fist, and when it opened, Jude Ward stood there. Callie's father looked older, with more lines around his eyes. More grays in his hair. But the same stern expression on his face.

The older man stared him down. "You've got some balls showing up here, son."

"Is she here?"

"Why would I tell you that?"

The muscles in his biceps flexed. "Because I love her. And I need to fix this." The words sounded hollow even to his own ears. Fix this? It wasn't something that *could* be fixed. It was trauma, a scar that would forever live within both of them.

"Haven't you hurt her enough?"

"I've hurt her too damn much. I'm not gonna lie and say I haven't. I own my actions. I thought I had a good reason for what I did, but now..."

"Now what?"

"Now, I would give anything to be able to do things differently. If I had that time again, I *would* do things differently. Please. Let me see her."

Jude looked at him so closely, Lock wondered what he was looking for. What could the older man see just by staring at him?

Finally, Jude's chest rose on a deep inhale. "She's in the unit out back."

Thank fuck. "Thank you."

"You make this right," Jude said before closing the door with a resounding slam.

Lock moved around the house.

Jude had an accessory dwelling unit on the back of his land. Lock should have guessed she was there, probably seeking solitude.

The second the little building came into view, his heart began to pound. It beat so hard that he could hear it, blocking out the rest of the world around him. When he stopped at the door, it took a moment to lift his fist and knock.

When no movement sounded, he called out to her. "Callie. It's me. Lock."

Then he waited, hoping like hell he had a shot at redemption.

* * *

CALLIE SHOT up in the bed, her pulse thumping, sweat coating her skin.

Another nightmare. This one so real it felt like she was there again. Back in her bed. Hurting. Lonely. Needing him. Only this time, the nightmare had twisted into something else. Lock *had* answered her call. And when she'd asked him to come, he'd said no. He'd reminded her that they were over. Then he'd hung up, the echoing click of the call ending still loud in her ears.

Jesus. She leaned forward, dropping her face into her hands, trying to catch her breath. Just needing one deep breath to wipe away the memory.

The scent of pine filled her nose, reminding her that she wasn't home, but rather in her father's rental cabin. It was one big room with a bed and a kitchen, with only the bathroom in a separate space. She'd originally gone home last night, but then Lock had shown up and she'd needed a night to clear her head. But it didn't feel like it worked.

He knew. Two years later, Lock finally knew.

She lifted her phone to see a dozen missed calls, all from Lock. She swallowed and clicked into the messages. Some from Aspen, but not all of them.

She looked at the messages from Lock.

Lock: I need to see you.

Lock: Please. We need to talk.

Lock: I need you to tell me where you are.

She clicked out and dropped the phone to the bed. She was just rising when the knock sounded at the door. Probably Dad. He'd been so worried about her when she'd shown up, cheeks stained with tears.

She took one step toward the door when the voice sounded.

"Callie. It's me. Lock."

Her feet ground to a halt, and she barely held in the gasp.

How had he known where she was? Did that even matter? He was here now. Of course he was here, they needed to talk. He deserved to hear everything that had happened.

"Callie. I need you to open the door."

Again, she stood there, hating that she was being a coward.

"I screwed up," Lock continued. "I screwed up so bad that there's no way to repair the damage. But I need to know you're okay. I need to know that at least *you're* still whole."

Whole? She hadn't felt whole for a long time.

Like her feet had a mind of their own, she moved toward the door but didn't open it. Instead, she clicked into the camera beside the door. And there he was, expression so sad, he almost looked lost.

He touched one hand to the wood before resting his forehead against the door. "Open the door, Callie. Please."

"I can't." The words were barely a whisper. So quiet that she didn't think he'd hear.

"You can. For me, honey."

His words had her eyes scrunching and her hand touching the wood on the other side of his.

When she didn't move to open the door, she expected him to leave. He didn't. Three entire minutes passed of them just standing there in silence, a couple inches of wood separating them, before he turned. But instead of walking away, he dropped to the ground and leaned against the door.

He wasn't going to go. He was going to wait for her.

She took a moment to suck in air. To summon that little bit of courage.

You can do this without breaking down, Callie. Talk to him.

Her mind still screamed at her to keep the door closed, but her heart was braver, urging her to open it and let him in.

Slowly, she unlatched the lock and pulled open the door.

Lock rose to his feet and turned, his gaze intense as he took her in. "Callie..."

"Come in."

Before he could respond, she turned and headed into the apartment. The door clicked closed, but she didn't turn, just went to the kitchen counter and got out the bag of coffee. Keeping busy felt better. Easier. A small distraction.

"That's what you were going to tell me that morning, wasn't it?"

She paused at his words before turning back to look at him. He was about five feet away, but it still felt too close. "Yes. I'd known for about a month, but I wanted to tell you in person. I was scared about how you'd take it. We'd only been dating a year, and even though I knew I loved you, and we were planning on living together, there was still fear because we'd never talked about kids."

His brows flickered. "When did you lose the baby?"

"Three weeks after you broke up with me. I was already asleep, and I woke up to..." She closed her eyes, the crack in her voice making her pause for a second before she looked at him again. "I woke up and I knew something was wrong. I called you, but when you didn't answer, I called Dad."

Pain twisted his features, and she almost wished she hadn't added that sentence. But God, she was tired of keeping it all inside her.

He stepped closer. "I wish I'd answered the call, Callie."

"Dad took me to the hospital. They called it 'early pregnancy loss.'" She shook her head, the words still feeling wrong in her head. "It didn't feel early. I'd known for almost two months by that point. It felt like I already knew this little person inside me."

His hands fisted. "How long were you in there for?"

"Only a night. It was when I got home that it really hit me… I'd gone from having you and expecting our child and having this vision of our future to losing absolutely everything. And the grief…God, it changed me. It changed the way I existed in the world. I don't know if that makes sense to you, but it does to me."

"Callie, I'm so damn sorry. I loved you so much, and I thought I was doing the right thing."

"I know that. But it's not about how much you love someone. It's about *how* you love them." If possible, his frown deepened. "I get why you did what you did, I really do. But it doesn't change anything. It doesn't change the fact that you weren't there, and I don't know how to…let that go."

"Then don't."

She frowned.

"Hold on to it. Remind me every day that I messed up, and that I need to do better. That I need to *be* better." He stepped closer again, this time cupping her cheek, and she couldn't pull away. "I *will* be better, Callie. For you, I will work every day to be the best version of myself."

He sounded like he meant it. And despite their past, despite the ache in her chest, she wanted to believe him. God, she wanted to believe him.

Callie pulled her car into her driveway and leaned back against the headrest.

Man, she was tired. She almost wanted to close her eyes right then and there. Screw the walk to her front door.

She'd spent the entire day in her studio teaching, working out, and deep cleaning the place...basically, doing anything and everything to keep busy after yesterday's talk with Lock.

But had it distracted her? That was a big freaking no.

She looked up at her house. It was her first night back here. She'd stayed one more night in her father's unit, telling herself she wasn't hiding, which she knew was a damn lie. But there was something about being close to her father when everything felt wrong that just made her feel safe.

But she couldn't hide out in his backyard forever. Besides, she missed Aspen. If there was anyone who could make her smile when smiling was the last thing she should be doing, it was her best friend, and man, did she want to smile.

As she was climbing out, a car down the street caught her eye. It was parked in front of the home of Mrs. Midson, an eighty-year-old recluse known for never having visitors.

Was there a person *in* the car? The windows were tinted, but...

Suddenly, the car lights turned on and it drove away.

Strange. A light chill skittered over her skin, and she walked quickly to her front door. Inside, she dropped her bag on the side table and stepped into the living room—only to stop.

"Aspen?"

Her friend sat on the couch wearing bright pink pajamas, with two tubs of ice cream on the coffee table and two spoons dug inside them. There were also containers of Chinese food and a neatly folded set of what looked to be more pajamas.

Aspen smiled. "Biscoff ice cream for you and chocolate brownie for me. Pajamas because comfort is a must. Chinese in case you feel like any sugar-free food, but that's not mandatory. And *Terminator 2* ready to go."

Callie's lips twitched. "That sounds awfully close to our breakup girls' night."

In fact, they'd had this exact evening eighteen months ago, when Aspen had broken up with her previous boyfriend, only it had been Callie on the couch ready and waiting for her friend.

"It's our whenever either of us has experienced a colossal kick in the gut."

"I kind of feel like I've been kicked in the chest too."

"Well, get your butt over here, woman."

Despite everything, Callie laughed as she crossed the room and lifted the pajamas. They were also bright pink, but with the word *Queen* underlined on the front. She dropped beside her friend. "Thank you."

Aspen lifted the Biscoff ice cream and handed it to her. "How are you doing?"

"Honestly, I'm not sure." She swirled the ice cream around. It was the perfect in-between state of frozen and melted. "Remember when I told you I saw a therapist after I left Misty Peak?"

"Yeah, you said she helped."

"She did…most of the time. But there was something she said that always stuck with me. She told me that instead of seeing our relationship as over, I should see it as complete." Callie shook her head. "But that never made sense to me, because the end of our relationship didn't *feel* complete. It felt messy and painful and…wrong."

Aspen tilted her head. "Maybe you always knew you'd find your way back to each other."

"I don't know. It hurt so much when he left."

"And now you're scared that if you take him back, you're vulnerable to him hurting you like that again."

"Yes." A thousand yeses.

"You *will* be vulnerable." Aspen gave a small smile. "But…you might also get everything you've ever wanted."

Her heart gave one of those giant kick-in-her-ribs thumps.

Could she? Could she and Lock finally have the future they'd once planned? "I don't know how to let go of the past."

Aspen leaned forward and lowered her voice. "You don't have to forget what happened. That will always be a part of you. You just have to decide whether or not to let it control your future."

"It's a risk."

"But don't the greatest risks have the greatest rewards?"

The corner of Callie's mouth lifted. "You want me to let him in."

"No. I want you to be happy. What you went through was heartbreaking, but before that, you *were* happy together. Happier than I'd ever seen you. I would give the world for you to have that again."

Callie pulled her friend into a hug. "Thank you. You've always been the best friend to me."

Aspen's arms wrapped around her. "Ditto." They separated and Aspen cocked her head. "Now, I need you to get your skinny butt into those queen pajamas so we can eat ice cream and watch Arnie kick some ass."

Callie chuckled, and God it felt good to laugh.

For the rest of the night, she ate way too much ice cream, followed by the Chinese—yes, dessert first. They watched the first two *Terminator* movies and belly laughed.

A few times during the night, Aspen's phone lit up, but every time Callie asked about it, her friend waved it off as nothing until she eventually switched her phone off completely.

Which was strange behavior.

The second movie had just finished when Callie turned to look at her friend. "How are you and Dylan doing?" There was a visible flinch from her friend, which made Callie straighten. "Is everything okay?"

One look at Aspen's face and she knew it wasn't. God, she'd been going on about her own problems all night and hadn't even realized Aspen had some of her own. Terrible. She was a terrible friend.

"Aspen, what is it?"

Her friend shook her head. "You're going through—"

"We've talked about my problems, now I want to talk about yours."

A heavy beat of silence passed. "We broke up."

Callie gasped. "Oh my God, what happened?"

"Nothing. We just...we had a fight the night of the party, and I broke up with him."

"The night of the party?" That was two nights ago. God, she felt like an ass. "What was the fight about?"

"Dylan..." She stopped and shook her head. "I don't want to talk about it right now. Not while you're in the middle of something so heavy."

"Aspen—"

"I'm fine. Dylan and I were never a great match, and it just took me a while to realize that."

"Still, you dated him for months. Are you sure you don't want to talk about it?"

Aspen laughed, but the sound was all wrong. "No. I definitely do not. But I *do* want to go to bed because I'm exhausted." She leaned over and kissed Callie on the cheek. "I hope you feel a bit better. And remember, I'm fine. Better than fine, actually, because I'm a single pringle again. Have a good night."

Her friend rose and headed to her room. Callie wanted to stop her. To ask a gazillion questions. But Aspen was an open book until there was something she didn't want to talk about, and then she closed up tight.

Maybe she just needed a bit of time to process.

With a sigh, Callie cleaned up their mess and went to her room. She was about to climb into bed when her phone vibrated with a text. Her pulse picked up speed when she saw who it was.

Lock: Can I see you tomorrow?

She bit down on her bottom lip, Aspen's words flicking back into her mind.

You might get everything you've ever wanted.

And she *did* want Lock. Even though she'd been fighting it. Even though their past was a mess. She loved him. Despite everything, that had never changed.

When a minute passed and she didn't text back, another message came through.

Lock: Please.

Callie: Maybe. Can I sleep on it?

Lock: The ball's in your court, Callie. I'll wait for your text. Have a good night, honey.

Honey...gah.

She dropped into bed, her head hitting the pillow with a thud. But when she closed her eyes, she didn't feel tired at all. Not even a little bit. Damn sugar overload.

Come on, Callie, sleep.

She squeezed her eyes closed and rolled to one side, then the other. Fifteen frustrating minutes later and she huffed before climbing out of bed.

Great. Now she had insomnia too.

Lifting her phone, she headed to the kitchen, where she grabbed a glass of water and downed it. Her gaze moved to her phone. She'd set it on the counter, but her fingers itched to pick it up again. Call him just so she could hear his voice.

She shouldn't. It was late. He was probably in bed.

She wrapped an arm around her waist as if that could somehow stop her.

Ten more seconds passed.

Screw it.

The phone only rang once before his gravelly voice sounded over the line. "Callie?"

"What would you do differently if you got a do-over?"

There was a pause. It stretched so long that, for a moment, she thought the line had cut out. Then he spoke. "I still would have temporarily broken up with you, but I would have *made sure* you knew it wasn't actually real. I would have made sure you knew I still loved you. I shouldn't have done what I did right after hearing about Winnie. I should have waited, calmed down, and figured things out."

She dropped her head, chin touching her chest. "You still wouldn't have been able to answer my call that night."

"I would have. Because if you knew what we were up against, then I would have known you'd only call if it was important. *Really* important. And I would have gone to you. Next time you need me, *I will* go to you."

She swallowed before opening her mouth…but before she could respond, a flash of movement in her backyard caught her attention.

Frowning, she turned to glance out the window. It was dark. Almost pitch black out there.

She was about to turn away when she saw it again.

Gasping loudly, she stumbled back a step.

"Callie? What's wrong?"

"Someone's in my backyard."

* * *

LOCK PRESSED his foot to the floor of his truck, but he wasn't moving fast enough, dammit.

Someone was in her *yard*. The same person who'd written her those creepy fucking notes? It had to be. And it meant they were escalating.

He should have stuck close to her. He should have camped out on her street and refused to leave.

When he finally reached her house, he slammed the truck into park and ran to the door. He was halfway across her lawn when another car pulled up in front of the house.

Eastern. Lock had called him the second he'd gotten off the phone with Callie.

He didn't wait for his brother, instead pounding his fist on the door. The couple of seconds he waited for her to open it felt like a damn lifetime. Then the door finally opened, and Callie stood there, hair down over her shoulders, pajamas on, and skin too pale.

He didn't care that they weren't together, that they had a past so complicated they weren't sure they'd ever find a way forward, he still stepped into her house and cupped her cheeks like she was his.

"Are you okay?"

"I'm okay. We both are."

Aspen came up behind Callie, squinting behind Lock. "You called Eastern?"

"Of course." Eastern didn't follow him inside, but then, Lock hadn't expected him to. "He'll check out the yard. Can I come in?"

Callie stepped back. His hands dropped, and all he wanted to do was touch her again.

The lights were on in the living room, mugs sitting on the kitchen island.

"I was making coffee for everyone to help keep us awake," Aspen said, arms wrapped around her waist. She cleared her throat. "I'll make another for Eastern."

"Thank you." Lock didn't take his eyes off Callie. All he'd been able to think about on the way here was, what if the asshole had gained access to her house? What if he was too late?

"It's not safe for you here," he said, barely keeping the growl out of his voice.

"They didn't get into the house. They didn't even try."

"If they *had* tried, it wouldn't have been hard to break a window."

"If they broke a window, the neighbors would hear, and someone would call the sheriff's office. Plus, with Aspen here, there's two of us."

Two untrained women against an unknown threat wasn't reassuring. "One minute. Maybe less. That's all someone needs to gain access and take you. Eastern or his deputies wouldn't have time to get here and save you." *He* wouldn't have time to get here and save her.

Her skin paled further.

Fuck. He didn't want to scare her, but he needed her to understand the situation. "Callie—"

The front door opened and Eastern stepped in, locking the door behind him before moving into the living room. "There's no one out there, but I did see some footprints in the flower bed by the back door. Large ones. Men's footprints."

Callie visibly tensed, and Lock slipped an arm around her waist, praying she didn't pull away.

She didn't.

Aspen handed everyone a coffee before Eastern continued.

"Did you get a good look at him?"

Callie shook her head. "It was dark. I just saw a shadow. My first thought was that it was a man, maybe because the shadow looked large. Tall. As soon as I got off the phone, I ran to wake Aspen, and by the time I got back, I couldn't see him anymore. I'm sorry."

Lock tightened his arm around her. "It's not your fault."

"Lock's right." Eastern took out a notepad and wrote something down before looking up. "You did the right thing in waking Aspen so you were both alert. Have you received any more notes?"

"Not since I made the report."

"Okay. This could be the same person. They have your address. They're interested in you. Their behavior could be escalating."

Lock's thoughts exactly.

Callie nibbled her bottom lip. "There was a car on the street when I got home."

He frowned. "A car?"

"Someone was in the driver's seat, but when I stopped and looked at them, they drove away."

What the fuck?

Aspen frowned, looking worried. "You didn't tell me that."

"I'm sorry. It slipped my mind once I got inside."

"Make? Model?" Eastern asked, remaining so much calmer than Lock.

"Um, it was blue, but I'm not sure of the make. Sorry. I didn't even think to notice." She scrubbed her face.

"Don't apologize," Eastern said. "A color is better than nothing."

Aspen cleared her throat. "Dylan drives a blue car."

Everyone looked her way, but it was Eastern who asked, "Who's Dylan?"

"My boyfriend. Or ex-boyfriend." She rubbed the back of her neck. "He, um, didn't take the breakup too well."

"What do you mean by that?" Eastern asked.

"I could just tell he wasn't happy."

"I'll need his details," he said.

While Aspen shared her ex's contact information, Lock lowered his head to Callie. "You're staying with me tonight."

She was shaking her head before he finished speaking. "No, I'm not leaving Aspen."

"She can come too."

"No."

"Yes. Callie—"

"I'm not being scared out of my home."

A muscle ticked in his jaw. Damn, she was stubborn. "You need more security on this house, and if you won't stay with me until you have it, then I'm staying here."

"Lock—"

"He's right, Callie," Aspen said, drawing their attention. "We'll be safer with him in the house. He can sleep on the couch."

Finally, someone seeing some fucking sense.

Callie sucked in a long breath before looking up at Lock.

Come on, honey. Trust me to look after you.

"Okay."

The air rushed from Lock's chest.

"You can stay on the couch. Thank you."

It was a step in the right direction. Hopefully one of many.

CHAPTER 14

"That brings us to the end of our class. You're welcome to stay and do some more stretches if you need, but otherwise, have a great day."

Callie smiled as she watched everyone put their shoes back on and pack up after the yoga session.

She loved her job. Massive could-do-it-every-day-and-not-get-sick-of-it kind of love.

Yoga and Pilates had always been passions of hers, and being able to share those passions with others gave her purpose. And today…today it also gave her the perfect distraction from everything else happening in her life. In fact, over the last three hours, she'd almost forgotten that she'd barely slept last night. And *not* because she'd seen someone prowling in her backyard. No, that's what would keep a normal person awake.

She couldn't sleep because Lock had slept on her couch, a mere few feet from her bedroom.

Then she'd woken to see his perfect chiseled chest when he was shirtless in her kitchen, making pancakes. Freaking pancakes! Oh, and bacon, because you can't be a perfect ex-boyfriend without also making bacon.

The guy knew she was a sucker for a good breakfast.

Gah.

She stepped behind the desk and waved goodbye to two women as they stepped outside.

At least some more security was being installed at the house today. An alarm and a camera that would feed to her phone. If some asshole was watching the house at night, what was their end game? To gain entry or just watch them? *Could* it have been Dylan?

She still hadn't told her father. He'd done a class earlier that day, and she hadn't said a word about it. She was going to put that conversation off for as long as possible.

"Hey. How are you?"

Her gaze shot up to Hamish. She hadn't spoken to him since the party. "Hi, I'm good." Well, she was kind of good, but Hamish didn't need her messy my-ex-slept-on-my-couch story. "You did great today."

"Thanks. I have a great t-teacher."

"Great? I'm not sure about that. Tired though? Absolutely, but you can probably see that from the bags under my eyes."

"You always look beautiful."

She swallowed, not sure what to do with that comment. Was it appropriate for a male client to call her beautiful? Was she overthinking everything because of Aspen's comments about him being into her? "Thanks."

"I, um, was w-wondering..." His gaze lowered to the floor, and Callie got an uncomfortable pit in her belly at what was about to come. "Would you...I mean, if y-you're free...I would love to, uh, have d-dinner with you some time."

Okay. Maybe Aspen had been onto something. Crap. "Hamish, that's sweet of you to ask, but I'm not really in the headspace to date anyone right now."

It was kind of true. She hadn't really been in the headspace to date anyone for years.

Hamish's face fell, and she suddenly felt like the worst human on earth.

"Th-that's okay. I sh-shouldn't have asked. Sorry."

"Hamish—"

But he was already hurrying out the door.

Oh, man. She hated upsetting people. Especially kind people like Hamish. But was there a way of turning down a date that *wouldn't* have upset him?

Hamish had only taken a few steps when two guys stopped in front of him on the sidewalk.

She frowned. The brunette...he looked familiar. Where had she seen him before?

A cocky grin spread across his face, and suddenly it hit her. The bar. It was the guy who'd grabbed her while she was dancing at Meridian. The same guy Lock had hit in the face.

The guy shoved Hamish in the shoulder.

Callie straightened. What the hell?

Hamish shoved him back, and he shoved Hamish a second time, but harder.

Assholes.

Callie ran outside and stepped in front of Hamish. "What the hell are you doing?"

The guy's brows rose, surprise flickering through his eyes. "Hey. You're the girl from the bar. The one with that alpha-dick boyfriend."

"Apologize to Hamish."

"Why? This another boyfriend of yours? He gonna hit me too?"

Asshole number two scoffed. "He could try."

The first guy's cocky grin widened before he stepped forward and touched her hip. "If I recall correctly, we had some unfinished business."

"Leave her alone," Hamish said, stepping forward.

Callie shoved at the guy's chest, but he didn't budge. "You have two seconds to drop your hands."

"Or what? You hurt me with your pretty face?"

"Or I kick you in the balls."

He held her gaze for one more beat before laughing and stepping back. "Luckily for you, I have somewhere to be."

The other guy shoved Hamish, who stumbled a second time as the two men walked away.

Jesus, why were they such dicks? She turned and touched Hamish's arm. "Are you okay?"

"Y-yes. Are you?"

"I'm fine."

Hamish scrubbed a hand over his face, bumping his glasses. "I'm sorry."

"Hey, it's not your fault they're jerks."

"But I should have..." He shook his head, red tingeing his cheeks.

He was embarrassed. He shouldn't be. "Hamish, they're bullies. You don't need to—"

"I should go. I'll see you next time, Callie."

For the second time that afternoon, he walked away before she could think of anything to say to make him feel better. And now she felt double guilty, even though she had no idea what she could have done differently.

Running her fingers through her hair, she realized she was trembling. Even though she'd played it tough, the guy had shaken her. If it wasn't broad daylight with people around, would he have done more than just touch her?

Argh, she hated that she was affected by those lowlifes.

She stepped back inside and moved to the desk. Lifting her laptop, she then took it to the back room, where she set it on the table before making coffee. Maybe some admin work would make her calmer.

Once her drink was ready, she sat at the small table and went through her emails. She was taking a sip of coffee when she saw an email from an unknown sender, untitled.

Frowning, she clicked into it.

He's not good enough for you. He's never been good enough for you.

She shot back from her computer like it was a bomb about to detonate.

He was sending her emails now? And about *Lock*? Because it had to be about Lock.

"What the fuck?"

She jolted at the voice, her coffee sloshing over the edge, sending boiling-hot liquid spilling over her hand.

* * *

Fuck.

Callie gasped again and Lock shot forward, taking the mug from her hand. Without a word, he led her to the sink and ran cold water over her skin.

He wanted to kick his own ass. What was wrong with him, scaring her while she was holding a cup of coffee?

"I'm sorry." The words came out through gritted teeth.

She shook her head. "It's not your fault. I'm jumpy."

It *was* his damn fault. He'd reacted without thinking.

He skimmed his fingers over her delicate skin, hating the redness on her hand. "Did you just get that email?"

"Yeah. He's never emailed me before."

"It's your work address?"

"Yes."

So, available to the public. Still, her home address wasn't, and he'd found that.

Lock's muscles tightened at the reminder, but he was careful to keep his features neutral. "I'm sorry I was late." He'd driven her to work and told her he'd be here to pick her up, but his last job had run longer than he'd thought it would.

"It's okay."

Their gazes met, and he got caught in the green of her eyes. The way it reminded him of the grass in spring, when it was that vibrant color after plenty of rain.

"You're so beautiful."

Her eyes widened, and yeah, maybe he shouldn't have said it. But his intentions had always been clear—he wanted her back.

"Lock…" Her mouth opened and closed, like she couldn't get the next words out.

The action drew his gaze to her lips. Her very full peachy-red lips. "The need to kiss you is killing me." It was fucking torment.

This wasn't the right time…but was there really ever a *wrong* time to kiss the woman he loved?

Her breathing caught, her chest pausing on its rise. "If you do…I don't know if I'll have the strength to pull away again."

His chest contracted, the hand on her wrist sliding down to her waist. He lowered his head, time almost slowing in that fraction of a second.

Then his mouth covered hers, her sweet lips welcoming him.

When he kissed her, it almost felt like something returned to him. Something he'd lost long ago. A part of himself, maybe. A little bit of sanity.

His hand slid up her waist. She gasped, and he slipped his tongue into her mouth, tangling with hers while palming her.

She groaned, and the sound threaded itself inside him, like a song composed just for him.

"God, I've missed you," he growled, turning to push her to the wall, pressing his body into hers so her soft pressed to his hard.

Her leg lifted, slipping around his waist, drawing him closer. And the feel of her against him…God, it was breathtaking. Made time stand fucking still.

They were made for each other. No matter what had happened in their pasts, what damage he'd caused, they would always belong together.

He spun them and lifted her to the edge of the kitchen counter before stepping between her thighs, hands on her knees. Every inch of her made him want to explore more. Touch and taste.

He was just sliding his palms up her thighs, when the ringing of a phone sounded…*his* phone.

"I'm ignoring it," he whispered against her lips.

But her body stiffened, and it was as if the call pulled her out of the fog and back to reality.

Goddammit.

Her hands slid out from beneath his shirt and pressed to his chest. He bit back a growl as he forced his mouth back from hers. It took him two breaths to look up at her.

"You should answer that," she whispered.

It was the last damn thing he wanted to do.

With a click of his jaw, he gripped her hips and lifted her down from the counter. "This isn't over."

Her eyes flared.

He turned and moved back into the studio room and took out his phone.

Antwan. Well, fuck. He couldn't be mad at his friend.

He waited one more second to get his breathing back to normal and then answered the call. "Hey."

"Lock…did I catch you at a bad time?"

The worst fucking time possible, but it wasn't like he could tell him that. "No such thing. You doing okay?"

His friend took a few deep breaths. "I just needed to talk to someone who understood."

Lock straightened. "What's wrong?"

"I'm struggling. Being here, in our old apartment, without her…it's harder than I thought it would be."

Lock ran his fingers through his hair. He was talking about Hollie. Antwan had kept the lease on their apartment because he couldn't give it up. But now that he'd been discharged and had moved back there, he probably couldn't handle the memories.

If the team hadn't already killed Malone, Lock would have hunted him down and killed him a second time. "What can I do?"

"I don't know. Talk to me?"

"I'll do you one better. You still coming to visit with Jesse?"

"Yeah, flights are booked for the week after next."

"Pack a bigger bag."

There was a pause. "What?"

"Stay in Misty Peak longer. Hell, stay a year. Being in the same town where you lived with Hollie can't be helping anything."

Lock's phone vibrated with a text, but he ignored it as he waited for his friend to respond.

"You sure that's okay?"

"Hell yeah, I am. I've got four bedrooms and I'm only using one, so there's plenty of space." In fact, his house felt pretty damn empty right now.

"Okay. Thanks. I'll see you soon."

Lock hung up to see a text from a local asking him to patch a hole in a wall. He was about to respond when Callie's voice sounded.

"Did I hear right? Was that Antwan?"

Lock turned to see Callie's lips still red from his kiss. Fuck, that made him want to kiss her all over again. He clenched his fists to stop himself from grabbing her. "Yeah. He and Jesse are visiting in a couple weeks. Antwan might stay for a while."

Callie's brows shot up. She'd spent time with his team when she'd visited their base between missions. She knew all the guys.

"That's great. It will be good to see them again."

He stepped closer. "You know I'm sleeping on your couch again tonight, right?"

She shook her head. "The extra security should be in and—"

He touched her hip. "Please...one more night."

She nibbled her bottom lip. "Fine. On one condition."

"Anything." He'd give this woman everything he owned if she asked.

"No more kisses…for now. Let's just be friends for a while, like you suggested at the party."

Could he do that? "That will be hard."

"I know. I just…I want to go slow."

Slow…that meant they were going forward. Hope lit his chest. "Slow it is."

CHAPTER 15

*L*ock stepped back. Done. He'd spent the better part of the day installing a new window in Hamish's living room. A window Hamish had ordered a while ago but never installed. The crack in the glass of the old one had apparently been there for almost a year. Usually just the glass could be replaced, but the wood had also been rotting, so he'd wanted the entire thing changed.

Lock was outside, having just finished the last of it.

His phone vibrated in his pocket, and he pulled it out to see a text.

Antwan: You better be excited to see my pretty face because I just started packing my shit. See you in a week.

Lock smiled. He was looking forward to seeing the guys. He just wished his entire team could make it. They'd gone from seeing each other every day to being too damn far from each other, but Lock was counting on seeing them soon.

Lock: Don't know which pretty face you're talking about, but I'll get the spare rooms ready.

Antwan: You can't have forgotten. You only looked at it every day for the last ten years. Try not to fangirl when you see me.

His lips twitched. Antwan joking around was a good sign.

He shoved his cell back into his pocket as footsteps sounded behind him.

"You're finished."

Lock turned to see Hamish. "I am. Was a pretty bad break in the glass. How'd it happen?"

A flash of anger passed over Hamish's face, but it was gone as quickly as it came. "Some jerks threw a r-rock at it."

The *fuck*? "Who?"

"Doesn't matter."

"Of course it matters. Did you tell Eastern?"

Hamish shook his head before pushing his glasses up his nose. "Can I ask you s-something?"

"Shoot."

"What does it feel like?"

Lock frowned. "What does what feel like?"

"B-being you."

Okay, now Lock was really fucking lost. "I've really got nothing to compare it to. Why are you asking?"

"People don't mess with you b-because you're strong and tough. W-women trust you to keep them safe. I'm not like that."

Lock stepped forward. "Hamish. What's going on?"

"I..." He shook his head. "Nothing. Life's just kicking my ass at the m-moment. Send me the bill for the window, okay?" He turned and headed toward his front door, but before he made it inside, Lock called out to him.

"Hamish." He looked at Lock over his shoulder. "We all have our rough patches. You're doing good."

His brows flickered, and he looked like he wanted to say something. But he just dipped his chin. "Thanks." Then he stepped inside.

Poor guy. It seemed like everyone was having a tough time right now.

Lock blew out a breath as he packed up his tools. He'd just climbed into the truck when he cursed at the time.

Shit. He was late to pick Callie up and take her home. Again. And he still needed to drop by Mrs. Agar's place and fix her lock. It would only take him twenty minutes, but he wanted to get to Callie. At least she wasn't alone. She'd texted that her dad was staying for pizza after the last Pilates session.

He drove faster than he should have and ended up fixing Mrs. Agar's lock in half the time.

When he reached the studio, he parked on the opposite side of the road. He was about to climb out of his truck when something in the rearview mirror caught his attention. Or, less something as some*one.*

Was that…was that a fucking person standing at the mouth of the alley? Were they watching the studio? There were shadows over the person's face, so Lock couldn't make out features, but he was tall. Definitely a man.

The veins in Lock's forearms pulsed. He shot one glance at the studio window. The lights were on, but he couldn't see anyone inside. Her father's Chevy was out front though. They were likely in the back room.

Instead of heading toward the studio, he walked the sidewalk toward the alley, keeping his head down and hands in his pockets. He tried to keep his body language casual so it wasn't obvious what he was doing. But if the guy was watching Callie, he'd recognize Lock—and he'd probably run.

Like he'd read Lock's mind, the man suddenly turned and disappeared into the alley.

Fuck.

Lock ran, his feet pounding against the concrete and following the guy into the alley. The asshole was fast. Just as fast as Lock.

Dammit, he wasn't closing the distance.

The closed gate at the end of the alley would hopefully slow him down. It was high and would be hard to climb.

The guy reached it—and Lock watched as he climbed and jumped over to the other side in one fluid move, like he'd done it a thousand times before.

Who the fuck *was* this guy?

The guy exited the alley, turning right.

Lock sped up and jumped the gate. He followed him onto the street…only to stop.

He was gone. Where? There were a few cars on the road, some parked, some moving. He could be in or hiding behind any of them. There were also a couple of businesses still open.

Lock's chest heaved, air rushing in and out of his lungs. He wanted to keep going. To scour the streets, searching every car and business to find the asshole.

But he also didn't want to be away from Callie for too long.

Gritting his teeth, Lock jogged down the street, going the same way the guy did, circling back to Callie's studio.

Still nothing. He was gone.

There was a chance the guy had nothing to do with Callie or the notes she was receiving. That he was just a lurker who'd run scared at the sight of Lock.

But the guy hadn't moved like some random person who'd run scared. He was too fast. Too agile. And no part of Lock wanted a guy like that close to Callie.

* * *

CALLIE LAUGHED at something her father said.

It felt good to spend time with her dad and think of something other than Lock.

He'd spent the last week sleeping on her couch while she pretended to be unaffected by the sight of his muscled chest. By the day-old stubble on his face each morning that she itched to run her fingers over. Hell, even the scent of him in her house was driving her wild.

She was pretty sure she'd done a terrible job at the pretending-to-be-unaffected part. He might even have caught her staring once or twice.

Great. It was just great.

"She told you she was going to put a camera on your house?" Callie asked. Her dad had a wacky neighbor. It wasn't the normal level of crazy. It was the door-knocking-at-six-a.m., daily-empty-threats, and death-stares-from-the-living-room-window kind of crazy.

"Not on my house," her dad pressed, "*in* my house."

"What?"

Her father nodded. "Apparently, I would never find it, but she'd always be watching just to make sure I wasn't plotting to take one of her ten cats."

"What did you say?"

"I told her she'd never find the devious plans that I'd printed and hidden in the house."

Callie threw back her head and laughed. A big belly laugh. She could just imagine the older woman's reaction. Not only was she unhinged but she couldn't take a joke to save her life. "Maybe you need to move. I'm a bit worried about your safety."

"That woman's all empty threats."

It was true. She was about ninety years old and probably going senile.

Her father leaned back. "I'm full. Ordering pizza was a great idea."

"Well, I'm on strict instructions from Lock to stay here until he comes to get me, and I couldn't think of a better way to spend my time than eating pizza with my favorite person."

The second she brought up her safety, she regretted it. She'd told her father about the notes and the person in her yard, and of course he was worried.

The laughter cleared from his face, replaced with concern. "Are you safe?"

"Lock's been sleeping on my couch. I couldn't be safer."

"Good. You tell me if that changes."

She'd actually do everything she could *not* to, but she nodded anyway.

Her father cleared his throat. "I'm actually glad you called. There's something I've been meaning to talk to you about."

Callie's belly gave a little dip, even though she wasn't sure why. "What about?"

"I want to sign my properties over to you."

And there it was, the crash back to reality. The reminder that her father was sick. That there was no cure. That even though they could sit here, eat pizza and laugh while they pretended everything was fine, it wasn't.

"Dad, we don't need to talk about this right now."

"We do. I know this is hard for you, but we can't dance around the fact that I have a neuro-degenerative disorder, and it's going to get worse."

Her chest squeezed.

"My properties were always going to go to you anyway. My diagnosis has just…fast-tracked things." He reached down and lifted a folder he'd walked in with that she intentionally hadn't asked about. "I asked my lawyer to prepare everything. All you need to do is sign." When he held it out to her, there was a shake in his hand. Another reminder of the ugly disease.

She didn't move to take it. It felt like she couldn't. She didn't *want* his properties to be signed over to her. They were his. They would always be his.

He leaned forward and gently took her hand to place the documents in her palm. "Please, Callie. I love you. I need to make sure everything's in order before—"

"Dad, stop. Parkinson's itself isn't fatal. You could live ten, fifteen, twenty years or more with the disease."

"Callie—"

A distant knock sounded from the other room, and she blinked away the tears before standing and moving to the studio area to see Lock outside.

She set the folder on the desk while her dad opened the door. "Hi, son."

Lock dipped his head as he stepped inside, his jaw visibly tight and hair windswept.

Something was wrong.

Lock gave her a once-over before looking back to her father. "It's good to see you here looking after your daughter, Jude. Thank you."

"No, it's Callie who looks after me." Her dad turned toward her. "I'll see you next time, sweetheart." He leaned down and kissed her cheek.

The second the door closed after him, she sucked in a breath and looked up at Lock. "What's going on?"

He opened his mouth like he was about to tell her something, only to stop and frown. He studied her face, making her want to turn away and hide.

"What's wrong?" he finally asked.

"Nothing." A lie if she'd ever told one.

Before he could ask anything else, she headed into the back room. Making sure to keep her back toward Lock, she closed the pizza-box lid. "There's half a pizza left if you want it."

"Callie—"

"My dad barely ate anything. I, however, ate far too much."

"Callie, stop."

She grabbed a cloth from the sink and wiped the table. "We should get out of here before it gets too late. It's already getting dark and—"

Strong, warm arms wrapped around her waist, halting her, making her drop the cloth to the table. His mouth moved to her ear as he gently whispered, "What's wrong?"

Her chest moved quickly, grief tugging at her heart. "He was shaking."

There was a small pause. "Your dad?"

"Yes. He was shaking. And even though I told him he could live twenty years or more, the reality is, the complications from Parkinson's can be fatal. People fall because of mobility issues. They get infections they can't fight. And it makes me think that I can't hold on to people. I can't save anyone I love. I can't—"

She was turned and pulled against him.

Five seconds. That's how long she held it together before the tears began and she let herself fall apart, knowing Lock would save all the pieces. Trusting him to put her back together later. He held her so tightly she felt safe. He was warm and familiar, and right now, he was the only thing keeping her on her feet.

He didn't say anything, just let her cry for the losses she'd already experienced and the losses that were still to come.

She wasn't sure how many minutes ticked by before she finally stopped. God, his top was drenched with tears—again—and her eyes had to be puffy. When she looked up at him, it was to see concern in his eyes.

He didn't ask if she was okay though. He knew she wasn't. Instead, he said three healing words. "I've got you."

How did he know exactly what to say?

"I know you do. Thank you." She shook her head. "I've got to stop falling apart on you."

"No, you don't. I'll hold you whenever and for as long as you need." He swiped a tear from her cheek.

Too sweet. He was too sweet.

Pull yourself together, Callie.

She pushed her hair back from her cheek. "What was wrong when you walked in here?"

His gaze shifted between her eyes. "It can wait. Right now, I just need to know you're okay."

CHAPTER 16

Callie climbed out of the car, the fresh air brushing over her skin as she faced the mountains.

Man, they were beautiful. The kind of beautiful that sucked up all your worries. Or at least tabled them for later.

Aspen climbed out from behind the wheel. "Beautiful, aren't they?"

This was why they were best friends, because they read each other's freaking minds. "Gorgeous."

Her best friend had picked her up from work to take her to the Misty Peak Visitors Center so they could do a quick trek in the mountains. It was mostly for Aspen, who claimed she needed inspiration for her book, but Callie was pretty sure the breakup with Dylan was weighing on her more than she was sharing.

When Callie had told Lock about her plans, he'd reminded her that two of his brothers, Kayden and Jace, both worked here, in case they ran into trouble. They wouldn't. Or at least, she hoped they wouldn't.

Aspen rounded the car and linked her arm through Callie's as they headed toward the café. "So…he's really leaving?"

"Why do you say that like you can't believe it?"

"Because he's been sleeping on our couch for over a week. Playing protector super well. Plus, he's been making us breakfast and coffee every morning, so if I got a vote, it would be for him to stay. Why don't I get a vote?"

"Because he's not your ex."

"Pfft. Small detail."

Callie sighed. "I know it's been good having him there…for safety."

Aspen scoffed.

"I haven't received any more notes, and no one's shown up in our yard since. He can't stay there forever."

"What about that guy in the alley?"

Callie tried not to tense. Lock had told her about that a day later. She understood why he hadn't shared right away, and there might be a tiny part of her that wished he hadn't told her at all. But that was silly. If someone was in a freaking alley watching her, she needed to know.

"We don't know that he was watching me. If you saw someone who looked like Lock heading toward you, you'd run too."

"Uh, but I can't scale a fence like he did."

"We have great security on the house now." A new alarm. New locks. Their house was like Fort Knox…well, kind of.

Aspen cocked her head. "You think some random was just hanging out in the shadows of an alley near your studio and when they saw Lock, they thought they'd run even though they had nothing to hide?"

Okay. It was a far-fetched theory. "I just need a little bit of space from him."

"Now we're getting to the truth. And now you can tell me why. Neither of you have any secrets anymore. He's been there for you a hundred percent since he found out about the pregnancy loss. And he loves you."

Callie's breath caught as they stopped in front of the café

door, not stepping inside yet. Love...God, it felt so big. "Honestly, I'm not sure why I'm still hesitant. Maybe because I've spent so long thinking he broke my heart for no good reason, and it's hard to believe my heart's now safe with him." She needed more time. How *much* time, she wasn't sure.

Understanding crossed Aspen's features. And something else. Something Callie couldn't quite place.

"I understand being hurt and struggling to trust," Aspen finally said. "Hopefully you can learn to trust again." There was almost a sadness to her tone.

Callie opened her mouth, but before she could ask about it, her friend entered the café.

Elle smiled at them from behind the counter as they approached. "Callie. Aspen. Hey."

"Hi," Aspen greeted her.

Callie smiled. "Hi, Elle."

"What can I get you ladies?"

"I would love a double shot mocha latte in a to-go cup," Aspen said.

"I'm not that fancy." Callie laughed. "I'll just have a regular latte."

"You got it." Elle turned to the espresso machine.

"How're things with Jace?" Callie asked. Elle was dating Lock's youngest brother. Apparently, they'd been best friends in high school but hadn't dated until recently.

Elle turned her head, a smile on her face. "We're great. You'd probably assume we bicker less since dating, but I've found out that's not the case. The bickering has possibly increased actually. Luckily, he makes me laugh."

Callie chuckled.

"I need to get to another yoga class," Elle added.

"Anytime."

"I did Pilates this morning." Aspen shook her head. "I don't know how I'm still walking."

"That's why I like yoga," Elle said. "On another note, Dylan was here the other day. Ordered a few coffees and sandwiches."

Aspen tensed.

Eastern had questioned Dylan about the night they'd seen someone in their yard. He had an alibi. The fact Aspen thought it might be him was a red flag though. Because you'd only suspect someone was stalking you if they'd shown some warning signs already, right?

"We're not together anymore," Aspen said quickly.

Elle's brows shot up. "Oh. I'm so sorry. I shouldn't have—"

"It's fine."

Once the coffees were ready, they paid and thanked Elle before stepping outside.

Callie waited until they were on a path before bringing it up. "Is there anything you haven't told me about your breakup with Dylan? I know you said you just realized he wasn't the right guy for you, but was there something that tipped you off?"

Aspen sipped her coffee, gaze on the path in front of them.

Stalling. Aspen was stalling. She never did that.

"He just turned into kind of an asshole," Aspen finally said vaguely.

Callie frowned. "An asshole how?"

"He just..." She shook her head. "He wasn't the guy I thought he was, and he certainly wasn't the guy for me. Sorry, can we talk about something else? I don't like thinking about him."

There was more her friend wasn't telling her...and they usually told each other everything. What made this situation different?

"Okay, but you know you can tell me anything, don't you?" Callie asked softly. "I'm always here to listen."

Aspen gave a jerky nod. "I know."

They were just coming up to a bend in the path when voices sounded up ahead. Men's voices.

"He's moving back into his place today."

Was that Lock's brother, Kayden?

"They'll sort things out. He bought a damn *house* for her, for God's sake. One that she apparently chose."

And Jace. Who were they talking about?

"Yeah. I've never known Lock to be one for big romantic gestures, but obviously Callie changed him. To buy a house for her, keep it for two damn years when he didn't even know if he'd ever see her again, then fix it up…that's love."

Callie's steps faltered. Lock had bought her a *house*?

The men rounded the bend—abruptly stopping right in front of her.

Jace's eyes widened. "Callie."

"He bought our house?" she whispered.

* * *

LOCK HAMMERED the last nail into the railing.

Finished. The deck was finally finished, and the inside of the house was almost there too. He was just waiting on the new oven, which was being delivered later this week, and then he'd have a fully renovated house.

He stepped back and looked up, the phone conversation from that day more than two years ago flicking back to him. Toying with him.

"This is it."

Lock laughed, phone pressed to his ear as he looked over the online ad for the place. She couldn't be serious. "It's a dump, Callie."

"Our dump. I went to look at it with Dad over the weekend, and he thinks it has potential."

Yeah, potential to be knocked down. Because that was exactly what whatever unlucky bastard who bought it would do.

"I can hear you thinking, Lock."

"You can't hear thoughts over the phone."

"I can hear yours. You're thinking it needs to be knocked down. But

what you forget is, you are amazing with your hands. All those summers spent with your uncle out of state. You learned how to make any old pile of wood into a home, and you can do that to this one."

"It would be a huge venture."

"But after the venture, it would become our home." There was an almost whimsical note to her voice. Maybe because she knew what he knew. That their future was already locked in, even though they weren't engaged. They had no kids. But they both knew they were it for each other.

"Lock...I felt something when I walked inside. It was like I knew this house was ours."

Fuck...how was he supposed to say no to that? Hell, she hadn't even needed to say it. He would buy this house for her simply because she wanted it. Simply because she asked. "I'll contact the real estate agent."

"Really?"

"Yeah." Didn't she know he'd do anything for her?

She made an excited high-pitched sound. "Thank you."

"I love you, Callie."

"I love you more."

"Not possible."

Lock's chest contracted as he forced the memory away. How often had he remembered that conversation? Sometimes it made him smile. Other times it dragged him so deep into his grief and loss that he had to push it down. Forget about it just for a little while.

Six weeks after that call, Hollie had been killed. Then Winnie and Remi. And just after that, he'd lost Callie. And with her, he'd lost a huge part of himself.

He was just taking his tool belt off his waist when a car engine sounded behind him. He turned to see Callie in her blue Kia, pulling into the driveway.

What the hell? How did she know he was here?

When she climbed out, she didn't say anything. Not immediately. Hell, she barely looked at him at first. She scanned the front of the house, her chest rising and falling with fast breaths, eyes wide with disbelief before landing on Lock.

"It's true," she whispered. "You bought our house."

He dropped the tool belt to the ground and stepped toward her. "How did you—"

"Kayden and Jace. I overheard them talking about it." Tears filled her eyes. "When?"

"The same day you told me you wanted it. Called the agent the second we hung up."

Her chest moved faster. "You didn't sell it when I left. Why?"

"Because it was always supposed to be you and me. Even when I couldn't find you, I had faith that we would work our way back to each other. That it was always going to be us in the end."

A tear rolled down her cheek.

He took another step forward. "I screwed up. I should have found a way to tell you the truth. I should have found a way to be there for you when you needed me."

"I should have stayed," she whispered. "But it hurt, Lock. Losing you hurt so much, then losing him… I didn't know how to deal with the pain. And I guess, a part of me wanted to blame you and us and our love, because it was easier. And holding on to that blame…it felt safe. Safer than admitting that something really awful happened for no reason. Safer than saying out loud that such painful things can happen, and no one can tell you why."

"Callie—"

"Hiding from you, from us, protected me for a while…but I can't hide anymore, Lock. I love you."

The house, the mountains, it all faded beneath her words repeating in his head, rolling around, pushing everything else aside. "You love me?"

"I've *always* loved you. I'm sorry I ran."

He closed the distance between them and cupped her cheek. "It's you and me, Callie. It's always been you and me."

Then his mouth crashed to hers.

CHAPTER 17

Everywhere...Lock was everywhere. Against her lips. Pressed to her body. It was intoxicating. And it was also everything she'd craved for so long.

She buried her fingers in his hair, the strands soft.

God, how did this man still feel like home after two years apart?

"Lock." She breathed his name. It sounded important and intimate and right on her lips.

He slipped his tongue into her mouth, sweeping it against hers. He tasted of spices and mint.

She slid a hand beneath his shirt, then up, running her fingers over all the hard ridges of his body. Every inch of him was pure muscle.

A growl rumbled from his throat and he lifted her. Immediately, she wrapped her legs around his waist, still not quite feeling close enough, always wanting to be closer.

Air shifted around her as Lock moved, carrying her up the steps and inside the house like she weighed nothing. Like carrying her was the easiest thing in the world.

The soft thud of the door closing sounded, then he was

moving again, only stopping once inside the bedroom to press her to a wall. His mouth moved down her neck, making awareness spiral throughout her limbs and a deep ache throb in her lower belly.

She opened her eyes, but everything was a blur. The room. The walls. She couldn't focus on anything but Lock. On the sweep of his lips against her skin. The thick cords of muscle in his shoulders.

He tugged her top over her head, and she pulled his off just as quickly.

Desperate…they were desperate for each other.

Her breath caught at the sight of his chest. So big and powerful, just like she remembered.

She grazed her fingers down his skin, onto his flat stomach, pausing on a small scar. "This is new."

His mouth returned to her neck, nipping and sucking. "Training. Antwan caught me with a knife."

His head lowered, his hands moving behind her back and unclasping her bra. There was the soft sound of it hitting the floor before Lock made a low, sexy moan as his gaze moved over her breasts.

"I've missed these. I've missed *all* of you."

She couldn't even feel self-conscious because when he looked at her like that, he made her feel beautiful and desired.

He swooped, taking one pebbled nipple between his lips and sucking.

A cry ripped from her chest, and her head dropped back against the wall. She grabbed at the strands of his hair as if that could somehow anchor her while his tongue swirled around her nipple, nudging it back and forth. He was the only person in the world who could do this to her. Make her feel so much and push her so close to the edge so quickly.

He switched to her other breast, and she whimpered, heart beating so fast she was sure it would punch right out of her chest. His teeth grazed her nipple while his hands slid down her sides.

How had she known that this existed and *not* sought it out for two years?

"Lock," she whispered. "I need all of you."

He released her nipple and lifted his head, his blue eyes almost black as they seared into hers. "You have me. You've always had me."

One more kiss on her lips, this one softer. So gentle and slow, she almost thought time had paused.

He turned and lay her on the bed, his weight pressing her into the mattress. She'd missed that weight. And the heat and the hardness that was Lock.

Again, his head lowered, trailing a line of kisses down her neck and chest. He stopped at her breast and sucked hard, causing her back to arch and her eyes to scrunch. He released it with a pop before continuing down her body. When he reached the top of her leggings, he slipped his fingers into the waistband and pulled down. She toed off her shoes moments before he made it to her ankles. Even when the pants hit the floor, he didn't rise. His lips returned to her skin, touching her ankle before slowly making his way up her leg.

It was like he needed to be touching her at all times.

He groaned. "God, I dream about these thighs."

At her hips, his fingers moved to the band of her panties while his mouth pressed to her hip bone. Her breath caught. She couldn't breathe. Not while he was so close to her core.

Torturously slowly, he dragged her panties down her thighs until she was completely bare beneath him, but again, she didn't feel self-conscious. She couldn't. Not with the way he looked at her.

The second her panties were gone, he parted her thighs and his head dipped. When he swiped her clit with his tongue, she arched a second time, her cry loud as it cut through the room. He swiped again, this time moving his tongue in a circular motion and causing her pulse to speed up.

Oh God. She grabbed the sheets, clutching them in her fists.

Too close. She was too close. But she didn't want to finish like this.

He kept swiping and licking, and she kept trying to arch off the bed until, with desperate fingers, she grabbed at his arms, tugging him up.

He rose from the bed, his powerful body glistening. His hands went to the buckle of his jeans as he kicked off his shoes. He didn't take his eyes off her as he pushed down his jeans and briefs.

Her mouth went dry. God, there was so much of him.

The second he returned to her, she reached between their bodies and wrapped her fingers around his cock. Huge. He was freaking huge.

The thick cords of muscle in his chest contracted, and his head hung as she began to explore him. Moving her fingers from base to tip. Gliding over him in a rhythmic motion.

She'd always loved touching him. It made her feel powerful and desirable. It was the one time she always felt she had a complete hold on him.

All too quickly, he grabbed her, tugging her arm up and kissing the inside of her wrist. Then, slowly, his eyes trailed down her body, fire flashing in their blue depths.

"God, you're gorgeous," he whispered. "Sometimes I thought the real you couldn't possibly live up to my memory. That you couldn't possibly be as beautiful as I remembered. But you are."

She cupped his cheek. "And you, Lock Walker, feel like home."

His eyes closed, his temple touching hers. "You *are* home."

He kissed her again, tongue tangling with hers, before he reached over and opened his side drawer. Using his teeth, he tore open the foil before leaning to the side and slipping the condom over himself.

Then he returned to her. "Thank you."

"For what?"

"Coming home to me."

His mouth returned to hers and he kissed her as he sank deep inside. Filling her. And for the first time in years, that hollowness disappeared.

* * *

LOCK SEATED himself deep inside her.

Fuck, she was tight. Blood roared between his ears, and every part of him screamed to move. To take this perfect woman. But he forced himself to remain perfectly still. To give her time to adjust to him. To just be connected in stillness for a second longer.

His eyes were still closed when she nibbled his bottom lip, teasing him.

"Mine," she whispered, breath brushing his skin.

Possessiveness punched through him. "I've always been yours."

He lifted his hips and thrust back inside. She cried out, her fingers digging into his shoulders as her walls hugged his cock. He did it again, and again she screamed for him.

He wanted to bottle up every sound she made, because they were fucking glorious.

He cupped her breast, thrumming her nipple back and forth. He hadn't been lying—he'd missed these breasts. Damn well dreamed about them. He continued to play with them as he thrust. Taking everything. Giving even more.

He moved his mouth to her neck, sucking her delicate skin. She tasted sweet, like candy. He'd never understood how she could always taste so good to him, like she'd been carefully designed just for him.

Her leg wrapped around his waist, and she met him thrust for thrust, pulling him deeper. Closer.

One more roll of her nipple, then he trailed his hand down between their bodies, finding her clit. He swiped and was rewarded with a cry that was so fucking sweet it made his blood pump harder. He rolled her clit with his thumb, applying just enough pressure that her breathing quickened. Her hips started to lift more frantically, quickening the pace of the thrusts.

"Oh God, Lock."

In his darkest moments, he'd wondered if he'd ever hear his name on her lips again. But he'd refused to lose hope. And it was hope that had kept him going. Hope that had brought him here. Because the idea of *not* hearing her voice again, of not touching her, talking to her…it had killed him.

He took her deeper. Faster.

He knew the exact moment she was on the edge because her breathing shifted and her eyes closed tight. She was trying to hold off.

Not gonna happen. He grazed her cheek with his lips before setting his mouth to her ear.

"Come for me, honey."

One more swipe of her clit, and she arched and screamed, her walls clenching his cock. Throbbing around him.

Fuck.

He kept circling her clit with his thumb, wanting more from her. Wanting to stretch out this moment.

But he made a mistake. He lifted his head and looked at her. *Really* looked at her. He saw the loss of control. The way she gave herself to him so completely.

Two more thrusts and that was it. He tipped over the edge. He growled as he broke, dropping his temple to the crook of her neck.

He kept thrusting until everything he had was hers, with nothing left. Then there was stillness. He didn't want to move.

Being inside her, a part of her, made the moment so intimate. But eventually, he knew he needed to move.

He found her mouth again, pressing one more kiss to her lips before gently lifting and dropping beside her.

She snuggled into his side, and damn, she fit so well. Neither of them said anything, but they didn't need to. They both felt it. The importance of this moment. This was what they'd both been trying to work their way back to. It hadn't been easy. It had been fucking *hard*. But they were here now, and he wasn't letting anything tear them apart again.

CHAPTER 18

Callie ran her finger over the small scar on Lock's stomach. It was new, but everything else about him was familiar. The feel of his warm skin against her cheek. The hum of his soft breaths as he slept.

The morning sun had just slipped through the gap in the curtains, telling her it was time to get up. But she didn't want to. She wanted to remain exactly where she was, head against Lock's chest, leg slung over his body while memories of the previous night played over in her mind.

The kisses…the touches. She closed her eyes, letting everything that had passed between them sink inside her.

Over the last couple years, she'd tried to tell herself that she was fine. Maybe even happy. But being here, with him, she knew that wasn't true. She'd been surviving. Getting through life one day at a time, trying to force herself to forget.

"Keep stroking me like that and I'm not sure we'll ever make it out of this bed."

Her lips twitched at Lock's deep, rumbly voice. She should have known he was awake. He'd always had this freaky ability to wake at any small movement or sound.

She looked up to see him watching her closely, his eyes dark and intense and focused solely on her. "How long have you been awake?"

"A while. I knew the second you woke."

The sneak. "So you've just been lying there, not saying anything and letting me touch you?"

"Mm-hmm. It's been torture. I think I deserve a reward." He rolled them and nuzzled her neck.

She laughed, grabbing at his shoulders as his lips moved over her skin. Jesus, she was getting hot and bothered already.

When he raised his head, the smile only lasted another second before it slipped.

"What is it?" she asked, frowning.

"Will you tell me something?"

Why did she get a pit in her belly at that question? "Sure."

"How did you feel when you found out you were pregnant?"

Her lips parted in an "o." Nope, she certainly hadn't thought he'd ask *that*. "Honestly? I was excited because I knew I loved you, but I was also scared."

"Why were you scared?"

"Because we'd only been dating a year. Plus, it was long-distance. And even though we talked about you getting out and us buying a home, nothing was set in stone. I was worried the baby would change things. Maybe make you question us."

"Never."

He said it like a vow. Like the idea of questioning anything to do with them was ridiculous.

She nibbled her bottom lip hesitantly. "How *would* you have reacted?"

"To the news that you were expecting our baby? A whole human being that was half you and half me, who would bind us together for life and make us a family?" Another darkening of his eyes. "It would have been the best day of my life."

The old ache returned to her chest.

A deep frown cut into his brow. "When you lost me and the baby…when you were hurting…did you regret us?"

Gosh, that was such a loaded, heavy question. "Honestly? On my darkest days, I wondered if I would have been better off never loving you."

His jaw clicked, pain skittering over his features before she continued.

"But every time, I always realized the same thing."

"What?"

"That even though the pain of losing you hurt like nothing I'd ever experienced, I'd do it again and again, just for one more day of loving you."

His head dropped, his forehead touching hers. "I needed to hear that, Callie. You have no idea how much I needed to hear that."

He kissed her, and it felt like every painful bit of their past faded just for a moment.

When he lifted away, she cocked her head. "Dad said you went to him and asked where I was?"

"I did. I didn't get any information, and he gave me a pretty big black eye for my effort."

She gasped. "No, he didn't!"

"He did. My team had just finished debriefing and all that shit after eliminating our target. I got last-minute leave to come home and make things right with you, but I couldn't find you. So I went to his house, and the second he opened the door, he hit me. Told me to never come back."

"And you let him." There was no way her father could have gotten the drop on a man like Lock without him allowing it to happen.

"I deserved it. I deserved worse." He slipped a lock of hair from her face. "He told me you were gone. That you weren't coming back and the damage I'd done couldn't be reversed. I didn't understand at the time. I thought after a few months, you'd return."

She swallowed, thinking about the day he'd broken things off with her. What that period of time must have been like for Lock. "That must have been hard for you, losing me *and* Winnie. I'm sorry that you lost him. He was a good guy."

"He was the best guy. I was so angry for so long. I lost him and you in the span of an hour. It was a great motivator for me to find the asshole who killed him and end him."

"Who was he? The guy who killed Winnie?" She wasn't sure if she truly wanted to know, but once the question was out, she couldn't take it back.

"His name was Malone. He was an IT expert in a terrorist organization. An organization my team had been tasked to take down."

The idea of Lock being involved with such dangerous people made fear curl in her belly. "After killing Winnie, Remi, and Hollie, he must have known you were coming. He would have been prepared."

Lock frowned. "That's the thing I always found strange. He was easy to find, and he almost looked surprised when we breached his apartment. Surprised we'd found him or surprised we'd come...I wasn't sure."

"Did you question him?"

"He reached for a weapon and a team member eliminated him before he could talk. Kill shot to the head."

She shuddered at the thought.

Lock ran a soothing finger down her arm. "Sorry. I shouldn't be telling you this stuff."

"No. I'm glad you are. I want to know. I—" She stopped when her phone vibrated on the side table. Lock reached over and handed it to her, and she gasped when she saw who it was. "Dang it."

"What?"

"It's Dad. I forgot he's coming to my house for breakfast this morning—in ten minutes. Crap!"

"Want me to drop you off?"

She frowned. Did she want him to drop her off?

She shook her head. "No. I want you to join us."

* * *

LOCK SHOT a glance at Callie as she ran her finger over a seam in her leggings in the passenger seat. It had been a mad rush to shower and throw on clothes before heading to her house, and even though she'd said she wanted him to come, he wondered if she was changing her mind.

"You're nervous."

Her gaze shot up. "No. Not nervous. I…okay, maybe a little nervous. I just don't know what he'll say about us. He was fine when you picked me up from the studio yesterday, but that was you protecting me. I don't know what he'll say when we tell him we're back together."

"Will it bother you if he doesn't approve?" Shit, would that be a deal breaker for her? The thought tasted like acid in his mouth.

"It's not that it would bother me. Dad just…he worries about me. More since everything happened. And I don't like worrying him after his diagnosis."

Lock reached over and slipped his fingers through hers. "Guess I'd better show him I'm the best man for you then."

She smiled but it wasn't wide enough to convince him that she was okay.

He pulled up in the drive of her house to see her father's car already on the street. He climbed out of his truck and moved around to her side.

"I just need you to know one thing before we go in there," she said quietly as they stopped at the front door.

Shit. Was it something bad? "Anything."

"I'm okay now. I wasn't back then, but now, after some time has passed and being here with you, having you know the truth…I am."

Was she telling him this because she'd been worse than he could have imagined, and her father might tell him that?

Fuck, he hated that thought.

He cupped her cheek. "You sure you're okay now?"

"The past will always hurt. But it won't stop me from being happy now."

The door opened, and Aspen stood on the other side, a huge-ass smile on her face. "Well, hello. It's so nice of you two to finally grace us with your presence."

Callie rolled her eyes and slipped around Aspen to go inside. "Are you saying that because you missed me?"

"Of course. I missed you too, Lock, or at least your morning coffee." Aspen's smile widened at him. "Good night last night?"

His lips twitched, but luckily the question didn't require a response, because Aspen was already turning and heading into the house.

Lock stepped inside and closed the door after him.

The smell of bacon and eggs hung in the air, a plate of waffles already on the table.

"While you two have been…sleeping, I made waffles," Aspen sung as she moved to the kitchen.

Jude rose from a stool at the counter and kissed his daughter on the cheek before studying her. "Are you okay?"

"I'm great, Dad. In fact…" She turned to look at Lock, bottom lip disappearing between her teeth. "Lock and I have something to share." She stepped beside him, and he slipped an arm around her waist. "We're back together," Callie said quietly.

There was a small beat of silence where her father didn't speak. His expression didn't even change. Jesus, the man was unreadable.

Aspen stepped forward. "Congratulations." She tugged Callie into a hug, then Lock. "Be good to her if you want to avoid some bruised balls," she whispered into his ear.

His lips twitched as they separated. "Always."

Jude's gaze went to his daughter. "Are you happy?"

"I am." Callie's response was instant.

"Well, that's all I want, baby."

He hugged his daughter before shaking Lock's hand. The handshake was too firm for Lock to believe he was really on board, and the look in the man's eyes told Lock this conversation wasn't over.

They spent the next half hour preparing the rest of breakfast. The women filled every one of those minutes with talk, and it was only when they were about to sit down to eat that Callie left the room to change her clothes. Aspen slipped out at the same time to take a call.

Lock was the first to break the silence. "Say it, Jude."

"She was a mess after what you did to her."

"I know."

"No. You don't. You weren't here."

The knot in his gut tightened. "You're right, I wasn't. And it's something I'll always regret. Something I will spend my life trying to make up to her. I wish I *had* been here. I would give anything to turn back time and do things differently."

Jude's frown deepened. "Son, I'm gonna be frank with you. I'm getting older and my tolerance for bullshit is low. I just need to know one thing. Do you love her?"

"Yes." The single word came quickly, like a reflex. "I have loved her since the day I met her, and I'll love her until the day I die."

"What if there's another threat in your life, and you think she'll be safer away from you again?"

"We'll figure out a way forward together. I will never hurt her like I did before, ever again."

Jude seemed to take a moment to consider that before finally dipping his chin. "Good. I'm going to hold you to that, son."

"I hope you do."

CHAPTER 19

Callie smiled at her class as they packed up from the yoga session. Hell, she'd been smiling all morning. And it was all because of one man.

A week had passed since she'd slept with Lock. And in that week, they'd spent every night together. Mornings. Car trips to and from work. Actually, it was only while she was teaching that they were apart.

The only thing she didn't like was being away from Aspen. Sometimes they stayed at her place so she could be with her friend, but Aspen hadn't been home much. She was out all day, every day, finding somewhere to write or researching something for her book. And there'd been a few nights she'd stayed at her mother's, something she hated doing but her mother tended to guilt her into it.

Callie missed her. And it almost felt like her friend was avoiding her. Why, she had no idea. Did it have something to do with Dylan? Her gut told her yes.

She moved into the back room to grab her phone from the table and sent a quick text to Aspen while she had a minute.

Callie: Hey! Want to get lunch today? We could eat in the park.

It was one of Aspen's favorite things to do. Her friend said people-watching gave her inspiration for her books. Ideas would run wild in her head about who they were and the kind of lives they lived.

Honestly, she had no idea how Aspen came up with all the ideas for her stories. Callie could barely think of what she wanted for dinner, let alone come up with entire fictitious worlds and characters and story arcs.

She watched the screen for a few seconds, waiting for a response. Aspen was usually quick at getting back to her. Another thing that had been off this last week.

When no reply came through, Callie sighed and turned, only to run smack into a chest—Hamish's chest.

"Oh, gosh." She grabbed his arms to steady herself. "I'm so sorry."

"No, it was my fault. I s-snuck in behind you."

It was true. He should be gone by now. Everyone else who'd done the class probably was. "Is everything okay?"

"I just wanted to tell you that you l-look nice today. Happy."

She swallowed. Her last few encounters with Hamish had made her a bit more cautious around him, just because she didn't want to lead him on. "I *am* happy. Thank you."

"Is it because you're back with Lock?"

Her mouth opened. She hadn't been expecting such a direct question, but maybe she should have. "I'm back with him, yes, and he does make me happy."

Disappointment flashed in his eyes, making Callie hate herself for being honest. But at the same time, she didn't want to lie to the guy. And maybe it was good for him to know she was taken.

"You deserve to be happy."

He quickly turned and headed toward the door, making guilt slither in her belly. She *shouldn't* feel guilty, but she couldn't help it.

"Wait." She chased after him and grabbed his arm. When he

turned, she softened her voice. "Your perfect woman will show up one day, Hamish, and you'll realize that she's the one you've been waiting for all along. I promise."

He swallowed. "Th-thanks."

"In fact, there's this girl—" She stopped at the sight of two men leaving a store across the road. One of them looked up and caught her eye through the window, a smirk on his face.

Argh. It was those bullies, the ones who'd shoved Hamish and laughed about it.

Hamish turned his head to follow her gaze.

"Just wait in here until they leave," she said quietly.

He frowned. "I'm not scared of them."

"I never said you were. I just think avoiding them is best."

For some reason, that response seemed to make him almost angry. Without a word, he swung toward the door.

"Hamish—"

But he was already outside and crossing the street toward them.

What was he doing? She chased after him, but man, his long legs made it hard.

"What's your problem?" Hamish shouted from halfway across the road.

One guy's brows rose. "What?"

"You were smirking at us. You think you can just treat people however you want?"

"Actually, I know I can."

Hamish shoved him against a car. The guy shoved Hamish back, but unlike last time, Hamish didn't move.

Immediately, the jerk's friend rounded the car. "Hey, you got a problem with us?"

"Yeah, I do," Hamish snarled.

"Don't know why," Asshole One scoffed. "We're not the freak with the stutter."

Hamish swung a fist, but the guy dodged it and caught his

arm. The second guy grasped his other arm, and the two of them pushed him so he was bent over the hood of the car.

Callie gasped. "Let him go." She gripped the first guy's arm, but he was too strong.

Hamish tried to buck them off, but it was two against one. The first guy shoved Hamish's head to the hood of the car, hard. "Hey, do you like that, freak?"

"Stop it!" She tried to grab him again, but it didn't seem to matter how loud she shouted or how hard she tugged; he wouldn't listen.

"You're pathetic," he yelled at Hamish. "You know that? Doing yoga and Pilates like a little bitch to get this whore's attention."

"Get off him," Callie cried. "*Now!*"

Asshole Number One lowered his head. "You're a sad excuse for a man." He shoved Hamish's head against the car a second time, and Hamish growled in pain.

"Stop!" she shouted louder, yanking at his arm again.

He swung his arm, sending Callie flying. She screamed as she hit the road, and a car came around the corner. Its wheels squealed, and it screeched to a halt inches from hitting her.

Her heart beat hard as two doors opened.

Callie's jaw dropped when she saw the two men climbing out. One blond shaggy-haired guy, the other with dark hair and tattoos down his right arm. Both men were large, with thick arms and chests…and familiar.

Antwan and Jesse, members of Lock's former Ghost Ops team.

Antwan raced forward and grabbed the asshole by the back of his shirt before slamming him hard against the driver's-side door. "What the fuck is wrong with you, throwing her to the ground?"

The guy tried to get out of Antwan's hold. "I didn't—"

"You *did,*" he growled, not releasing him.

The second bully released Hamish and stepped back.

Jesse held out a hand, helping her up. "Are you okay?"

"I'm fine. These guys are just being jerks."

"We can see that," Antwan said through gritted teeth. "I should throw *you* in front of a moving vehicle and see how you like it."

The guy's jaw clicked.

"What's your name?" Antwan asked. When he didn't answer, Antwan got louder. "*What's your name?*"

"His name is Lucian," the second guy said, almost looking scared that he was next.

"Fucking fitting. I've never met a Lucian I liked. *Go.* But if I see you messing with her again, you won't get away unscathed." Antwan let the man go and he straightened, a scowl on his face, before he slid into the car.

They stepped back as the two guys drove off.

She looked at Hamish, seeing the red bruise already forming on his temple. "Are you—"

"I'm fine," he said, cutting her off. "Thanks for the help." He didn't look at any of them before heading down the street.

Her heart hurt for him as she watched him walk away. He was embarrassed. He shouldn't be, but he was. God, she hated those bullies. And why on earth had Hamish approached them? To prove he could? He didn't need to prove anything.

Jesse touched her arm. "Are you sure you're okay?"

"I'm all right." Her frown turned into a slow smile. "And you're here." She tugged Jesse into a hug. "How are you?"

His long arms wrapped around her. "I'm good."

Next, she turned to Antwan, her smile turning a little sad as she hugged him. "Hey. I know it was a while ago, but I'm so sorry about Hollie."

He embraced her a little tighter. "Thanks, Callie." He pulled away but kept hold of her upper arms. "It's good to see you."

"You too." She tilted her head. "Have you seen Lock yet?"

"Nope. But I heard he's somewhere called Sugar and Spice, so that's where we're headed."

* * *

"So no more notes or seeing people in her backyard?" Eastern asked.

Lock lifted his mug. Eastern's partner, Sadie, had made the coffee, and it was damn good. No surprise. She was also the granddaughter of Mrs. Sandler, who owned the bakery.

"No more notes," Lock finally answered, "but she hasn't been home the entire time to *see* anyone in her yard."

One side of Eastern's mouth lifted. "Is that right? And where has she been staying?"

"With me."

The smile widened. "You two back together then?"

He hadn't told his brothers yet. He hadn't seen much of them over the last week, but even if he had, it felt good keeping the news to themselves for a few days. Intimate.

"We are."

Eastern closed his fingers around Lock's shoulders. "I'm happy for you, brother."

"Thanks. I'm glad she's taken my sorry ass back. It also means I can be around to protect her."

Eastern frowned. "What about her roommate, Aspen? She seen anyone suspicious around the house?"

"I don't know. She and Callie haven't seen a lot of each other this week. Callie hasn't said anything, but I'll ask her again today."

"It's hard to think someone who's stalking her would have just backed off."

Lock's fingers tightened around the mug. "I know. I want to find the person responsible, and I want to find them fast."

"We will."

Lock needed a change of subject before the frustration ate into his mood. "How's Avery?"

Eastern's features softened at the mention of his eight-year-old daughter. "Amazing." His gaze lifted to Sadie behind the counter. "And watching Sadie and Avery together is just…shit, I don't know how to describe it. It's magic. She's Avery's mother, even if it's not by blood."

Sadie had been Avery's nanny for most of the girl's life, and she'd always loved her like she was her own…while Avery's biological mother had never treated her the way she should have.

"You're a family."

"We are, and it feels good." Eastern's gaze lifted to the counter. "Looks like Sadie has a break in customers. I might go talk to her."

And by talk, of course his brother meant do a lot more than that.

Eastern stepped behind the counter and pulled Sadie into his arms to kiss her.

Yep, there it was.

Lock was just turning away when he noticed Callie climbing out of a blue Ford outside.

He rose to his feet. What the hell? What was she doing here…and whose car was that? He was supposed to be picking her up in half an hour, after she did her own Pilates session.

Then the front doors opened and two men climbed out. A smile cracked Lock's mouth.

Jesse and Antwan.

Callie stepped inside first, and he tugged her into his arms, planting a kiss on her lips before pulling back. "What's going on?"

"I found a couple of your friends."

Hell yes, she did. He looked up and pulled Jesse into a hug, then Antwan. "You're early!"

Antwan lifted a shoulder. "I changed my flight to an earlier one and found Jesse at the airport."

Lock shook his head. "Fuck, it's good to see you both. Missed you." He'd missed all the members of his team.

"We missed you too," Jesse said.

Eastern returned to the table, and Lock turned to him with a grin. "Eastern, these are two of the men from my team, Jesse and Antwan. Guys, this is one of my brothers, Eastern."

"The better-looking brother," Eastern said with a smile as he held out his hand.

"You're the sheriff?" Antwan asked, inspecting Eastern's uniform.

He dipped his head. "I am."

"Then you should probably know what just happened." Antwan's gaze shifted to Lock. "You too."

He tensed. "Something happened to you already?"

"We almost hit Callie with our car because some jackass shoved her down onto the street," Jesse said.

"What?" It was almost a damn shout from Lock, but he couldn't fucking help it. He looked down at Callie. "Who shoved you?"

"Just some guy who's been bullying Hamish. He had a friend with him. They're really awful to Hamish. Today, they slammed his head into their car."

"You get a name?" Eastern asked, sounding a hell of a lot calmer than Lock.

"Lucian," Antwan said.

"He's the guy you punched at the bar," Callie added.

Eastern cursed. "Lucian Tate. We've had complaints about him before. He's an asshole to a lot of people. Works for the local electric company. I'll have some of my guys talk to him."

Lock's hands fisted. He should have done more than hit the guy that night he'd touched Callie.

"That won't help," Antwan said, seemingly more to himself than anyone else. "He likes the power trip. One look at him and I could see that."

Lock turned to Callie and cupped her cheeks. "Are you okay?"

"I'm fine. Just worried about Hamish."

He was more worried about *her*. He scanned her body, lifting her hands, only to growl at the scrapes on her palms. "Callie—"

"I'm okay. Really. Come on. Let's focus on your friends being here."

Lock was glad his friends were here. But he also wanted to kick this Lucian's ass for touching Callie *again*. And he would if he ever saw the asshole.

CHAPTER 20

"Tell me about Amber Ridge," Lock said as he lifted the beer to his mouth. "Is it still as perfect as you described it?"

Antwan, Jesse, and Callie stood around him at a bar table at Meridian having some drinks.

Amber Ridge was in Montana, less than an hour west of Bozeman, and it was Jesse's hometown, where he'd grown up with his brother and sister. The town he'd just moved back to.

Jesse's lips twitched. "It's still your classic small town. No secrets are secrets for long, and everything remains exactly the same. Even the terrible pizza at Burt's Pizzeria hasn't changed."

"I still don't understand how a place with widely known terrible pizza can stay in business for longer than you've been alive," Antwan said as he lifted his beer for a drink.

Jesse shrugged. "We like Burt, so we band together and make sure he stays in business. I've been taking the first of the month."

"And you eat the pizza?" Lock asked.

"Every scrap of it. It's terrible. It's an act of love."

Callie sighed. "That's really sweet."

"You've always been too much of a softie," Antwan said with a laugh.

"That's how I attract the ladies."

"Ladies? What ladies?" Lock joked.

"Haha." Jesse sipped his beer. "Becket and Clara are in Amber Ridge, and so's Mom, so I'm happy."

Lock knew that Jesse had missed his mother, brother, and sister.

"What's Becket doing since he left the SEALs?"

"Fire chief. And from what I understand, a damn good one."

"Of course he is, because when would a Hayes ever *not* be good at something?" Antwan said with an eye roll.

It was true. Jesse had always been the perfectionist in the group.

"You're right, I'm good at almost everything," Jesse replied, receiving a shoulder shove from Antwan.

"Modest too," Antwan scoffed.

As the two continued to banter, Callie lifted her phone and typed something.

Lock slipped an arm around her waist. "Everything okay?"

"I'm trying to get Aspen to come down here tonight. It's a harder sell than it should be."

He glanced at the screen to read the text.

Callie: I need proof you're alive. Either come to Meridian or I'm coming to you.

"We're making a trip to your place tonight?" Lock asked.

"If we have to." She set her phone down with a light thump. "I'm sorry, I know tonight's a celebration because your friends are here." She looked up at Jesse. "What are *you* doing for work now that you're home?"

He lowered the beer to the table. "I'm a deputy."

"Wow, impressive." Callie smiled

"Thanks. I might need to talk to your brother and get some tips."

"You'll be great." Callie looked at Antwan. "What about you?"

There was a flicker of his brows. "Since leaving the military, I've just been having some time off. Finding my feet has been…hard."

It could definitely be hard settling back into civilian life. And it would be particularly hard for Antwan, who'd lost the woman he loved.

"You think any more about my offer to move here?" Lock asked.

"Actually, I sold most of my stuff and what I packed is basically all I own. So even if I don't settle here, I'm not going back home."

Wow. That was huge.

Callie leaned forward and touched Antwan's hand. "That's great. Sometimes a new environment is exactly what we need."

"I'm hoping."

Over the next half hour, they talked about anything and everything, until Callie went to step away from the table.

Lock grabbed her arm. "Hey, you. Where're you going?"

"Aspen just got here."

He looked up to see her friend by the door. "I'll come with you."

She rolled her eyes. "We're a few feet away. You can watch us the entire time without being right there."

Yeah, but he *wanted* to be right there. But she might want to talk to her friend without him hovering. "Don't be gone long."

"From you? Never." She kissed him before stepping away, but he kept his eyes on her the entire time.

"I'm glad you two made it work again," Jesse said once it was just them.

Lock looked back at his friends. "You have no idea. It was hell until she forgave me."

"You look happy," Antwan said.

"I am."

Jesse dipped his head. "Good."

He looked back at the women to see them deep in conversation. When they finally reached the table, Callie introduced everyone.

"Jesse, Antwan, this is my best friend, Aspen. Aspen, these guys were on Lock's Ghost Ops team."

Was it just him, or did Aspen seem a bit paler than usual? Not only that, but her smile wasn't quite so wide, and there were dark circles under her eyes.

The guys nodded before Jesse stepped away from the table. "I'll get you a drink."

Aspen shook her head. "You don't have to do that."

"I know. I want to."

"All right. But I'm coming with you."

When the two left for the bar, Callie's frown was deep. She was worried about her friend, probably because she'd seen everything Lock saw. He opened his mouth to ask her about it, but Antwan spoke first.

"You two should be dancing."

Callie shook her head. "We don't need to dance."

"Speak for yourself." Lock pulled her closer. "I'd love to dance." Then, as if to prove his point, he nuzzled her neck, getting a soft laugh in response.

"Go," Antwan said. "Before you make me sick."

He tugged Callie to the dance floor and waited until his arm was around her waist and she was flush against his chest to ask, "Everything okay with Aspen?"

"I don't know. She says she's fine but something's obviously going on with her, and I think that something involves Dylan. I don't know why she won't tell me. We usually tell each other everything."

"Maybe she just needs some time."

"Maybe." Her frown deepened. "Is Antwan okay?"

"He looks better than I thought he would, but it would be easy to appear okay without actually *being* okay." He hadn't been okay since Hollie died. Or at least, he hadn't been how he used to be.

He lowered his mouth to Callie's ear. "You know who's better than okay?"

A shudder rolled down her spine. "Who?"

"Me." He kissed her neck. "Because I have you. I'm never letting you go. You know that, right?"

She softened against him. "I wouldn't let you if you tried."

* * *

CALLIE PEEKED around Lock's body. Aspen was talking to Jesse and Antwan at the table. Well, mostly Jesse. In fact, the two looked like they were getting along *very* well. While she'd been talking to him, it was like she'd transformed into a different person entirely from the one who'd walked into the bar.

What was going on with her?

It was Dylan. It had to be. Man, she hated that guy. She didn't even have a reason to hate him—he'd never done anything to her. She just did. Call it gut instinct.

"Stop spying."

She jumped at Lock's whispered words and looked up, way up, into his beautiful eyes. "I'm not spying, I'm…watching."

"Is that different?"

"Yes. It sounds better." She shot a look at her friend again. "Does it look like she's flirting with Jesse? It does, doesn't it? But that would be crazy, because she just split from Dylan."

"They're just talking. But if you're worried about her, you could talk to her."

"I told you, I've tried. She won't tell me anything."

"All you can do is keep trying."

"I know. I'm just impatient." She glanced back up at Lock. "When did you become so…"

"Wise? Good-looking? Strong?"

She scoffed. "You were probably born good-looking and strong. Maybe even wise."

He chuckled, and she wanted to bottle the sound.

"She'll come around," Lock said, sobering.

Probably, but that didn't stop Callie from pushing. She couldn't help herself.

When the song ended, she slipped her hand into his and headed back to the table.

"I need a drink, and you need to get one with me," Callie said, interrupting her friend mid-conversation with Jesse.

Aspen frowned. "Callie, I'm—"

"Coming with me." She tugged Aspen toward the bar.

"Jesus, how are you so strong?"

"Give a girl a reason, and she becomes superwoman." They stopped at the bar. "Are you flirting with Jesse?"

Aspen's eyes widened. "What? No. I was being nice. You know, getting to know a new person."

"All right, but if you were, it would be okay. Dylan's your past, not your future."

Something flickered in Aspen's eyes.

Callie frowned. "What was that?"

"Nothing. I just…he's been calling me nonstop. And texting. And showing up at our house."

"He's been showing up at our house?" Okay, now she felt even worse for not being home much. "Maybe we should get Eastern to talk to him."

"No." The answer came quickly. Far quicker than Callie would have thought. "I just…I want him to go away."

"Okay. But if he doesn't want to—"

"He'll get the message eventually."

Eventually? Callie didn't like that. How long would it take him? And what would happen to Aspen's mental health in the meantime? "Is there anything I can do?"

"Just keep being my amazing best friend."

"Always." Callie tilted her head. "Just so you know, you deserve to be happy. And he didn't make you nearly happy enough. I'm glad you ended things."

"I should have done it sooner. I feel like an idiot for staying with him when he…"

Callie frowned. "When he what?"

"Nothing." She shook her head. "Can we just order a drink and have a good night, please? I need a distraction from thinking about it all."

Callie squeezed her friend's arm. "Okay. But I'm here for anything you need, got it? To listen. To laugh. To cry. To drink into oblivion."

Aspen's mouth cracked into a small smile. "I know you are. Thanks, Callie."

They each ordered a cocktail and were just stepping away from the bar, when Aspen stopped abruptly. "You've got to be kidding me."

Callie followed her gaze to the door, and her heart sank. Dylan. And he was looking straight at her friend.

Had he known she was here? He had to. He hated bars. Aspen had told her that on more than one occasion when he'd refused to meet them here.

"Do you want me to—"

"No." Aspen handed Callie her drink. "Can you take this to the table? I'm going to tell him to leave."

"Want me to come with you?"

"No. I'll be fine."

Callie took the drink back to the table, but her eyes barely left her friend. The second Aspen reached him, they were embroiled in what looked to be a heated conversation.

"Is she okay?" Jesse asked, standing a bit straighter.

"I hope so. They broke up a few weeks ago, and he's an ass. *King* of the asses actually. But she'll let us know if she needs help." At least, Callie hoped she would.

Jesse nodded, not looking completely convinced, but then Lock said something to pull his attention away from the scene.

Callie turned to Antwan. "I know I've said this already, but I am *really* sorry about Hollie."

His jaw clenched, and he looked down at his beer, fingers tightening around the glass. "Thanks. I kept our apartment because I couldn't let it go. All our memories were there. I thought after two years I'd be able to return. But I couldn't. She was everywhere. And while everyone else had a family in a different town to return to, I didn't."

She touched his shoulder. "I'm so sorry, Antwan."

He nodded as he looked at her. "Thanks. I—"

She didn't catch what he said next because from the corner of her eye, she saw Dylan take Aspen's arm and pull her toward the door.

What the hell?

Alarm raced through her system, and she moved on instinct, pushing through the crowd and racing toward the door. She heard the shout from Lock behind her, but her entire focus remained on the door. On the way Dylan's features had been twisted with anger and the tight grip he'd had on her friend.

She sprinted outside.

"Get your hand off me *now*!"

It was like Dylan didn't hear Aspen's shouted words or feel her attempts to pull free. He just kept marching them forward.

What the hell was wrong with him?

Callie reached them and grabbed his arm. "Let her go!"

He kept moving down the street, ignoring her.

Desperate, she kicked him in the back of the knee.

"Fuck!" He stumbled and released Aspen before swinging toward her.

Callie tried to back up too fast and would have fallen, but strong arms slipped around her waist, catching her. Then Jesse was between her and Dylan—and he swung, nailing Dylan in the cheek.

Callie's jaw dropped.

Dylan had just hit the ground when Jesse grabbed him by the shirt and yanked him back up, shoving him against the wall of the neighboring business.

"You think it's okay to grab a woman and drag her outside against her will?"

Dylan tried to pull away, but Jesse held him too firmly.

"What was the plan?" Jesse growled. "Drag her to your car and take her to your place?"

Callie wanted to know the answer to that question too.

"Get off me," Dylan growled.

"Jesse, step back," Lock said from behind her.

A few seconds of silence passed where no one moved, but eventually, Jesse let him go and Dylan straightened his clothes. Dylan took a step to the side, but Lock spoke again. "Wait." He looked at Aspen. "You want to press charges? I can call my brother."

Aspen's gaze shifted to each person around her before landing on Dylan.

Say yes, Callie whispered in her head. *Teach the jerk he can't treat you like that.*

Aspen shook her head, making disappointment skitter through Callie's veins. "No."

Dylan smirked at Lock before looking at Aspen. "We'll talk later."

Asshole.

When Dylan was gone, Jesse stepped in front of Aspen. "Are you okay?"

Callie missed her answer because Lock turned narrowed eyes on her. "You need to stop doing that."

"Doing what?"

"Grabbing aggressive men. That's twice in one day."

"I'm not just going to let people hurt my friends."

Lock glanced at the sky like he was searching for…something. Composure maybe? When he finally looked at her again, he appeared a bit calmer. "Fine. But don't run out on me again. Next time, tell me what's going on and I'll take down the bad guy."

He was right. Shit. She hadn't been thinking. "You're right. You can take care of the bad guy. I'm sorry."

He kissed her, and in that kiss, she felt his desperate need to keep her safe.

allie's gaze shifted from the reformer machine beneath her to the note on the desk. It had been waiting for her at the studio this morning. She hadn't opened it yet. She'd told herself she'd open it when she finished her classes, but she hadn't. Then she'd told herself she'd open it when she finished *her* Pilates session, and, well, she was almost done and *still* didn't want to open it.

She paused at the end of her set of triceps extensions to glance out the window.

Even though it was the middle of the day, she'd still locked the doors. Lock had told her to, but she would have done it anyway. Between the notes and Aspen and Dylan, there was so much going on.

She began her stretches. She hadn't finished the workout, but her mind was anywhere but on what she was doing.

Usually, Pilates and yoga were her escape from the real world. They took her mind off everything she had going on around her and let her turn inward.

Why was it not working today?

At least Antwan and Jesse were here—extra people in town to

keep an eye out for anything that could go wrong. They were staying at Lock's house. With her there too, it was a nearly full home. She'd tried to convince Aspen to stay with them as well—heck, there were enough bedrooms—but her friend had refused. Why, exactly, Callie wasn't sure.

Fifteen minutes later, she rose and moved to the desk. The note was mocking her. Just sitting there, waiting for her to open it.

Still, she didn't touch it, not yet. First, she texted Aspen.

Callie: Hey! How'd your writing session go? Get much done?

How her friend could concentrate on anything other than that awful ex of hers, she had no idea. He'd *grabbed* her last night, forced her outside.

What would he have done if he hadn't been stopped? Forced her into his car? Dragged her to his house? Then what? And why hadn't she wanted to involve Eastern?

A shudder skittered down her spine as her phone pinged with a response.

Aspen: I couldn't concentrate so I decided to drown myself in cake at Sugar and Spice. Then Jesse showed up and we kind of spent the day together.

Callie's brows rose. She'd spent the day with Jesse?

Aspen: Just as friends. We walked around. Talked. He's sweet.

A small smile stretched Callie's lips. Now, Jesse and Aspen were a relationship Callie could get behind. Not that her friend was in the headspace for dating right now.

She was glad Aspen had spent the day with him. He *was* sweet. He was also big and intimidating, so if Dylan approached Aspen, he wouldn't be afraid to hit the guy a second time.

A knock on the glass made Callie jump, and the phone dropped from her fingers. The air rushed from her chest when she saw Antwan outside. Good God, she was edgy.

She opened the door.

"Sorry," he said as he stepped inside. "I didn't mean to scare you."

She shook her head. "It's not your fault. I was distracted."

"Everything okay?"

She locked the door after him. "It's fine. Actually, Aspen was just telling me she spent the day with Jesse."

"Yeah, he ran out to get us coffees this morning, and after an hour, I started to wonder just where the hell he'd *driven* for this coffee, but then he texted that he was with Aspen. I assumed he wasn't coming back."

Callie cringed. "So, no coffee?"

"I had to fend for myself."

"What a tragedy."

"You have no idea."

She laughed. "Is that why you're here? Jesse deserted you, Lock's doing a job, and you eventually got bored?"

"Actually, Lock got caught up on his job and asked me to drive you home. Is that okay?"

"Oh. Of course. Thank you. I'll just wipe down the machine I was using and pack up my stuff."

She'd just started cleaning the reformer when Antwan lifted something from the desk. "What's this?"

"It's another note."

He scowled. "Lock mentioned you've been receiving them. What do they usually say?"

"Silly stuff about my looks and how Lock's not good enough for me. I've been trying to forget about them."

Another narrowing of his eyes.

"The person hasn't actually done anything," she added. Once the machine was clean, she moved over to Antwan and slipped the letter from his hold. "Let's see what they have to say this time."

Because she was no longer alone, opening it felt easier. Or

maybe it was because she was trying to prove that she was unaffected when, in reality, that was far from the case.

The same familiar handwriting stared back at her.

He doesn't keep you safe the way I do. He doesn't love you like I do.

Keep her safe? How on earth was this person keeping her safe?

Her phone rang, and she jumped again.

Jesus. She needed to get a hold of herself.

Antwan put a warm hand on her shoulder. "Hey. It's okay. It's just a call."

She blew out a breath, only to frown when she saw the unknown number on her screen. "Hello?"

"Callie. It's Eastern. Are you with Lock?"

Eastern? Why was he calling? Something cold and uncomfortable skittered down her spine. "No, I'm with Antwan. Why? Is something wrong?"

"Actually, yes. We need you to come down to the station and tell us about all of your encounters with Lucian Tate."

She straightened. "Lucian. Why?"

There was a small pause. "He was murdered last night."

LOCK PULLED into the parking lot of the sheriff's station. He was pissed. He was *beyond* pissed. Eastern had called Callie in for questioning after a damn murder, and he hadn't told him. It had been *Antwan* who'd messaged him.

Lock stepped inside.

Antwan rose from a seat. "You got here fast."

"Where is she?"

"Eastern still has her in a room in the back."

His hands fisted and he took a step forward, but Antwan gripped his shoulder. "Hey. I don't think your brother thinks she did anything wrong. I'm sure he just wants to know about their interactions."

"He should have called me."

"I'm sure he had his reasons not to."

The click of a door opening sounded down the hall. He looked up to see Callie step out of a room, closely followed by Eastern and a deputy.

He met her halfway and cupped her cheeks. "Hey. Are you okay?"

She nodded, but her complexion was pale.

Shit, he was even angrier now. He turned to his brother. "Why didn't you call me?"

"Come into my office, Lock."

He didn't want to go into a damn office, he wanted to kick his brother's ass.

Eastern held open the door of his office, and Lock placed a hand on Callie's back and led her inside.

"I'll wait out here," Antwan said before lowering back to his seat.

"I didn't tell you," Eastern began, once the door was closed and he was behind his desk, "because I needed to talk to Callie alone and I knew you'd fight me on it."

"Damn straight I'd fight you on it. I should have been with her."

Callie touched his arm. "Lock. It's not your brother's fault. He's just doing his job."

Eastern lowered to his seat. "I don't think she had anything to do with the murder, of course." He waved a hand at the two seats opposite his desk.

Lock helped Callie into a seat, then sat beside her. "How was he killed?"

Killed...fuck. Someone had actually *killed* the guy. Yeah, Lucian was an asshole, but he shouldn't have died.

"Looks like someone entered his house through an unlocked

back door and struck him in the back of the head. They then kicked him until he wasn't breathing any longer."

Jesus Christ. "They were angry."

"My thoughts exactly. He was killed in a rage."

Lock reached over and wrapped his fingers around Callie's thigh, suddenly feeling like she was too far even though she was right next to him. "Any idea who did it?"

"They didn't leave any evidence. No prints or witnesses. His brother got home this morning after being out all night and found his body."

"Brother?" Callie asked.

"Oscar Tate, the guy who's always with him."

She frowned. "I didn't know they were brothers."

Eastern nodded. "They are, and they live together."

"Is Oscar a suspect?" Lock asked.

"He claims to have been at his girlfriend's house the entire night, and she corroborates the story."

"So what did you want with Callie?" Lock asked, still angry that she'd been dragged into this.

"We needed the details of her interactions with him."

"I told them everything I remembered about the bar, and then the two incidents with Hamish," she said softly, her hand slipping on top of Lock's as she looked at him.

"Hamish," Lock said softly. "They were bullying him, right?"

She shook her head. "No...well, yes, they were, but like I told Eastern and his deputy, I don't think he could have done this."

"How well do you know Hamish?" Eastern asked.

Her brows rose. "I mean, not super well. But I see him a few times a week and have conversations with him all the time. He's kind, and the least-violent guy I know."

"Has he ever shown a romantic interest in you?"

At Callie's beat of silence, Lock turned to look at her. He obviously had. But then, that wasn't a huge surprise. Lock had suspected the guy had a thing for her.

"He asked me out," she finally said.

Lock frowned. "Why didn't you tell me?"

"Because it didn't seem important. I let him down gently and that was that." She looked back at Eastern. "Him showing an interest in me doesn't mean he'd kill someone though. That's crazy."

Eastern leaned forward. "Did you know him before you left town?"

"Yes."

"And you were receiving notes then too, right?"

Callie squirmed in her seat.

Fuck. Could it really be him? Lock had always liked the guy. Sure, he was odd, but Callie was right—he'd never come across as violent.

Eastern rubbed the stubble on his jaw. "He asked you out, and you've been receiving notes from someone who's interested in you. There have been two incidences involving you, Lucian, and Hamish, both of which turned violent, and this morning you receive a note from your stalker, claiming he's keeping you safe."

Lock tensed. "You did?"

She swallowed before looking at him, her expression giving her away before her nod.

Shit.

"And now," his brother continued, "Lucian's dead."

"I still don't think Hamish could have done it," Callie pushed. "He's not like that."

Eastern leaned back in his seat. "We'll talk to him."

"Can I take Callie home?" Lock asked, ready to get the hell out of here.

Eastern nodded, and both he and Callie stood. He could feel her energy. She was sad. Maybe a bit scared. He hated both.

He tugged her into his side before stepping back into the waiting area. "It'll be okay," he whispered into her ear, needing to do something to help.

She nodded but didn't look convinced at all.

Antwan stood as the door opened. Immediately, Callie tensed at the sight of Hamish being escorted in by two deputies.

"I don't understand w-what's going on! I didn't—" Hamish stopped when he looked up and his gaze locked with Callie's. "Callie! I didn't do this. P-please believe me. I didn't kill anyone. I w-wouldn't do that!" He tried to veer toward her, and both Lock and Antwan shifted in front of her as the deputies guided him toward the hall.

"I believe you." Callie's words were quiet, but when Hamish's features eased, Lock knew he'd heard.

Lock frowned. Her words, and her words alone, eased Hamish's fear...as if all that mattered was that she believed him.

Was it true? Could he have killed someone to protect her?

He tightened his hold on Callie's waist, suddenly wanting her as close as fucking possible.

CHAPTER 22

*C*allie glanced in her rearview mirror. Her father only lived five minutes away, but right now it felt longer. Maybe because she was so on edge. Had been on edge for days.

Dead. Lucian was dead. Because someone had murdered him.

It didn't feel real.

Lock was supposed to come with her to see her dad, but he'd been called out on a last-minute job. He'd wanted her to wait, but she'd said no. Why, exactly, she wasn't sure. Because she didn't want to hide? Because she didn't want this person to scare her or impede her life?

Christ, she just wanted Eastern to find the guy and be done with it.

This is why she needed to see her dad. He was her calm. He'd *always* been her calm.

She frowned at the gray BMW in the rearview mirror. Had they been there since she'd turned off her street? Or was she just being paranoid because of everything that was happening?

Instead of taking the next left like she was supposed to, she continued straight, turning right when she reached the end of the road. The car turned right with her.

Her pulse picked up speed as her breathing came out a bit shorter. She took another right, watching the road behind her more than the road in front.

But this time, the car continued straight.

The air whooshed from her chest.

Good God, Callie. Get a grip. The whole world is not out to get you.

She turned around and headed back to her father's house. When she arrived, she took a moment to deeply exhale before getting out of the car. She didn't want her dad to see her so on edge. She'd already caused him enough stress with the notes and the guy in her backyard—he didn't need this too.

After picking up the tray of cannelloni from the passenger seat, she climbed out and headed for the front door. Instead of knocking, she used her spare key to enter the house. She'd just stepped inside when she heard a crash from the kitchen.

Her heart shot into her throat, and she ran toward the noise. "Dad?"

She stopped inside the kitchen, breath catching at the sight of him pushing up from the floor behind the island.

"Dad! Oh God, are you okay?" She set the tray on the counter and helped him up.

"I'm okay."

He was out of breath, pale, and didn't sound like himself.

"What happened?" she asked.

Once he was on his feet, she helped him over to a stool.

"I just tried to move too fast and fell."

Muscle stiffness. Impaired balance. Loss of automatic movements. All symptoms of Parkinson's disease.

"I'll get you some water," she said once he was seated. She turned toward the fridge and grabbed a bottle, using the moment away from her dad to pull herself together. His diagnosis wasn't about her. He needed her to be strong.

Once the lid was uncapped, she turned and set it in front of him. There was a tremor in his hand as he lifted it. Her father looked into her eyes once the bottle was down...like, *really* looked at her.

"It's okay to not be okay with what's happening to me, Callie."

She blew out a long sigh of air. "I want to be okay for you."

"I know you do, honey. But I've accepted my diagnosis. And I'm choosing to focus on the good. *You're* my good. The years I've had with you. The years that are still to come."

She slipped her hand into his. "You're my only family."

"I don't know if that's going to be true for long."

"What do you mean?"

"*Lock* is your family too. And his family will become your family. And you'll eventually start one of your own."

A family of her own...maybe with babies. She swallowed the lump in her throat, because the idea scared the crap out of her. "We've just started dating again. I'm trying not to look too far into the future."

"That's fair enough, but I want you to promise me something."

"Anything."

"Don't shy away from building a life after your loss."

Her heartbeat did one of those little stumbles. That was her dad...always seeing her fears even when she hadn't voiced them. "I'll do the best I can."

"That's all we can do. And just so you know, *you* are the best thing that I ever did. So I'm all for creating family."

"And you're the best thing to happen to me." She wrapped her arms around her father's shoulders. "I love you, Dad."

"I love you too, honey."

She stayed for an hour. Talking to her dad. Being told off for attempting to cook and clean.

When it was time to go, it was too soon. But she had to make a quick stop at the studio to pick up her laptop to do some admin, and she'd promised Lock she'd be home before dark. If she was going to keep that promise, she had to leave now.

On the way to the studio, she checked her rearview mirror a million and one times, but there was never anyone there.

Yeah, because no one was following her, and no one *had been* following her. She was just losing her mind.

She'd just climbed out of her car in front of the studio when her phone rang. Lock. "Hey."

"Are you almost home?"

"I just pulled up at the studio. I'll grab my laptop and come home."

"Callie, I told you I'd pick up what you need if you left your dad's too late."

"It's not late." She jogged across the street and took out her key. "I'll be home in two seconds. I just need—"

Something shoved her into the studio door, and she cried out in shock and pain. The phone fell from her fingers, the hard body behind her close. Way too close.

"It was one of your friends, wasn't it?" a male voice snarled.

She tried to breathe, but fear tightened her throat. "What?"

He yanked her head back, then slammed it against the glass. Pain whipped through her.

"You know what I'm talking about," he shouted. "Your friends *killed* my brother!"

* * *

CALLIE'S CRY made shock waves of fear rush Lock's body. "Callie?"

The hum of a male voice sounded, but it was distant, and he couldn't make out a single word.

Fuck!

Blood roared in Lock's ears as he pulled out of his driveway. The tires squealed against the asphalt, and he pressed his foot to the floor.

He sent a quick message to Jesse and Antwan, asking them to get to the studio. Maybe they were closer.

The second he'd seen her car missing, he'd gotten this pit in his gut.

Why had he agreed to take that last job? He should have gone to her father's with her. He should have been by her damn side!

He took a hard right, the tires screaming a second time.

He'd been going to say no, but it had been a single mother who'd called needing her front door fixed. He hadn't wanted her and her child to sleep through the night with a broken door.

Using the Bluetooth on his phone, he called Eastern.

"Lock—"

"Get to Callie's studio! *Now.*"

Air rushed over the line. "What happened?"

"Someone attacked her."

He hung up as he turned onto the street of her studio, pushing his truck to move faster. Then he saw them. A man pressing Callie against the studio door, his hand on the back of her head, his body against hers, trapping her.

Fury pummeled his limbs, blinding him. Consuming him.

He slammed his foot onto the brake and jumped out of the truck, leaving it on the street as he sprinted toward them. Another car jerked to a stop behind him, but he ignored it as he gripped the attacker by the back of the shirt and pulled him off Callie. Lock punched him, his fist slamming so hard into the asshole's cheek that he dropped straight to the ground.

Immediately, he lifted the guy back up and slammed him into the glass. "What the fuck are you doing?"

He groaned, head lolling to the side.

"Answer me!" Lock shouted.

Muffled voices sounded behind him. He turned to see Antwan kneeling in front of Callie, checking her face. Her *bruised* face.

Lock saw red.

He punched the guy a second time, not caring that he should calm the fuck down and step back. He kept a hold of the asshole's shirt as he got really fucking close to his face. "I said, *what are you doing?*"

More cars pulled up on the street. He turned to see his brother getting out of one of them, deputies climbing out of the other.

Eastern rushed over and stopped beside Lock, placing a hand on his shoulder. "Release him."

Lock's chest rose and fell, his fingers remaining tight on the guy's shirt. He should let him go. His nose was clearly broken, there was blood all over, and he wasn't going anywhere, not with Eastern and his deputies there.

But he was so fucking angry that he couldn't untangle his fingers.

"Lock," Eastern said firmly, "Callie needs you."

Callie…

He stepped back, fingers unclenching, and Eastern swooped in to cuff the guy.

Lock dropped beside Callie, on the other side of Antwan. Her skin was too pale, and the fucking bruise on her head was already too dark.

He gently touched her chin, tilting her head up. He barely bit back the growl at the sight of her purple and red skin. He should have hit the asshole a third time. "What happened?"

"I don't know where he came from. One minute I was on the phone with you, the next, he was shoving me against the door, saying that my friends killed his brother."

Brother…? He looked up to see Eastern had already dragged the man to his patrol car.

Lucian's brother, Oscar.

He looked back at Callie, forcing himself to stay calm as he studied her eyes, noticing there didn't seem to be signs of a concussion. "You're okay."

It was like he needed to say it out loud to remind himself that it was true. That she was here. No one had taken her or seriously hurt her.

Her green eyes burned into him as she repeated, "I'm okay."

CHAPTER 23

allie studied the navy specks in Lock's ocean-blue eyes as the chill from the bathroom counter seeped into her skin. She'd always loved his eyes. A light blue that darkened with different emotions. She swore she'd always been able to see his every mood…and right now, she saw anger. And pain. Maybe a bit of guilt.

She set a hand over his where he held the ice pack to her head. "Are you okay?"

"You're the one who was attacked." His voice was low, that anger in his eyes slipping into his voice.

"That doesn't change my question."

There was a beat of silence before he responded. "I just got you back."

"You did."

"I can't lose you again."

She tugged at his wrist, pulling the ice pack down. "You're not going to lose me."

"Someone was killed. Someone connected to you."

"You're right. It looks like my stalker murdered Lucian because of the way he treated me, which means if anyone should be worried, it's *me* about *you*. If the person writing those notes wants me, you're in his way."

"I can take care of myself. And I wasn't the one who got hurt today."

"What happened today was a grief-stricken brother lashing out, not a stalker trying to get to me." She reached up and traced the lines beside his eyes. "Do you remember the night we met?"

He blinked, looking confused at her change in topic. "You took my Biscoff ice cream."

She pulled back, feigning shock. "No. You *tried* to take *mine*."

They'd both reached for the tub at the same time. The last tub. She'd had a crappy day, and the thought of Biscoff ice cream had been the only thing that had gotten her through. She'd only been mad at the potential loss of the ice cream for a fraction of a second—because then she'd looked up and spotted the most gorgeous man she'd seen in her life and had almost forgotten about both the ice cream *and* the crappy day.

His hands went to her hips, his fingers skirting below the material of her shirt. "I wanted Biscoff, and it was the last one."

"I tried to convince you that coffee bean blast was just as good."

His gaze shifted between her eyes, voice lowering. "I didn't want coffee bean blast."

"Neither did I. So we shared."

Yep, she'd agreed to share with a stranger. Heck, she'd invited him *back to her place*. It was the most reckless thing she'd ever done.

But there'd been something about him that had made her feel safe. Which was ridiculous, because anyone with two eyes could see he was huge and likely dangerous. But she'd just had this gut feeling that he wouldn't hurt her.

Her hands slipped around his neck. "We shared the ice cream that night, and it worked out pretty well for us...so let's share the load tonight. It's heavy. I feel it too. But together, we'll be okay."

He lowered his head, his breath whispering against her ear as he said, "I hated wondering if I'd get to you in time. I want you safe, in my arms, always."

When his mouth grazed her cheek, she shuddered. Then his lips trailed down her neck, and she felt the hem of her shirt rising.

"Lift your arms for me, honey."

She did, and he tugged her shirt over her head. A second later, her bra hit the floor with a small thud, and air brushed against her breasts.

"Perfect," he whispered before his head dropped and his lips wrapped around her nipple.

She groaned as he sucked, her head tipping back, fingers digging into his shoulders. There were other people in the house, so she couldn't scream, but God, she wanted to. To let the entire world know what this man did to her.

His tongue flicked her hard bud back and forth, his fingers spanning her waist. He switched to her other breast, his tongue drawing circles around her nipple, while he reached for the button of her jeans.

"Up."

She had to roll his word around in her head a couple of times before it made sense. Everything was a haze. Eventually, she pushed up and he slid her jeans and panties down her thighs. His mouth returned to her nipple, sucking it like it was candy, as his hand moved between her thighs.

He stroked her clit, and she gasped. He did it again, but this time the noise from her lips was more of a groan.

God, he knew her body so well. What she liked...what she needed.

His thumb started a circular motion around her core as he continued to suck and tug and lick her nipple. It was torture and ecstasy and a million other things.

Then his fingers slipped inside her, and she barely held herself together. He started a deep thrust of his fingers, his thumb continuing to circle and massage.

Jesus, she needed to touch him.

She reached for his jeans, her movements almost desperate. When she finally pulled out his cock, he stilled, fingers inside her, thumb pressed to her clit.

She slid her hand over his length. That's when his chest started moving again, but this time fast, his breathing coming out almost as a hiss. She explored every inch of him, adjusting her speed and pressure to what she knew he liked, rolling her thumb over his tip.

Every little sound he made, he made for her and what she did for him. And that made her feel hot and powerful and like *his*.

He lifted his head and his mouth found hers, his tongue plunging inside.

She'd barely released him before he positioned himself at her entrance.

"I love you." Her whispered words dropped into the air, heavy and important. "From that first day when you tried to take my ice cream, I knew it would be you and me."

His fingers curled around her neck, his forehead touching hers. "I love you so much it hurts, Callie. Your absence created a hole inside me. I was empty. And now I'm not."

She lifted her head and kissed him as he plunged inside her. She tried to cry out but he swallowed the sound. He started moving, sliding in and out of her. Deep, even thrusts, setting a rhythm that drove her wild.

His fingers dug into her hips, likely the only thing keeping her on the counter.

When his mouth shifted to her cheek, she threw back her head, biting her bottom lip in an attempt to silence the sounds that threatened to break free.

He tugged her closer to the edge of the counter, thrusting deeper. Harder. Hitting a new point inside her.

Oh Jesus. She couldn't hold on much longer. But she wanted to. God, she wanted to stretch out this moment. Make the bubble they'd created last just that bit longer. It felt safe and good and intimate, everything she so desperately needed.

His hand slipped between her thighs, and he rolled her clit with his thumb while his mouth closed over her nipple again. He sucked hard and she shattered.

* * *

LOCK LIFTED his head and watched as ecstasy washed over Callie's face. As her eyes closed and her head tipped back.

Fucking perfect. All of her.

He kept thrusting, even when her walls throbbing around his cock made him want to lose it. When the sounds tearing from her chest were so sweet he wanted to bottle them up.

It was because of him and what he did to her. Because *she* was it for him.

He lifted her off the bathroom counter and turned, pressing her to the wall. He pumped deeper, his mouth crashing back to hers as he tasted her.

His Callie, so fucking sweet.

Her fingers dug into his shoulders, and he welcomed the pain. He welcomed every fucking thing about her.

"Lock..." His name on her lips was more of a groan. And it made blood roar between his ears. He tried to hold on, but her head dipped and she bit into his shoulder, and he fucking lost it.

He growled as he broke, his body convulsing, legs barely holding him up. Three more thrusts, and he was finally still, their whooshing breaths the only sounds in the room. The rise and fall of their chests the only movement.

He looked down to see her eyes hooded, her lips a rosy pink.

"Say it again," he whispered, almost desperate for it.

"I love you, Lock Walker. I've loved you for as long as I've known you."

Each beat of his heart crashed into the next, and he kissed her again. But this kiss was slow. Soft. A gentle reminder that he finally had everything he ever wanted and needed after so long going without. And this time, he wasn't going to lose it.

He moved away from the wall and carried her to their attached bedroom. Once she was under the sheets, he stripped off and joined her in bed. He still needed to check the house. Antwan and Jesse were out there somewhere, but he wanted to give everything another once-over...after he'd finished holding her, that was. Why was letting her go so hard?

Like she'd heard his thoughts, she snuggled into his side. "Thank you."

He frowned. "For what, honey?"

"Fighting for us."

He kissed the top of her head, his lips lingering. "I will always fight for us."

Her head rose, eyes colliding with his. "You never lost faith."

"And I never will."

Her eyes heated, and she reached up and kissed him again before laying her head back down on his chest, right over his heart.

He wasn't sure how long they lay there. He didn't move until her breathing had evened out and her chest rose and fell in slow succession. Then he gently untangled himself from beneath her, pulled his jeans back on, and left the bedroom.

He found Antwan and Jesse in the kitchen, both looking angry. Maybe even as angry as him.

"I need eyes on Callie at all times," Lock said quietly, teeth gritted.

The guys nodded, and it was Antwan who responded. "We'll keep her safe, Lock."

*R*inging pulled Lock from dead asleep to awake and alert in an instant.

His eyes flashed open to see the top of Callie's head as she lay on his chest, the sheets tangled around them.

He could answer the call, but then he'd have to get up, something he did not want to do.

The phone silenced but immediately started up again.

Shit. That meant it was important.

Carefully, he slipped out from under her, almost groaning when she made a sexy moan and cuddled into the pillow.

Jesus Christ, if this wasn't important, the asshole would get an earful. He tugged on jeans, grabbed his cell, and snuck out of the room.

Eastern's name flashed on the screen. His brother would only call this early if he had information. Information about Lucian? Had he found the killer?

He didn't answer the call until he was outside on the back porch. "Eastern."

"Hey. Sorry to call so early."

"What's going on?"

"Oscar didn't show up to his shift at the gas station this morning."

A muscle in Lock's jaw tensed. "What time was he supposed to start?"

"Four."

Lock pulled the phone down. Seven. Shit. "I assume you made sure he didn't just sleep in."

"We're at his house now. The front door was left ajar and the lock's broken. No one's here but it looks like there was…an altercation."

"What do you mean, an altercation?"

"The coffee table legs are broken like someone fell onto it. There's other broken shit on the floor." Wind blew over the line. "He lives in a pretty remote part of town, so we're going to check the mountains around his place in case he ran on foot, but I'm not sure how long that will take us."

"Lucian shoves Callie and ends up dead. Oscar attacks her and goes missing." Lock wrapped his fingers around the porch railing. "He's watching her."

"It definitely seems that way."

"You said Hamish didn't have an alibi for the night Lucian was killed?"

"Correct. And up until this point, I thought maybe it was him."

"But you don't think that anymore?"

"Oscar doesn't seem like a great athlete, but I still think he'd beat Hamish in a fight."

"Hamish is tall and broad—"

"He's also awkward. Doesn't really seem like someone who'd win a fight against another guy who's awake and alert."

It was true. But there were also too many reasons it made sense for this to be Hamish. "I don't want you to discount him."

"We're keeping an eye on him. In the meantime, stick close to Callie."

"Was planning on it."

"I'll let you know when we have an update on Oscar."

"Appreciate it."

When Lock stepped back inside, it was to see both Jesse and Antwan standing in the kitchen.

"We overheard. Oscar's missing." Jesse pushed off the counter. "This asshole's escalating."

"Correct."

"Who's Hamish?" Antwan asked.

"He was the guy Lucian and Oscar were pushing around that day you got to town, outside Callie's studio. He does a lot of her classes and has shown a...romantic interest in her."

Antwan's eyes narrowed.

"It might not be him though," Lock added. "I'm not sure he's capable of what this guy's doing."

"What do you need from us?" Jesse asked.

"Remain aware of your surroundings. Check the house while you're home. And if I can't be with Callie—"

"We're there," Antwan cut in, nodding.

"Thank you." He squeezed Antwan's shoulder as he passed, grateful to have them here during this difficult time.

When he returned to the bedroom, it was to see Callie's eyes still closed, her chest moving up and down evenly beneath the sheet. She hadn't moved an inch since he'd left, and she looked like a damn angel.

He crossed the room and perched on the bed beside her, grazing a lock of hair from her cheek and tucking it behind her ear.

Her eyes scrunched before sliding open, her green gaze meeting his.

"Hey, beautiful."

The corners of her lips tugged up. "Hey, yourself. You're awake."

"I am."

The smile on her lips faltered. Fuck. Had he given himself away or was she just too good at reading him?

She pushed up into a sitting position. "What is it?"

He didn't want to tell her. He wanted her to feel safe, like nothing and no one could touch her, but he also couldn't hide this from her. "Lucian's brother, Oscar, never showed up for work this morning."

She frowned, her gaze shifting between his eyes.

"And it looks like there was an altercation in his house," Lock finished.

She nodded quickly. Too quickly. "First Lucian after he shoved me, then Oscar after he attacked me. This basically confirms it's my stalker."

Lock's back teeth ground together. "It looks that way. I'm sorry."

"It's not your fault. You don't need to be sorry. I just…I hope he's okay. He was a jerk, but I don't want someone else dying because of me."

"Hey. Even if the worst-case scenario eventuates, and they do find a body, it *is not* because of you. It's because of *him*, the asshole who won't leave you alone."

"But if—"

"No," he cut in. "You didn't ask for any of this. Not the notes. The attention. The fucking watching you."

"Oh my gosh, you're right. He must have been watching me!" She straightened. "Wait, when I was driving to my dad's yesterday, I thought someone might have been following me."

"Did you get a license plate?"

Disappointment dulled her eyes. "No. Sorry. It was a gray BMW though."

"I'll let Eastern know."

She touched a hand to her stomach. "I feel sick."

He hated this. All of it. "I'm not leaving your side. Okay?"

"I have classes to teach. I can't just sit around the house."

"I'll join your classes."

Her head tilted, a small smile curving her lips. "I'm teaching two Pilates and a mat yoga class this morning. Then I'm doing my own workout."

"I'm due for a good workout."

"You're going to do four hours of Pilates and yoga this morning?"

"Sounds like it."

The smile widened before it slipped again. "Thank you for looking after me."

"You don't need to thank me. I will *always* look after you."

* * *

CALLIE SAID goodbye as the last client left the studio.

Two classes down, one to go.

She turned back to see Lock standing with his arms crossed.

Why didn't he look tired? Not even a little bit. Her classes were hard. They were *known* for being hard. What was he, made of steel? He'd just done an intermediate reformer Pilates class followed by an advanced class, and he hadn't even broken a sweat. Surely his glutes were on fire?

She crossed the room and slipped her arms around his waist. "Are you in pain?"

He frowned at her question.

Clearly, he wasn't.

"How are you so fit?" Part of her almost wanted to be annoyed. Or maybe not so much annoyed as offended that he didn't find her classes challenging.

"Didn't you know? I have gladiator genes."

She grinned. "No wonder you and your brothers all look the same."

"By the same, you mean I'm the better-looking and stronger one, right?"

Her grin widened, only to falter when someone walked past the glass. It was a stranger. Someone who didn't even look their way. But every time someone appeared outside, she wondered if it was *him*.

Basically, she was losing her mind.

"You haven't seen anyone suspicious today?" she asked, looking back at Lock.

He'd done a few perimeter checks, and she'd also seen his gaze moving over the glass every few minutes.

"No one," he said quietly, fingers grazing her side. "So, yoga next?"

He was trying to distract her. All day he'd been ridiculously discreet about what he was doing, so much so that she could almost forget why he was here.

And that's why she loved him. Or one of the reasons.

"Yes, yoga." She turned her head and eyed her laptop on the desk. "I haven't had a chance to check who signed up for the class yet and whether there'll be a spot for you."

"You'll just have to kick someone out."

He was joking, but she'd be tempted. "Aspen usually does this one, and I am *not* sending her away. I've barely seen her lately."

As if her words conjured her friend up, the door opened and Aspen strolled in. Only, her friend wasn't smiling, as usual. In fact, she almost looked scared.

Callie crossed the space to her best friend. "Hey. Are you okay?"

"I just saw Dylan."

"What did he do?"

"Nothing. Well, I mean, he was walking out of a shop, and he saw me and wanted to talk. I didn't want to talk to him, so I tried to walk away."

"Tried?"

"He grabbed my arm and told me we needed to talk. I started yelling at him to leave me alone, and I think that's why he let me go, because I became a little hysterical and people started staring."

"What an *ass*." God, ass didn't even do him justice. "I'm so sorry."

Lock stepped forward, anger darkening his features. "Is he still out there?"

Aspen shook her head. "He left. But *God*, I hate him. I don't even care if that makes me a horrible person. I hate him and the way he makes me feel, and I hate that I can't escape him in this small town."

"What can I do?" Callie asked. Because she needed to do *something*.

Aspen closed her eyes and sucked in a long breath, as if trying to calm herself. When her eyes flicked open, she looked a bit calmer. "Give me some Zen with this yoga class, please."

"Of course. But—"

"I'm sorry. I shouldn't be dumping this on you. Are you okay? Any more notes?"

Because they hadn't seen a lot of each other, and Aspen had this stuff going on with Dylan, Callie hadn't shared anything about Oscar. "Everything's fine. And Lock's here to make sure it *stays* fine."

Aspen's brows flickered.

Callie tugged her friend toward the mat. "Come on. Let's get you a mat before the class starts."

Aspen looked like she wanted to push, but instead headed over to a mat. A few seconds later, three other girls walked in. Was the fifth place booked? Usually, this class was full, but she could easily pull out a sixth mat for Lock.

She went to her laptop and pulled up her schedule...and sucked in a quick breath at the fourth name on the list. The class *was* full, and the last person booked was—

The door opened, and Hamish stepped in.

Lock took a step toward him, but she rushed forward and cut him off, shaking her head as she whispered, "Don't."

"He can't be here," Lock growled quietly, words only reaching Callie's ears.

"We don't know that he has anything to do with what's going on, and we can't just kick him out because it's a possibility."

"I sure as hell *can* kick him out."

She pleaded with both her eyes *and* words. "Please. I believe he's innocent. Eastern wouldn't have released him if there was enough evidence to hold him. And I don't want to kick him out if it's just a maybe."

Lock's jaw tightened.

"Lock," she whispered. "I don't want to hurt him any more than he's been hurt already."

Because she'd seen his face when he'd been hauled into that station. Heard the pain in his voice. He *had* been hurting. And probably deeply embarrassed.

Lock's chest rose on a deep inhale. "Fine. But I sit next to him."

"Done." She rose to her toes and kissed him before whispering against his lips, "And no glaring at him."

That got a small smile out of him. "When do I glare?"

That was a question best left unanswered.

She turned and crossed the room toward Hamish, who was already taking his shoes off beside the last mat. "Hey, Hamish."

He shot to his feet and started wringing his hands in front of him. "Callie. Hi. I-I hope it's okay I'm here. I didn't—"

"I know you didn't. And you're welcome to be here."

"Okay. G-good. I..." He frowned before swaying slightly on his feet.

She touched his arm. "Hey. Are you okay?"

"Yeah. I just suddenly don't feel very good."

Was it stress-related? She looked at him closer, noticing his face was a bit pale and there were small beads of sweat on his brow. "If you're not feeling well, you don't have to—"

"No. I'm okay." He shook his head. "I'm okay. I want to be here."

A part of her wanted to insist that he sit this class out. She had a duty to care for her clients. But he might think she was trying to send him away because of what had happened. "Okay. But you let me know if you feel any worse, all right?"

He nodded.

She released his arm and turned to see Lock watching them closely. Jesus, not the most calming environment for yoga. She grabbed another mat and set it beside Hamish's, making sure Lock wasn't too close. The last thing she wanted was a physical altercation.

She moved to her own mat in front of the class. "Welcome, everyone. Thank you for joining us today. I—"

She stopped when Hamish swayed on his feet a second time.

Nope. He wasn't okay. "Hamish, I think—"

He dropped to the floor.

There was a collective gasp around the room. She ran to him, but Lock got there first.

"He's not breathing," Lock rushed out. "Call nine-one-one!"

CHAPTER 25

Callie's gaze shifted from her lap to the hospital hallway.

It was busy. And the noise of people moving and talking was loud. Aspen's body heat penetrated her side. Her friend didn't need to be here...hell, *she* didn't either...but she wanted to know that Hamish would be okay. And when he was, she wanted to know what had happened to him.

Her nails bit into her thigh, her feet itching to get up and ask someone for information. It would be pointless. She wasn't family, so they wouldn't tell her anything. Exactly why Eastern was on his way. Well, one of the reasons.

Her gaze lifted to Lock. He was pacing and he looked nervous. Probably because he'd thought the stalker was Hamish, and if it wasn't, that left them with no suspects.

"You okay, Cal?"

She turned to look at Aspen. "I'm worried about Hamish."

"He's going to be all right," Aspen said quietly.

"You don't know that. He stopped breathing." If another person died because of their connection to her...

No. Hamish wasn't going to die. He'd be fine.

"Yes, he did stop breathing. But now he's here, in the best

hands." She tightened her fingers around Callie's arm. "Thank God he was in that class, and we were able to get him help."

Trust Aspen to see the positive. And she was kind of right. It *was* lucky that he'd been in her class. If he'd been anywhere else, he might not have gotten any help at all.

A shudder rolled through her.

Aspen slipped an arm around her shoulders. "Stop worrying."

"I don't want another person to die because of—"

"Don't finish that sentence. None of this is because of you. Not Lucian. Not whatever's happened to Oscar—which I still wish you'd told me about. And not Hamish."

She laid her head on her friend's shoulder. "Thank you."

Aspen rested her head on Callie's. "I'm always here for you."

She was, and Callie knew exactly how lucky she was to have her. Her gaze caught Lock's. He'd stopped pacing and was watching her. He was always watching her. She was lucky to have *all* the people she had in her life.

She didn't realize she was digging her nails into her thigh again until Lock sat on the other side of her and covered her hand with his own.

His lips grazed her ear. "It'll be okay."

Just those three words did so much to ease her anxiety.

She didn't know how long they waited, watching the doors. It was only when Eastern stepped inside the hospital with a deputy behind him that Callie straightened.

Lock rose and talked to his brother in a hushed voice. Eastern's body language gave nothing away, and a few seconds later, he headed down the hall and Lock sat back down.

"We weren't the only ones who called him," he said quietly.

Her stomach dropped. "You mean—"

"The hospital called."

So it was likely a criminal case, and Hamish wasn't just sick.

She nodded quickly like that news didn't devastate her, when really, it felt like the walls were closing in.

Hold it together, Callie. Don't make this about you.

A few minutes later, the door opened, and a woman stepped inside. She was older, with short gray hair and lines beside her eyes. But it was the expression on her face that had Callie frowning…she looked worried and scared.

The woman stepped up to the counter. "My son, Hamish Evergreen, is here."

Callie shifted to the edge of her seat. Hamish's mother.

The nurse typed a few things on the computer before turning back to the woman. "The doctor will be out to talk to you soon."

"No! I need to see someone *now*. My baby is in there. I need—"

A doctor approached the nurses' station. "Mrs. Evergreen?"

Eastern and the deputy followed close behind him.

Hamish's mother rushed toward them, but they spoke too quietly for Callie to hear what they were saying. It was only when the mother started crying and the doctor led her down the hall that Callie's stomach dropped.

Hamish wasn't okay.

Emotion clogged her throat, but she swallowed it down.

When Eastern headed over to them, she, Lock, Callie, and Aspen stood.

"What's going on?" Lock asked, arm around her waist.

Eastern shifted his attention to the hall, then back to them. "There's a possibility this is connected to what happened to Lucian and Oscar."

Callie tried to calm her fear. "What do you mean, 'a possibility?'"

Eastern met her gaze. "They found GHB in his system."

"What's that?" Aspen asked.

"It's a drug commonly linked to date rape. But when it's used in a high dosage—"

"It's lethal," Lock finished.

"Yes." Eastern ran his fingers through his hair. "It's a flavorless liquid, so easy to slip into someone's drink."

The fine hairs on Callie's arms stood on end. "So, whoever drugged him got close to him just before class."

Eastern frowned. "Maybe. There's also the possibility he takes it himself. In small doses, it induces euphoria and relaxation. Maybe the stress of being questioned caused him to overdose. His mother insisted he doesn't take drugs, though."

Callie's finger dug into her palm. "How much did he consume?"

"Enough to put him in a coma."

Her jaw dropped. *Oh God.*

"We need to find out where he was before the class," Lock said.

Eastern turned to his brother. "We know where he was. He was getting a drink with his mother at Sugar and Spice, but she said they didn't talk to anyone else. I need to talk to Sadie and her grandmother and see if they remember who else was in the café." His gaze shifted to Callie before returning to Lock. "There's something else."

"What?" Lock asked, voice low and dangerous.

"We found Oscar's body."

Callie's heart thumped. "His body?"

Eastern's gaze returned to her, voice somber. "He was beaten to death in the woods behind his house."

* * *

Lock's fingers tightened around the wheel as they drove away from the hospital.

Drugged. In a coma. And Oscar was dead.

Jesus, things were going from bad to worse.

Eastern believed that Oscar being beaten to death made it less likely Hamish was the culprit and more likely a victim. Lock wasn't convinced. Not enough to write him off anyway. Hamish could still be involved. Just because someone didn't appear capable of something didn't mean they weren't. Lock had run into plenty of dangerous people during his time in the military who'd played the part of an innocent but really knew a hundred ways to kill someone.

And overdosing on a drug was something a guilty person might do.

They'd have to wait until Hamish woke up and Eastern could question him to know for certain. His brother was good at what he did, so if anyone could get to the bottom of this, it was him.

He shot a glance over at Callie. She was blaming herself for everything, and he fucking hated it.

He took a left, then a right turn.

Callie frowned. "This isn't the way home."

He'd been wondering when she'd realize. "We're not going home."

"Where are we going?"

"You'll see."

Callie opened her mouth like she was going to argue, only to sigh and put her hand on his thigh. He kept driving until he reached the spot.

Callie leaned forward. "This is the lookout."

"It is." It was the highest point in Misty Peak. You could see almost the entire city from up here. He climbed out and circled the truck to open her door. She spotted the blanket immediately with the picnic basket and cooler bag beside it.

"You did this?" she gasped.

"Cody owed me a favor, so technically he and Harper did under my instruction. You need a break from everything."

She wrapped her arms around his waist tightly before seeming to breathe him in. "Thank you."

"I'd do anything for you." He meant that. Whatever she needed, he would find a way to give it to her.

They settled on the blanket, and he took cheese and crackers out of the cooler. There were grapes and olives. Even wine.

Callie cocked her head. "Wait, this is the stuff we ate that first night we met."

Ah, she was putting it all together. "It is."

Not only had they shared the tub of ice cream that night, Callie had taken out an entire board of picnic-type food to go with it from her kitchen.

"But there's no—" She stopped when he took the tub of Biscoff ice cream from the cooler bag. Her smile was wide as she looked at him, and he fucking loved it. "You're amazing, you know that?"

"Not amazing, just completely and utterly besotted with you."

Her smile softened. "I'm kind of besotted with you too." She eyed the ice cream. "Would it be crazy if I ate dessert first?"

He took out two spoons and set the tub between them. "I was counting on it."

She laughed, and as they ate, they watched the sun set. Neither of them brought up the notes or the Tate brothers or Hamish. In fact, they barely spoke at all. It was like they both needed a bit of silence together.

It wasn't until they'd finished half the food and she was lying on his chest that she asked a question that pulled them out of the bliss. "Do you miss him?"

He knew exactly who she was talking about. Even thinking about him felt like a punch in the gut. "I miss Winnie every day. But I know he's up there with Remi and Hollie, probably blasting some music and laughing at us unlucky bastards who still have to figure out this life shit."

She smiled as she traced a line down his chest. "Do you ever wonder how someone was able to get close enough to kill him with his training?"

"Every damn day. He was as aware of his surroundings as the rest of us. And he was a great fighter. But then, so was the guy who killed him. Maybe Winnie was so busy trying to protect

Remi, he couldn't protect himself. That was Winnie, always looking out for others."

"I wish things had been different."

He wished that so many times it had become a broken record inside his head. "Can I ask you something?"

"Anything."

"Do you see kids in our future?"

She tensed. And he immediately regretted the question.

She rolled onto her belly to look at him, a crease between her brows. "Honestly...I don't know. The idea of being pregnant again kind of terrifies me."

He shifted a lock of hair from her face. "I can understand that."

"The pregnancy loss was unexplained. There was never any indication of why it happened. If it happened again..."

The pain on her face felt like a physical blow. "I hope like hell it doesn't. But if kids are what you want, I'll support you through all of it, no matter what happens."

"Do *you* want kids?"

"Yes." The answer was immediate, and he wasn't sure if maybe he should have paused or hesitated or looked like he needed time to think about it. "But I want you more. So if you can't do that, we don't have to try."

She nodded, but the line between her brows remained, her eyes focused more on his chest than his face.

"Callie."

She finally looked up.

"If our future is just you and me, then I will be the luckiest son of a bitch on the planet. Kids are something I want. But *you* are all I need."

Some of the worry eased from her features. "What if one day you wake up and resent me for not giving you kids?"

"That will never happen."

"You don't know that."

"I do. Because I know what it's like to not have you, and I would always choose the other option. I would always choose you."

A small smile touched her lips. "Okay, but you could get sick of just me."

"Not possible."

"I don't know. I can be pretty annoying when I'm hungry or tired."

"Then I'll feed you and force you to rest."

"Will you rest with me?"

He leaned up, hovering his lips a mere inch from hers. "I'll hold you the entire time." He kissed her, feeling for the first time that day like everything was going to be okay.

CHAPTER 26

Callie leaned into Lock's side, a smile on her lips.

Man, it felt good to smile. To sit outside with Lock, Jace, and Elle, the warmth of a fire in front of them and a glass of red wine in hand.

A week had passed since the incident with Hamish. He was home and recovering and, according to Eastern, had vehemently denied taking the GHB. Although, he'd also said he had no idea who could have slipped it into his drink. Sugar and Spice had been busy that day, but he claimed he hadn't gotten close to or spoken to anyone.

She hadn't seen Hamish since he'd gotten out of the hospital. She wanted to, but Lock had insisted they wait until they found the person responsible for everything that was going on.

Everything had been quiet over the last week, and she'd felt safe with Lock by her side. Or as safe as she could feel with a crazy stalker on the loose.

"You really took his clothes so he had to walk out of gym bare-ass naked?" Lock asked Jace, pulling Callie's attention back to the conversation around her.

It was Elle who nodded. "He did. Casper was so mad, but he never found out who did it."

"Trust me when I say he deserved it," Jace said, sipping his beer. "The guy was a dick ninety percent of the time."

Callie looked up at Lock. "Did you do stuff like that in high school?"

Jace scoffed. "Mr. Serious over there? He didn't have my balls *or* my charm."

"Charm?" Lock laughed. "I think you're mistaking your big ego for charm, buddy."

"I can have both ego and charm." Jace grinned.

Callie laughed. "So you two were best friends in high school but didn't date?" It sounded unbelievable, because looking at them now, you'd think they'd loved each other for years.

Elle nodded. "Yeah. It took us a while to get our act together."

"It took *me* a while." Jace slipped his arm around her and tugged her closer. "But we got here in the end."

As the two kissed, Callie smiled up at Lock. "Sounds a bit like us."

"I like it when you do that," Lock whispered.

"Do what?"

"Smile."

Her smile widened. "It's what you do when you're happy. And I am happy. Which is crazy right now, isn't it? I *shouldn't* be happy."

"Yes, you should. And I'm glad you are." He lowered his head and kissed her, and she sank into that kiss.

Elle handed her wine to Jace and stood. "I'm just going to use the bathroom."

"I'll show you where it is," Callie offered, handing her own wine to Lock.

Lock shook his head. "I can do it."

"Don't be silly. Catch up with your brother. We won't be

long." She bent down and kissed him one more time before heading into the house with Elle.

"Jesse and Antwan are staying here, aren't they?" Elle asked.

"They are. Although they've gone to Meridian with Aspen tonight. I told them to stay, but I think they sometimes feel like they're intruding. Which they're not. We appreciate them extending their stay." When all three men were in the house, she felt ridiculously safe.

"Does Aspen go out with them often?"

"She's actually been hanging out with Jesse quite a bit." Callie had pushed for more information on what was going on between them, but Aspen had insisted they were just friends. She'd then gone on to insist that she planned to be single for the next ten years and adopt five cats.

It wouldn't happen. Her friend was young, funny, and gorgeous, with long blond hair most women would kill for. There was no way she'd stay single for long.

Callie glanced at Elle as they moved through the kitchen. "You and Jace look happy."

"I've loved him for so long that sometimes I need to pinch myself so I know I'm not dreaming, and he really does love me too."

"He definitely loves you. Anyone can see that."

"Thank you. You and Lock seem to be doing great as well."

"I'm really lucky to have him." She stopped in front of the bathroom off the hall. "Here you go."

"Thanks."

The door closed after Elle, and Callie was about to head back outside when a cool breeze brushed the back of her neck.

Frowning, she turned. It was coming from Lock's bedroom. Had he left a window open?

She walked into the bedroom, and sure enough, the window was pushed all the way up. She took a step toward it, only to stop, common sense slamming her in the face.

What the hell was she doing? Lock wouldn't have left a window open. He was too safety conscious. And *she* definitely hadn't.

The hair on her arms stood on end. It wouldn't have been Jesse or Antwan—their rooms were at the end of the hall, and they never came in here.

So…who had done this?

She was about to turn and rush back outside when a hand slammed over her mouth and a strong arm banded around her waist.

She froze, fear paralyzing her. It took an entire second of being dragged toward the window to realize it wasn't a hand over her mouth. It was a cloth. And that cloth had something on it. Some sort of chemical that made her dizzy and light-headed.

Shit.

She thrashed her legs, trying to kick the guy behind her. Stomp on his foot. *Anything.* When that didn't work, she grabbed at his shoulder, pulling on material and hearing a small tear.

It wasn't enough. A couple more steps and they'd be at the window.

Her head started to grow fuzzy, a deep exhaustion settling into her bones.

Noise. She needed to make noise! Even the smallest sound could alert someone that something was going on.

Before she was lifted out the window, she used her last scrap of energy to kick the bedside table. A small lamp fell, and the crash of the ceramic breaking echoed through the room.

Then another noise sounded—this time from outside the room. Footsteps.

"Callie, are you— Oh God!"

Elle. The other woman's voice was the last thing Callie heard before her world went black.

* * *

"It's so good to see you happy, man."

Lock leaned back in his seat and smiled at his brother on the other side of the fire. "I *am* happy. I've loved Callie for as long as I've known her."

"That's damn beautiful. It reminds me of me and Elle." His brother sipped his beer. "Eastern any closer to finding the psychopath who killed the Tate brothers?"

His fingers tightened around his beer. "No. But I'm still not fully convinced it's not Hamish."

"Why do you say that?"

"The notes started over two years ago when she was living here in Misty Peak. They align with about the time she met Hamish in a class she was teaching. Then she leaves, locals don't know where she is, and the notes stop. Right when she gets back into town, they start up again, and Hamish expresses his interest in her."

"Okay. But Oscar was beaten to death after being chased through a forest. Hamish is big, but he doesn't strike me as a fighter."

"Do we really know what anyone else is capable of? Maybe he's had training we're not aware of. Or maybe he's just really fucking strong and fast."

Jace blew out a long breath. "You're right. Hell, I almost got shot by this granddad in a bakery during a mission once. Underestimated him for a second and that was all it took."

Exactly.

Jace leaned forward. "Are you watching *your* back?"

"Of course."

"Good. Because if it's not Hamish, then he was targeted simply for showing an interest in Callie. I hate to think what that could mean for you, the man who's actually dating her."

"I can look after myself."

"I know. I just don't want you to be so busy protecting Callie that you forget to protect yourself."

That was his brother...hell, it was his entire family—they watched each other's backs. "I appreciate it. But even if I miss something, I have Antwan and Jesse here to back me up."

"I'm—"

A scream suddenly pierced the air. Not Callie's scream—Elle's.

Lock shot to his feet and sprinted into the house, Jace right on his heels. They reached his bedroom just in time to see Elle slam into a dresser and a figure disappear out the window.

Jace ran to Elle's side as Lock flew across the room and leaped outside. The cool evening air hit him in the face as he spotted the asshole in a balaclava halfway across his yard—Callie's limp body slung over his shoulder.

Motherfucker!

Lock took off toward them, then dove and crashed into his legs just before he reached the street.

Callie hit the ground, and as much as Lock wanted to check on her, he had to focus on the abductor. He flipped the guy over, but before he could pull off the balaclava, or even get a good fucking look at his eyes, the asshole threw a punch that Lock barely managed to dodge.

He grabbed the fist and threw an elbow toward the guy's jaw, but he turned his head just in time, then lifted a leg to kick Lock off his body.

Lock was only on the ground for a second, but that was all the guy needed. He ran.

"Go after him!" Jace shouted from the window as he dropped to the grass. "I've got Callie."

Fuck, he didn't want to leave her, but he needed to catch this guy. He needed this to be over.

He rose and ran, sprinting down the sidewalk. The guy was fast, almost a shadow as he disappeared around a corner. Lock pushed his body to move faster, feeling the slap of concrete beneath his shoes. The whip of air across his face.

His hands fisted, and he forced himself into a sprint as Callie flicked into his mind. Her body strung over this asshole's shoulder, completely limp.

The guy turned another corner, and it made Lock see red. He needed to get his hands on this guy. To know his fucking identity.

He turned the corner again—only to stop at the sight of a disappearing car, its lights off. It turned the next corner so quickly, Lock didn't even get a license plate.

Fuck!

He ran frustrated fingers through his hair, every muscle in his body tight as rage punched through his limbs.

Gone. The asshole was *gone*. And Lock still didn't know who he was, which meant he was still fighting blind. And tonight, he'd almost taken Callie.

With fisted hands, Lock turned and ran back to his house. He had to get back to her. Was she okay? Was she hurt? Why had she been so lifeless?

He reached his front yard to see Jace on his cell, as Elle knelt over Callie's body.

A sick feeling churned his stomach. She still wasn't moving, and as he got closer, he could see her mouth was red.

He dropped to her side. "Callie?"

"He drugged her," Elle said quietly.

"Chloroform," Jace said as he hung up the phone. "Paramedics are on their way, and Eastern's meeting us at the hospital. You didn't catch him."

It wasn't a question.

Lock shifted his gaze back to Callie, focusing on the rise and fall of her chest. She was alive. That's what he needed to concentrate on.

"No," he finally said. "But I will. And when I do, he's a dead man."

CHAPTER 27

*L*ock's eyes moved over Callie's still body. The doctors had said she'd wake up at any moment. It wasn't soon enough. He wanted to see her eyes. Hear her voice. And fuck, he hated seeing the oxygen mask over her face.

His fault. This was his fault. Someone had broken into his home. Drugged her. Tried to take her. And he hadn't caught the bastard.

He should have gone into the house with her. But he hadn't, because he'd thought his house was safe. He hadn't counted on the asshole breaking the fucking lock on his window. How long had the guy been waiting in there to get her alone? And why hadn't he been worried that it would be *Lock* who went in there first?

Was he that ballsy, or had he been watching them in the yard and Lock hadn't noticed?

He had to have been watching and entered when the women went inside. No way would he have just broken in and waited, risking the possibility of Lock or Jace going in first.

He wanted to punch his damn hand through the wall. Let the pain dull out the other emotions. The anger. The frustration. The helplessness. That was probably the worst of it all. He wanted to do more. To take action and fix this. But he couldn't fix *anything*. He couldn't even protect the woman he loved.

The door opened and his brother poked his head in. "Can I come in?"

Lock dipped his head as he stepped toward his brother, his throat feeling too tight to get words out.

Eastern's gaze moved to Callie. "How's she doing?"

"No sign of respiratory issues. The doctor said she might just feel nauseous and light-headed when she wakes up."

"That's good. How'd you get in here?"

"I told the nurse I was her husband." He would have told them whatever was necessary to make sure he was by her side. "Tell me you found something."

"The stolen car was dumped a few miles from where you last saw it. My guys are going through it for prints, but they're not hopeful."

"Where was it stolen from?" Lock asked, gaze returning to Callie and the rise and fall of her chest.

"The parking lot of the Thai restaurant here in town. Owner left the keys inside."

Lock scrubbed a hand over his face. "He was fast, Lock. The same fast fucker I chased down in that alley opposite Callie's studio."

"Good. So we know this is one person."

Something on Eastern's face made Lock straighten. "You suspect someone. Who?"

Eastern's chest rose on a deep breath and, for a second, Lock thought his brother might not answer the question. "I'm just gonna ask this once, okay? And if you tell me to drop it, I won't bring it up again."

A sick feeling churned in Lock's gut. "What?"

"It couldn't have been Jesse or Antwan, could it?"

Lock flinched. "What the hell are you talking about?"

"They're both fast. Both well trained."

"They wouldn't do this. Fuck, they're like brothers to me, and they got to town after this started. But if you don't want to take my word for it, ask Cody. They were at Meridian tonight with Aspen."

Eastern nodded, not confirming nor denying whether he'd ask Cody. Knowing him, he would, and it made the anger inside Lock burn hotter. "Where was Hamish tonight?"

"Lock—"

"He was in the hospital for a week, and in that week nothing happened. He's out for a day and someone attacks her."

"He just got out of a coma. He couldn't have—"

"We need to stop assuming we know what he can and can't do. He matches the physical description of the guy I saw tonight, and he could have training we don't know about. Have you done a background check on him? Like a really fucking *thorough* background check?"

Something flickered in Eastern's eyes. Something dark.

His brother wasn't telling him everything.

Lock inched closer. "What?"

"He grew up with a dad who was a Marine. The dad died three years ago."

"So, his father could have taught him how to fight, and this whole awkward side of him could be one big fucking act."

"I'm not gonna lie, it's possible." Eastern's jaw clenched. "I plan to question him tomorrow."

"Good."

"I also plan to question Aspen's ex. Maybe he's still pissed about the altercation at the bar." Eastern's gaze moved to the door and back. "I'll man the hall until you leave."

"Thanks."

Eastern grasped Lock's shoulder before heading back into the hall.

Lock returned to Callie's bedside and lowered beside her. He threaded his fingers through hers and lifted her hand to his mouth to press a kiss to her soft skin. "Wake up for me, Cal. Let me see your eyes when I tell you I'm sorry. You should have been safe in my home, and you weren't."

He lowered his head so his temple touched her hand.

The slow rise and fall of her chest continued, and every second that passed made him want to yell that bit louder. Rage at the world that this had happened. That he'd come so damn close to losing her.

The door opened a second time, but it wasn't Eastern.

Lock rose to his feet. "Jude—"

"What the hell happened? Why is my baby in a hospital bed?" Jude stormed over to Lock, eyes narrowed and hands fisted.

Lock hadn't seen him this angry since he'd knocked on the older man's door two years ago, looking for Callie. "Someone broke into my house through the bedroom window. They drugged and tried to kidnap her."

"Where the hell were *you*?"

"I was out back." And he would hate himself for that for a long fucking time. Probably forever.

For a moment, Lock thought the older man might hit him. Lock would let him. He deserved it.

"You were supposed to protect her," Jude hissed.

"I know. I fucked up."

Jude swallowed hard. "Did you catch him?"

"No."

Jude's eyes darkened, and some of the anger shifted into something else…fear. Fear for his daughter. That this asshole was still out there.

"With all due respect, sir," Lock said quietly. "You couldn't say anything to make me angrier than I already am at myself."

Jude stepped closer. "I—"

"Dad."

They both turned.

Callie. Her eyes were open.

* * *

THE SMELL of cleaning products tinged the air. It was a familiar smell, but not in a good way. It reminded her of the night she'd lost her baby. Of lying in a hospital bed, feeling empty and alone.

She kept her eyes closed.

Why was she in the hospital? She'd been outside with Lock, Jace, and Elle, then what?

Voices pricked at her ears. Loud voices. Angry but also familiar.

"You were supposed to protect her."

Dad...what was he doing here?

"I know. I fucked up."

Lock. He sounded angry...angrier than she'd ever heard him.

She opened her eyes.

Ouch. Light hammered into her head.

Then it came back to her...the breeze from Lock's bedroom. The hand over her mouth.

Someone had tried to *kidnap* her. But he hadn't succeeded. He couldn't have. Because she was here, in the hospital, with Lock and her dad.

"With all due respect, sir, you couldn't say anything to make me angrier than I already am at myself."

She squinted through the light and forced her gaze to focus on Lock and her dad.

Her father stepped into Lock's space. "I—"

"Dad." She pulled the oxygen mask off her face as both men looked at her. "It's not his fault."

Lock rushed to her side and took her hand. "Callie! How do you feel?"

"My head hurts, and I feel a bit sick, but that's all." She squeezed his hand before turning to her father, who was now at

220

the end of the bed. "The person who broke into his house, *that's* who's to blame."

Her father's hands wrapped around the bed railing. "I hate seeing you like this."

"But I'm okay." She turned to Lock. "I am okay, aren't I?"

"The doctor said you'll be fine, you might just be a bit light-headed and nauseous."

Oh, she was definitely those things. "What happened after he grabbed me?"

A muscle in Lock's jaw twitched. "Elle screamed, and Jace and I ran in there. The guy had already carried you out the window, so I went after you. I grabbed him, we fought, but he got away."

He got away. So he was still out there. "Did you see him? Do you know what he looks like?"

"No. He was wearing a balaclava. But Eastern's looking into a couple of people."

She opened her mouth to ask who but stopped when a wave of dizziness washed over her.

Lock's fingers tightened around her hand. "Are you okay?"

"I'm fine." She wasn't. She felt terrible. But guilt already played over Lock's features, and her father was giving off the most intense worried vibes. There was no part of her that wanted to make them feel worse.

Lock's phone rang and he pulled it out, frowning at the screen. "Is it okay if I—"

"Answer it." She gave him a small smile, and he stepped back from the bed. She turned back to her father. "It's late. You should be at home, in bed." She had no idea what the time was, but by the darkness outside, it was either really late or really early.

"I'm exactly where I should be." He moved around the bed and touched her hand. "I'm glad you're safe, baby. You scared the hell out of me."

"I'm safe with Lock." She tilted her head and lowered her voice. "Please don't blame him."

"I know. I'm sorry. Fear makes me need someone to blame, and he was all I had."

She squeezed his hand. "Lock's on our side. And if there's anyone we want on our side, it's him and his brothers."

"I don't know what I'd do without you."

"Oh, Dad." She forced herself up into a sitting position, closing her eyes against the pain in her head, ignoring her father urging her to remain lying down. Then she looked her dad in the eye. "I'm not going anywhere. Okay?"

He blinked back visible tears. "I'm going to hold you to that."

"I'd expect nothing less." She looked down to see the slight shake in his hands. "You need to go home and get some sleep."

"I'm not leaving your side."

"What if I promise to visit you tomorrow?"

"No. I'll visit you. And I'm bringing a meal."

"Dad—"

"I'm bringing a meal, Callie."

She sighed. "Thank you."

Her father pulled her into a gentle hug.

He'd just left the room when Lock got off the phone.

"Everything okay?" she asked, not really sure she wanted to know if it wasn't.

"Yeah, just organizing a new lock on the bedroom window. Jesse and Antwan are working on it."

"They're good friends."

"They feel like shit for not being there tonight." He lowered to the chair beside her. "I'm sorry."

"Lock—"

"I should have gone into the house with you."

"You can't be everywhere, all the time."

"It's my job to protect you."

She reached up and cupped his cheek, letting the warmth of his skin seep into her hand. "You did. You protected me. I'm here and safe because of you."

"If Elle hadn't screamed—"

"But she did. Is she okay?"

He placed his hand over hers and turned his head to kiss the inside of her wrist. "She's fine. Worried about you."

The door opened and a middle-aged woman stepped in, red glasses on her nose and clipboard in her hand. "Miss Ward, you're awake. I'm Doctor Feldon. How do you feel?"

"Pretty good, considering what happened."

"Yes, being drugged with chloroform is more dangerous than a lot of people realize. Fortunately, the tests show you're both okay."

Callie frowned. "Both?"

"You and the baby."

Every muscle in Callie's body froze, sending a chill down her spine. There was a beat of silence where she wasn't sure if she or Lock even breathed. She didn't look at him. She couldn't take her eyes off the doctor.

"I'm pregnant?"

"Yes. The test is fairly accurate. You're early, but definitely pregnant." The doctor frowned. "You didn't know?"

Pregnant. A baby was growing inside her…and that was terrifying.

CHAPTER 28

Trees flew by the window, but Callie barely saw them. She barely saw anything. Her head was a mess, a million emotions competing against one another inside her, and none of them good.

Pregnant. She was *pregnant*. They should have been more careful. God, why hadn't they been more careful?

Lock had tried to get her to talk to him, tell him how she felt, but she couldn't speak. There was almost this desperate need inside her to keep her emotions locked away, as if that could somehow dull the fear of reliving the past.

She couldn't go through that again. She'd barely survived the first time.

Lock's hand rested on her leg, its warmth usually enough to calm her. Tonight, it wasn't.

He was worried about her. He hadn't said the words out loud. He'd said it with the deep frown etched between his brows. In the way he watched her so closely. Touched her with hesitation like he was scared she'd run.

And if she was completely honest…a part of her *wanted* to run. But this time, running wouldn't be an escape.

Lock and the doctor had spoken about her past pregnancy loss. Phrases like "high risk" and "extra observation" had been thrown around. She'd tried to listen, but every second that passed had made the walls around her feel that bit closer. Like the room was closing in on her.

Callie was so in her own head that she didn't even realize they'd arrived at Lock's house until his thumb grazed her thigh, tugging her back to the present.

"Callie. Talk to me, honey."

Lock wanted her to talk. But how was she supposed to articulate the pit in her belly? How was she supposed to put words to the fear and confusion and panic that swirled inside her?

"Callie—"

She turned toward him and he stilled. It was like one look at her and he saw everything. Every word she couldn't get out. Every emotion she couldn't convey.

He climbed out of the truck and moved around to her side, where he helped her out before setting a hand on the middle of her back and guiding her inside.

The second they stepped into his bedroom, her gaze shifted to the window, a shiver shaking her whole body.

There was the softest growl from Lock before he lifted her against his chest and carried her into the bathroom. She barely felt the chill of the bathroom counter beneath her thighs as he sat her down. Piece by piece, he helped her out of her clothes, his eyes never leaving hers.

His clothes dropped next, his bronzed skin on full display. Then he lifted her back into his arms and stepped into the shower. There was something about water and warmth and having the man she loved hold her that dulled some of the panic inside.

She tightened her arms around him and just let him hold her. Let the shower beat down on both of them. It almost felt like a circle of safety, a place where the grief of the past and the uncertainty of the future couldn't penetrate.

His mouth went to her cheek, his lips brushing her skin before he whispered, "It will be okay."

She wanted to latch on to his words and take them as truth, but he couldn't promise her that. No one could.

She burrowed her head into his neck. "Just hold me."

That was what she really needed. His warmth. His strength. *Him*.

* * *

It was still dark outside. Not even a sliver of light snuck through the gap in the curtains. What was it, four a.m.? Five?

They'd only gotten into bed at two. He hadn't slept. Not a single minute. He'd thought Callie wouldn't sleep either, but the second her head hit the pillow, she was out. Like the weight of the past twenty-four hours had left her without a scrap of energy.

His gaze lowered to the top of her head. To her torso, where it lay half over his.

Pregnant. She was pregnant…again.

It should have been an evening for celebration. They loved each other. They wanted to spend their lives together. But the weight of the past was heavy.

He'd wanted to talk to her about it. To hear exactly how she felt even if it was dark or ugly. But she hadn't wanted to talk. He didn't even think she'd been capable. And that fear on her face, in combination with her pale skin and the circles under her eyes… fuck, it had made him worry.

He stroked his thumb over her bare hip, wishing this moment could be different. Wishing, for the thousandth fucking time, that things had been different two years ago.

He lowered his mouth and kissed the top of her head.

At least she'd let him hold her. He needed that. It wasn't just the pregnancy announcement that had shaken him. It was everything that had come before with her almost being kidnapped.

His arm around her tightened.

He needed to know who the asshole was so he could rip him to shreds. Maybe that was why Eastern had kept the information about Hamish's father being a Marine from him. Because literally all the fucking signs pointed to it being him now. He fit the description of the guy. Same height. Same body type. And just because someone appeared non-threatening didn't mean they were.

He tried to close his eyes. To get a whisper of sleep, but a noise had his eyes shooting back open. It was a whimper. So quiet he almost didn't hear it.

Was Callie awake and upset? He held his breath.

Another whimper, this time louder, followed by a turning of her head into his chest.

"No," she gasped.

Lock frowned, his muscles flexing.

"Oh God, no!"

Jesus, she sounded terrified.

"Lock...I need you!"

His heart squeezed so tight it was painful.

He rolled Callie over so she was on her back, but her eyes didn't open. Her head started to thrash from side to side, tears streaming from her eyes.

Fuck, he had to wake her. "Callie."

Her head kept moving as she panted beneath him, the air whipping in and out of her lungs.

"Callie, honey, wake up."

Her eyes tightened, and for a moment he thought she might have heard him. Then she whispered, "Daddy...I need help!"

Lock's skin iced. She was dreaming about the night she'd lost the baby. He hadn't answered her call, so she'd called her father.

He didn't need her to wake up and tell him for Lock to know that.

He lowered his head so his mouth was near her ear, and whispered, "I'm here, C. Wake up for me."

He repeated those words three times, and slowly her movements stilled, the rise and fall of her chest slowing.

"Wake up for me," he repeated, voice soft, words just for her.

It took a few more seconds for her eyes to slowly open. But even then, they were glazed, like she wasn't really seeing.

She blinked. Once. Twice. On the third blink, she looked at him. *Really* looked at him, as if she was finally seeing him. "Lock."

"You're safe."

Her brows drew together, another rise of her chest before she pushed the blankets down and straddled his lap, digging her face into his chest.

The silence was thick as he stroked her back, the need to soothe her like a living, breathing beast inside him. Every part of him wanted to erase the past. Make it better. Easier. But he couldn't do that. He would never be able to do that.

"How often does that happen?" he whispered.

"Not as often as it used to."

"Tell me about it." It would kill him, but he wanted to know exactly what she was remembering.

"I wake up bleeding. I try to call you. You don't answer, so I call Dad." She nuzzled her face deeper into his chest. "Sometimes I almost swear I'm back there, living the nightmare all over again."

He lowered his mouth and kissed her temple, his lips hovering there for a long moment. "I'm sorry." He wasn't sure if he was saying sorry for the repeated nightmare or sorry the entire thing had happened in the first place. Maybe everything.

"Having a baby wasn't something I ever really considered," she said quietly. "But in the few short months I was pregnant, I started picturing my life with this child. Making space for them. Loving them. And then in one second, they were taken from me."

His arms tightened around her.

"What if it happens again?" she asked, fear now slipping into her words. "What if we lose another baby?"

"No matter what happens, I'll be by your side, and we'll tackle it together. You and me."

She blew out a long breath. "You and me."

"Always."

She drew a circle on his chest. "Because it was unexplained, I always wondered if…"

"What?"

"I was sad. So sad and so stressed. What if—"

"No." His voice was firm, leaving no leeway. "It was *not* your fault."

There was a small pause where even her finger on his chest stilled. "I started to blame myself. I felt alone and lost and angry at myself for being so stressed out. That was my rock bottom."

He would never forgive himself, not if he lived a hundred years. "You'll never be alone again. I'll make sure of it."

"Promise me." Her eyes clashed with his, almost desperate. "Promise me you'll never leave me again, even if the most dangerous, psychotic terrorist steps into your life and tells you to end things with me."

"Never." He said it like a vow.

She studied his face, searching for something. Then, as if she'd found what she was looking for, she lowered her head again, pressing her cheek to his chest right over his heart. "Good."

CHAPTER 29

*C*allie took a deep breath as she glanced at her reflection in the mirror. It was a new day, and it was going to be a better day.

Yes, she was pregnant, but this time things were different. She wasn't alone. Lock was with her, and he'd remain with her, no matter what happened. And every time she forgot that, every time she was dragged back into the past, she'd just remind herself again.

She tugged her hair up into a ponytail. Lock had left a few minutes ago. He'd said it was to work, but a part of her didn't believe that. Would he go to a job the day after she was almost kidnapped *and* found out she was pregnant?

Doubtful. But then, if not, where was he and why had he lied? Maybe Antwan or Jesse, her assigned babysitters, would tell her.

Her phone vibrated and she looked down at the text.

Aspen: I'm in the kitchen. Come out when you're ready so I can give you the biggest hug of your life.

Aspen was here. Good. She needed time with her best friend. She stepped out of the bedroom, listening to the voices in the kitchen.

"When are you going home?" Aspen asked.

"Home?" Antwan responded. "I don't really have one of those right now. I sold just about everything. But eventually, I'll find somewhere new to live. Jesse will probably leave before me. He misses Amber Ridge. A hell of a lot more than I miss my hometown."

"Why don't you like your hometown?"

"There's just not much there for me anymore."

Callie stepped into the kitchen, and they both looked up. Aspen was across the room in a second, pulling Callie into her arms.

"Oh my God, it's so good to hug you." Aspen pulled back, inspecting her closely. "Are you okay? And I want the truth, even if I'm not going to like it."

"I'm safe."

Aspen frowned. Callie hadn't really answered the question, and they both knew it.

"I'm sorry I wasn't here." Aspen pushed back a lock of hair from Callie's face. "I should have come over like you offered, not gone out. God, I was at the *bar* when you were almost kidnapped. I'm an awful friend."

"No, you're not. I'm glad you weren't here. You were safe at Meridian, and that's the most important thing."

"That's not the most important thing. Your safety is important too. I'm glad Lock got to you in time to scare the guy away."

"Me too."

Antwan cleared his throat. "You're really okay?"

She looked at him. "Better than I should be."

"Any idea who it was?" he asked.

"No. Lock didn't catch the guy, and he was wearing a bala-clava, so he couldn't see his face. He was also driving a stolen car."

"Argh. That makes me so angry!" Aspen shouted. "I hate men. Hate, hate, hate, *hate* them!"

"Hey! I'm a man, and you don't hate me," Jesse said, coming out from the hall with a grin on his face.

Aspen lifted her brows. "I don't hate you *now*… There's still time."

He playfully shoved Aspen's shoulder before turning toward Callie. "It's good to see you looking better."

He hugged her, and she returned the hug, grateful he hadn't asked her if she was okay like everyone else.

When he passed Aspen, he grazed her side, and she smiled as *she* gave *him* a big shove. The dynamic between the two of them almost made Callie smile.

"All right, we need you two to clear out so Callie and I can have a one-on-one," Aspen declared.

Jesse filled a glass with water. "I feel excluded."

"You can feel whatever you want. You still need to get out."

Antwan straightened. "Come on, man, let's go out front and cut that wood Lock's been bitching about."

Jesse met her gaze. "We'll stay close."

She nodded. She knew they would.

Before they left, Antwan stopped in front of her and hugged her. "I'm glad you're safe."

She pulled back and nodded. "Thank you."

As the two guys left through the front door, she saw Aspen frowning at them. Was her friend frowning at Antwan or Jesse? Probably Jesse. There was something going on there, even if she refused to admit it.

The door closed, and Callie stepped closer, touching her friend's hand. "How are *you*?"

Aspen's head whipped around. "Me?"

"Yes, you. Have you seen Dylan lately? And how's your mom?"

Aspen swallowed, her cheeks losing a bit of their color. "I see him every so often. Then I turn straight around and go the other way." There was strain in her friend's voice.

"I'm sorry."

"I hate living in the same town as him. I hate it so much. And Mom's…Mom. The same level of crazy as always. One minute she's gifting me a new bracelet and telling me she loves me, the next she's accusing me of stealing her rings."

"None of that sounds fun." Callie tilted her head. "Are you sure you don't want to talk about what happened between you and Dylan?" She'd never told Callie the details. Which still felt really odd.

Aspen swallowed. "I broke up with him. That's where the story starts and ends."

"Aspen, I want to be there for you, but I can't if you won't let me in." And there *was* information she wasn't sharing. She was starting to feel like she was nagging her friend about this, but she couldn't help her if she didn't have all the information.

Aspen frowned, and for a moment, Callie thought she might actually tell her something important. Then she blinked and shook her head. "You were almost kidnapped last night. I came to check on *you*, not the other way around. You went to the hospital, for Christ's sake. I'm assuming because they discharged you, you're okay?"

Callie lowered her gaze to her hands, the little bomb of truth on the tip of her tongue.

"What is it?" Aspen asked, inching closer. "Oh my God, you're not okay."

"I'm fine. I'm actually…pregnant."

Aspen gasped, and for a moment, she didn't move. Her mouth remained open, her eyes plastered on Callie.

"Pregnant?" she finally said.

"Yep. The doctor showed me the test result and everything."

Aspen nodded slowly. "Okay. And how do you feel about that?"

How did she feel? She felt a million things, but one word summed them all up. "Scared."

"Oh, Cal." Aspen pulled her into another hug. "You are strong and brave and loved. And you will make the best mother."

Callie bit the inside of her mouth in an attempt to stop the emotion clogging her throat. "Really?"

"Absolutely." Aspen pulled back and grabbed Callie's hand. "The past is not going to repeat itself. And before you say I don't know that, I do. Because the universe would not do that to you twice. I won't let it."

"You don't control the universe, Aspen."

"I absolutely do, and I've put in an order for only good things to come to you in your future."

God, she loved this woman. "Thank you. I needed to hear that. What would I do without you?"

"Probably the same thing I'd do without you. Drown in a bout of misery."

Despite everything, Callie laughed, because it was true, she probably *would* drown in a bout of misery without her best friend.

* * *

HE SHOULDN'T BE HERE. He knew he shouldn't be here. But the second he'd woken up, there'd been no keeping him away.

Lock climbed out of his truck and slammed the door before jogging up the couple steps to Hamish's front door. He banged on the wood, blood roaring between his ears as he waited for the asshole.

Hamish had barely pulled the door open before Lock grabbed him and pulled him outside. He slammed the guy against the wood, getting so close that he could see every fucking pore on his skin.

"Was it you?" Lock growled.

Hamish's eyes widened, fear turning them from brown to black. "W-what?"

"Don't fuck with me. Did you try to kidnap Callie last night?"

Hamish's mouth opened and closed, shock sweeping over his expression. "Someone tried to k-kidnap her?"

Was Hamish a really good fucking actor, or did he actually have no idea what had happened?

"It wasn't me," he gasped, almost sounding breathless. "I would never sc-scare her like that. I…I care about Callie."

Was he telling the truth? No, he couldn't be. Because if it wasn't him, then who the hell was it?

Hamish's mother stepped outside, phone in hand. "Get off our land. My boy's done nothing wrong."

A car pulled into the drive, and Lock turned his head, only to curse under his breath.

"I called the sheriff's office," his mother added.

Eastern had gotten here too quickly. He'd probably already been on his way to question Hamish.

"Lock," Eastern shouted. "Let him go or I'll be forced to cuff you."

Ignoring Eastern's words, Lock turned back to Hamish, looking him dead in the eye. "Tell me one more time you didn't do it. That you're not behind the notes she's been getting. That you've done nothing to scare Callie."

Hamish met his gaze. "I've done n-nothing to scare Callie. And I haven't written her any n-notes."

He was telling the truth. Lock stumbled back.

There was someone else. A blind goddamn threat. Someone with eyes on his woman. Someone willing to kill for her.

Eastern had tried to warn him, but he hadn't listened.

He stormed to his truck.

"Lock! Get the hell back here," Eastern shouted.

Lock wrapped his fingers around the door handle, only to have his brother grab his shoulder and spin him around. "You shouldn't be here."

"I know that. But what else was I supposed to do? Just sit around and wait for him to strike again?"

"I'm gonna find him."

"*When*? After his next kidnapping attempt?" It was a low blow. His brother was a former Navy SEAL and an excellent sheriff, but *fuck*, Lock was angry. Frustrated, he ran his fingers through his hair. "It wasn't Hamish."

"How do you know?"

"I asked him. I saw it in his eyes. He had no idea about the attack last night."

Eastern eased his hold on Lock. "So it's someone else." His brother looked as disappointed as he felt, because Hamish would have been an easy suspect. Lock had wanted it to be him... because then the case was solved.

Eastern stepped back. "Come with me to the station and we'll brainstorm."

Lock climbed into his truck, his mind moving at a million miles a minute as he drove. This person was watching her, so he had to be close. Was it someone she knew and trusted? Someone she *allowed* to be close to her?

For a single second, a thought popped into his head. Something he hadn't allowed himself to consider until now. The man last night had been strong, fast, and well trained...all the attributes the guys on his team possessed...just as Eastern had suggested.

No. It wasn't Jesse or Antwan. Even if they weren't like family, they'd been at Meridian last night with Aspen.

Hadn't they?

Before he could talk himself out of it, he hit the Bluetooth on the wheel and called his brother. Cody answered on the first ring.

"Lock. Everything okay?"

"Not really. I need you to tell me that Jesse and Antwan were at the bar last night."

His brother didn't hesitate. "Jesse and Antwan were at the bar last night. Although, we were busy, so I didn't have eyes on them the entire night. But I saw them arrive. Jesse and Aspen were together most of the night, and Antwan was chatting with a woman. And they all left together around eleven."

The weight on Lock's chest lifted. Callie's attack had occurred at nine thirty. "Thanks, man. I appreciate it."

He was just turning into the station parking lot when a loud bang sounded, followed by fire under his hood. Heat immediately cracked the windshield.

His truck swerved, and he couldn't get control.

Shit!

He clicked his seat belt off, threw open his door, and rolled out. His body hit the road hard while his truck crashed into a parked car.

Tires squealed nearby, and the door to Eastern's car flew open a second before his brother was out and running toward him.

"Lock! Are you okay?"

Lock rose to his feet, ignoring the scrapes on his sides. "Someone did something to my truck."

Eastern lifted his radio and called for both his deputies and the fire department.

Lock's blood pumped, the need to contact Callie and check that she was okay all he could think about. But his damn phone had been in his truck—and now the entire fucking thing was in flames.

What had it been? A bomb? Jesus. "I need your phone."

Eastern handed it over, and he hit Callie's name.

"Hey, Eastern."

The air rushed from his chest at the sound of her voice. "Hey, it's me. Are you okay?"

"Lock? I'm fine. Why are you calling from your brother's phone?" There was a small pause, and when she spoke again, she sounded panicked. "Something's wrong. Did something happen?"

He didn't want to lie to her, but he couldn't tell her the truth.

Not over the phone and not after everything that had happened in the last twenty-four hours. "I'm fine. I'll see you in an hour. You're keeping the doors locked, right?"

"Of course. It's just Antwan and me now, because Jesse took Aspen home."

"Okay. Make sure you stay close to him. I love you."

"I love you too."

He hung up and handed the phone back to his brother.

"Come into the station," Eastern said, already moving forward. "The deputies can look at the truck while I take care of those scrapes."

They'd just stepped inside the station when Aspen turned to look at them from where she stood by the front desk.

Lock frowned. "Aspen. What are you doing here? Jesse said he was taking you home."

"He did. Then I came here." Her gaze shifted from Lock to Eastern and back. "I think I know who's targeting Callie."

CHAPTER 30

*L*ock was hiding something.

Callie eyed the phone, tempted to call him back. Well, not him. Eastern. Or at least Eastern's phone. Another question she had…why had he called from Eastern's cell? She'd asked but he'd avoided the question.

Something had happened. What? And why hadn't he told her? Did he think she couldn't handle it?

She blew out a breath. He would have told her if it was really important, wouldn't he?

She turned and glanced at her yoga mat. She should return to her session. But there was no way she could concentrate now.

Maybe, if there was something going on, he'd told Antwan. Was it underhanded of her to try to get information from him? Did she care?

No. Desperate times called for desperate measures.

Deserting her yoga session, she left the bedroom and stepped through the living room and into the kitchen. Empty.

Strange. He'd been in here when she'd gone to the bedroom.

She headed down the hall, passing the first two bedrooms and stopping at the end one. She knocked.

Twenty seconds passed, and no answer. She knocked again, this time a bit harder, and the door creaked open.

Should she stick her head in? What if he was changing? But if he was changing, he would have heard her knock, right?

She stepped inside. "Antwan?"

Her gaze shifted to the closed bathroom door, the distant sound of the shower echoing throughout the room.

She checked her watch. Ten. It felt a bit late for a shower. But then, he and Jesse had been chopping wood before Jesse took Aspen home.

She was about to turn and leave when something poking out of his luggage caught her attention. Frowning, she moved toward it, her steps slow. She lifted the black shirt. It had been shoved under the other clothes, with just the edge sticking out. But it wasn't the shirt itself she was focused on.

She ran her finger over the small tear in the shoulder.

Callie had heard the material of her attacker's clothing tear at the shoulder last night.

She dropped it like it had burned her.

No. God, why did that thought even enter her head? This was Antwan, one of Lock's best friends. And besides, he'd been at the bar last night.

But it *was* strange.

Nibbling her bottom lip, she spared a quick glance at the closed bathroom door before rummaging through the bag. She'd clearly lost her damn mind, but she couldn't bring herself to stop.

She paused when she found the small compartment in the side of the suitcase. It was so small, she almost missed it.

She slipped her hand inside and pulled out a phone. Not Antwan's phone. Or at least, not the one he usually used. That was a Samsung, and this one was an iPhone.

She glanced up at the closed bathroom door a second time. The shower was still running, but that didn't stop the shaking in her fingers. Her heart started to beat faster as she opened the phone, surprised to find she didn't need a code or password.

A voice in her head screamed to put it down and get out. Not just out of this room but out of the house.

But another part of her needed to know why Antwan had a different phone hidden in his bag.

She looked at the messages first. There were none. Next, she looked at the contacts. Again, they were empty. Who had a phone with an empty contact list and no text exchanges?

She clicked into the photos—and her heart stopped.

It was her.

All of the photos were of her. Some of her crossing the road. Some of her in her studio, taken through the window, both teaching and doing her own sessions.

Nausea swamped her belly, and she almost dropped the cell when she saw the one of her in bed, sleeping. But not in Lock's house. In *her* house.

He'd watched her sleep. How?

Then she remembered…the broken back door.

Jesus.

Bile crawled up her throat, threatening to break free.

"Callie."

She jumped, her gaze flying up to see Antwan standing in the bathroom doorway, shirtless, his jeans hanging low on his waist and a towel slung over his shoulder.

She'd been so focused on the photos that she hadn't heard the shower turn off.

His gaze shifted from her face to the phone in her hand, then back to her. Nothing changed in his expression, but the energy in the room was thick and heavy and dangerous.

He stepped toward her. "You weren't supposed to see that."

Run. Get away. The words screamed in her head. But she'd never make it.

"It's been you all this time," she whispered, still not believing it.

"Yes."

Yes? *Really?* That was all he had to say?

"You *killed* people."

"For you. To protect you."

He said it so calmly, like taking a life was the most normal thing in the world.

"I can't…I have to go." She stepped back.

"Don't make me chase you, Callie. I don't want to hurt you."

What was the alternative? Let him do God knows what to her? He would never let her go now that she knew.

One heavy second of silence passed, and in that second, there was stillness. As if they were both waiting for the other to make a move.

Her blood pumped so fast it was all she could hear.

One more beat of silence—then she turned and sprinted down the hall.

She was a foot from the front door when Antwan's arms wrapped around her waist and he shoved her against the wall. Then his body was against her back, his mouth beside her ear.

"I told you not to run."

She tried to shove him back, but it felt like trying to shift a mountain…immoveable. "Get off me!"

"I can't do that, Callie. I won't hurt you, I promise, but I can't let you go." He wrapped an arm around her throat and pressed his other hand to the back of her neck. There was intense pressure, then the world around her hazed and she blacked out.

* * *

ASPEN WAS NERVOUS. One look and Lock could see that. Did she really know who was stalking Callie?

She paced Eastern's office, but so far hadn't said a word.

242

"Aspen," Eastern pushed, gently but urgently. "What do you know?"

"So, this morning I was at your house, Lock." She didn't look up or stop pacing as she spoke. "And there was this moment where Jesse hugged Callie, and Antwan…"

Lock's heart began to beat faster. "He what?"

"His eyes narrowed. It was only slight, but I don't know, it was…strange. And his muscles tensed. He didn't say it, but I could tell he didn't like Jesse touching her."

No. No fucking way. She was saying it was Antwan?

"What else, Aspen?" Eastern asked.

"Then *Antwan* hugged her, and he sniffed her hair. I swear, he closed his eyes and sniffed her hair. It was creepy." She blew out her breath and kept pacing. "It was all so strange that I thought I must've actually imagined it. I'm an author, so I often create stories in my head that aren't true. Hazard of the job. But then when I got home, I started thinking about last night."

"What about last night?" Lock asked through gritted teeth.

Aspen stopped pacing and looked at him. "Jesse and I were playing pool while Antwan was talking to this girl. He went to a corner table with her and the bar got busy. We didn't see him for, maybe an hour? When we *did* see him again, he was wearing a jacket. He didn't have one before and he was acting… I don't know. Different. Weird. I thought maybe things didn't go well with the girl, but now…"

"Antwan wouldn't do this," Lock said, as if still trying to convince himself. "I know him, and there's no actual proof."

Eastern turned to him. "Hamish and Sadie both said Antwan and Jesse were in Sugar and Spice the day he was drugged. Antwan could have easily walked past Hamish and slipped it in. He was also present at both altercations with the Tate brothers. And the car last night was stolen from Thida Thai, which is only a street away from Meridian."

"This person has been here, in Misty Peak, since before

Antwan even got to town," Lock pushed, desperate now. "There was a fucking note left at her house by hand."

"Did you actually get confirmation of when Antwan's flight got in?" Eastern asked.

"He got in the same day as Jesse."

"Who got in first?" Eastern asked.

Lock's jaw tensed. "Antwan. He waited for Jesse at the airport."

"So he could have gotten in a while ago and not told anyone. Gotten to the airport just before Jesse's flight to make it look like he'd just arrived." Eastern lifted his desk phone and pressed a button. "Paxley, I need you to look into a flight for me from Georgia to Misty Peak." Eastern glanced up at Lock. "When did they arrive?"

Lock closed his eyes, trying to recall. "July eighth."

Eastern relayed the information to Paxley.

The air started to feel too thick, the band around his chest tightening, suffocating him.

He grabbed his brother's cell from the desk and called Callie's number.

Come on, honey. Answer the phone for me. Let me hear your voice.

The call rang, then it rang some more. On the fifth ring, he knew she wasn't answering. He tried Antwan. The same damn thing.

Fear clawed at his insides. If what Aspen suspected was true, he'd just left Callie in a house with her goddamn stalker.

Fuck.

He quickly left his brother's office, ignoring Eastern's loud curse from behind.

Eastern caught up with him outside, just as Lock reached his brother's car. Eastern slid behind the wheel while he jumped into the passenger seat. As his brother drove, Lock called Jesse, who answered on the first ring.

"Lock—"

"Are you home?"

"No. I'm picking up coffee. Why?"

Shit. "Did Antwan disappear for an hour at the bar last night?"

"Possibly. I was playing pool with Aspen, and he was talking to a woman. I didn't have eyes on him the entire time, but I doubt he would have left."

"But you don't know for sure?"

"No, I don't. What's going on, Lock?"

Eastern took a hard right as Lock said the words he still couldn't believe were coming out of his mouth. "It might be him."

There was a small pause, and when Jesse spoke again, his words were slow and careful. "*What* might be him?"

"The guy who's fucking with us. The one stalking Callie and killing people. It might be Antwan."

"No," Jesse growled, just as harshly as Lock had. "We *know* Antwan. He's family."

Eastern's car phone rang, and he answered. "Paxley. You find something?"

"There were no flights from anywhere in Georgia to Misty Peak on July eighth."

Black specks began to haze Lock's vision.

He'd lied...

Eastern drove faster.

"Jesse, I need you to meet us at the house *now*," Lock said.

"Already in my car."

Lock hung up and the second they arrived at the house, he jumped out and sprinted toward the door.

"Callie?" he called once he was inside. The silence was so loud it was deafening. "Antwan?"

Nothing. Not even a whisper of movement.

Lock's heart raced, panic building inside him. He ran into his bedroom. A yoga mat sat on the floor, a water bottle beside it, but no Callie. Not in the bedroom or the bathroom or the walk-in closet.

He exited the hall to see his brother checking the living room and kitchen. Lock ran down the opposite hall to Antwan's bedroom. Jesse was already inside. All of Antwan's shit was still there, but he wasn't. Neither of them were.

CHAPTER 31

Callie rolled from her back to her side, sleep trying to tug her back under.

She squeezed her eyes shut at the light. What time was it? Surely it had to be time to get up if it was so bright.

She sucked in a deep breath, only to freeze…the sheets smelled different. Or maybe it was the room. Woodsy and earthy, nothing like Lock's room or her own.

Her eyes flicked open to see a wooden ceiling with an old light centering the space. She swung her gaze to the side to see wood plank walls and a wooden dresser.

Her skin grew clammy and her heart started to thump as she pushed up to see deep purple bed sheets that were nothing like the beige ones in Lock's room.

Panic seized her chest as she tried to recall her last memory.

It was the morning after her almost-kidnapping. Lock had gone somewhere. Aspen had visited, then Jesse took her home.

What had happened after that?

Antwan. She'd gone to his room to ask him something and found the shirt…then the phone.

Oh God.

What happened after the phone? Think, Callie.

She fought the clouds in her brain, recalling Antwan's large frame as he'd stepped out of the bathroom.

And the fear...Jesus, the fear had almost swallowed her. She ran...but she didn't make it. But then, she'd known she wouldn't. Antwan was big and trained, one of the most dangerous soldiers in the world.

A tremble slid through her limbs as she lifted the soft material of the lilac dress...a dress she'd never seen before in her life.

He'd changed her. Put clothes on her while she'd been unconscious.

Nausea pitted her belly, but she couldn't be sick. She had to figure out where she was and how to get out.

Carefully, she turned and set her bare feet on the wooden floorboards. Her gaze caught on a photo on the bedside table... A woman with a wide smile and green eyes eerily similar to Callie's. Antwan's arms were wrapped around her waist from behind, and they looked...happy.

Who was she?

Callie shook her head. It didn't matter. Nothing mattered except getting out.

On legs that didn't feel steady, she rushed to the window and pulled back the curtains to see nothing but trees. There was no fence. No other houses. She was isolated.

Shit, shit, shit.

Gripping the bottom of the window, she attempted to tug it up. She knew what would happen—of course she did—but she had to try.

It didn't budge, not even a little bit.

She pulled harder. Again, nothing.

Her gaze caught on the small key lock. With shaking fingers, she traced the hole with her finger before inspecting the rest of the window. It was new. Everything about this room seemed old except the window.

He'd replaced it to lock her in. Had he replaced all of them?

Fear twisted her belly before shifting into something else. Something harder but easier to manage. Anger. Red-hot anger that this man she'd trusted, who was supposed to be a friend, would do this. Scare her. Hide her somewhere with him.

She crossed the room and tried the doorknob. She expected it to be locked as well. It wasn't. Did that mean there wouldn't be any other escape routes in the house?

She'd find a way out. She had to.

She'd just inched the door open when she heard a sound from somewhere in the cabin.

What was that? A plate being set against a counter?

Slowly, she inched out into a short hall before stopping at a small kitchen and living room. Antwan's back was toward her as he lifted a plate from a rack and dried it with a tea towel.

He was doing dishes.

She almost wanted to laugh. A hysterical, you've-got-to-be-kidding-me kind of laugh, because it was absurd. Completely and utterly absurd that this man would *kidnap her*, then do a mundane task like drying dishes.

"I was wondering when you'd wake up."

She jumped at the sound of his voice. But she shouldn't have been surprised he knew she was there. He was just as perceptive as Lock, and Lock was always aware of his surroundings.

She wrapped her arms around her waist to chase off the chill. "Where are we?"

He turned, his black eyes staring into her. "Our cabin."

Our cabin?

He said it like this was some romantic getaway, when it was the furthest thing from that.

He reached into his pocket and pulled out a set of keys. "And there's no getting out, Callie, so don't try. It's you and me."

She swallowed the anger that threatened to break free. "Make this make sense, Antwan, because right now, I'm really confused."

"What are you confused about, darlin'?"

What was she confused about? Was he trying to get a reaction out of her? "We're just friends. We've always been friends."

"Not true. I've loved you since the day Lock introduced us. I understand you might not feel the same about me right now, but one day you will."

She flinched. Since Lock had introduced them? The framed photo in the bedroom flicked into her mind. "I saw the photo of you and that woman beside the bed. Who is she?"

Darkness flashed across his face before he shook his head. "She doesn't matter. What matters is that you're here now, and you're mine."

She wasn't his. She'd *never* be his.

The urge to scream at this insane man consumed her. But she had to be smart, not angry. "You can't just take someone and assume they'll become yours."

"You're not just *someone*. You're the woman I love." He went back to doing the dishes, like their conversation was completely rational. "When you disappeared, I thought I'd lost you forever. It killed me. But I bided my time, because I knew I'd find you eventually. Then, two years later, Lock tells me you're back in Misty Peak, and I knew then that nothing and no one would stop me from having you."

"But I don't love you."

He paused, glancing over his shoulder, the thick muscles in his biceps contracting and almost making her want to take back her words.

His jaw clenched, and he returned to the dishes. "I was hoping that while I stayed with Lock, you'd realize how strong our connection was and start to love me back. I killed for you. That's something Lock would *never* do."

Yeah, because Lock wasn't insane.

"It was only last night, after a few drinks at the bar, that I started feeling...frustrated. I started thinking maybe you'd never come to me…and I acted rashly. I was an idiot, I admit. I tried to take you with little to no plan. It was fucking stupid, and I knew the moment I did it that it was a mistake. I didn't even set the damn car bomb properly."

She stumbled back a step. "Car bomb?"

"It was supposed to kill Lock. It didn't. The asshole's been blowing up my phone with texts and calls."

The air rushed out of her chest, making her knees weak.

He was alive… Lock was alive.

Antwan's eyes narrowed on her. "But I'm going to try again, and this time, there'll be no mistakes."

"Don't." The word came so quickly that Antwan's narrowed eyes darkened. "I mean, you don't need to do that, now that you have me."

"He'll look for you. He'll scour every inch of the fucking earth to find you. He needs to be eliminated, something I put off for far too long because I let my emotions get in the way."

Her mind worked fast, protecting Lock all she could think about. "I'll end things with him."

"What?"

"I'll call him and tell him I want to be with you, not him. I'll make him believe me."

He turned, frowning. Was he thinking about it?

Say yes. You don't need to hurt Lock.

She forced her feet to move. To cross the distance between them and touch her hands to his chest. "Please. Let me do this."

Antwan's eyes shifted between hers, and when his hands went to her hips, she barely stopped herself from pulling away.

"I've loved you for so long, Callie." His head lowered, and when his breath brushed her neck, she bit her bottom lip hard to stop from cringing. "I never wanted to hurt anyone. I just wanted *you*. When I couldn't find you for those two years, I tried to forget you. But I couldn't. And when Lock said you were back…I knew I couldn't let you disappear a second time."

She frowned, something pricking at her mind. "But you were with Hollie when the notes started."

"She saw one of the notes I sent you."

Ice slid over her skin. "And what did you do when she saw the note?"

"She was going to tell you. She was going to turn you against me. We fought and I…I lost control."

"You killed her." Callie hissed out the words.

"It was easy to frame Malone. We were already looking for him, and he was pissed about his organization."

"What about Winnie and Remi?" Even as she asked the question, she knew.

His hands tightened on her hips. "I was staying with them a few days later. They didn't want me to be alone. It was my shoes…my fucking shoes. Winnie saw a small streak of blood. I made up some bullshit excuse. But that same night, Remi went into the spare room. She knocked over my bag and found my gun. It was the same caliber that had killed Hollie. He called me in and we struggled. I did what I had to do."

She was going to be sick. "You killed your teammate. Your friend."

"I didn't have a choice! I couldn't go away for killing Hollie. For a while, I didn't think I could live with myself after…but knowing you were out there kept me going."

Oh God, this would destroy Lock.

"But I'll let him live," Antwan said as he looked up. "If you end things and promise not to run."

There was no way in hell she wouldn't be attempting to run if she got the chance. But there was also nothing she wouldn't agree to in order to protect Lock. "I promise."

His eyes heated, and his gaze locked on her mouth.

He was going to kiss her.

Bile crawled up her throat as his head lowered. His mouth

was an inch from hers when a beep on his phone sounded, making him straighten.

Thank God.

He pulled out his cell and frowned. "Someone's in my room."

"Your room?"

"At Lock's house. I put a camera and a motion detector in there."

He stepped away from her and moved into the living room, tapping on his phone. The second his back was turned, she eyed the knives drying on the counter, one larger and a couple smaller.

She couldn't attack him. He was too well trained. And when she failed, he might go back on his word and attack Lock.

Desolation swirled in her mind.

"*Fuck.*"

She jumped at Antwan's curse and looked up to see him still staring at his phone. He was angry.

"They're going through my shit," he yelled. "They *know*! They'd only be in there if they knew. How the fuck do they know?" He scrubbed a hand over his face. "If Lock knows I took you, he won't believe you want to leave him. He'll search for you. I *have* to eliminate him. Then we can disappear. We'll just become another unsolved crime."

He nodded like it was already decided. Like he'd just planned out their entire future in a matter of seconds.

No. She wouldn't let him kill Lock.

She turned so she was facing Antwan, her back to the knives. Her movement was slow as she reached behind her, trying not to give away what she was doing.

His gaze suddenly shot toward her, and her heart stopped. "I need you to wait here while I go out for a bit."

"Now?" He was going to kill Lock *now*? He was insane. Completely and utterly insane.

"I have to do this now. If anyone can figure out where we are, it's him. He's smart. And he'll go to any lengths to get you back."

He crossed the space between them and cupped her cheeks. "I'm sorry. I know you don't want me to hurt him, but—"

"He thinks of you as family."

"I know. But I can't lose you! I'll make *any* sacrifice, go to any lengths, to make sure that you're mine."

He was sick.

He started to turn, and for a fraction of a second, Callie wondered if she could do it. But then the thought of Lock being attacked or killed flashed in her mind. The idea of never hearing his voice again…never seeing him…

She swung the big knife forward.

And at that exact moment, Antwan turned, eyes widening as he used lightning-fast reflexes to grab her wrist. "Callie—"

She swung her other arm, this time low, stabbing him in the side of his stomach and digging the smaller knife deep into his gut, then twisting.

He growled before swinging his elbow and making her world go black.

CHAPTER 32

*L*ock could barely breathe. Gone. She was gone. The words were on repeat in his head. It was like a nightmare he couldn't wake up from.

Jesse lifted a phone from the bag. "This isn't Antwan's phone."

Lock took it, noticing it was open to a photo album. His chest constricted.

Callie. Every fucking photo was Callie. Sleeping. Walking around town. Working in her studio.

Rage seared through his midsection, and he wanted to throw the goddamn cell. Either that or crush it in his fist. He probably would have if Eastern hadn't taken it from his fingers.

His brother cursed under his breath when he saw the images. Jesse continued rummaging through the bag.

Lock couldn't move. He'd put her stalker in the same damn house, right under her nose. He'd *introduced them.* Asked him to *protect* her.

"Who's this?"

Lock turned at Eastern's words and looked at the phone to see a photo of Antwan and a woman with green eyes and long dark hair. "Lola. They started dating in high school and got engaged a few years later, but she died of cancer four years ago."

Jesse stepped forward. "They look the same."

Lock frowned. "What?"

"I never thought about it before, but looking at her photo now…she looks like Callie. They have the same eyes. The same hair. The same build."

Lock's attention shifted back to the photo.

Was that what this was about?

"He used to talk about her sometimes," Jesse continued. "One night he told me that when Lola died, a part of him died too. I always thought it was strange that he never mentioned Hollie. She died while they were dating too, but he never really expressed how he felt about that, not once in the two years since. Not like he did with Lola."

"But he asked about Callie a lot over the years," Lock said, almost to himself. "Out of everyone in my life, he asked about her the most. About whether she'd come home. Whether I knew where she was." He'd thought Antwan was just being a good friend. He'd trusted him.

The rage on Jesse's face mirrored Lock's. They'd *both* trusted him.

"Any idea where he might have taken her?" Eastern asked, the only one with a semblance of calm in his voice.

Jesse frowned. "Antwan and Lola grew up not too far from here. North Carolina, I think. Maybe he has a place out there."

"What was Lola's full name?" Eastern asked, pulling out his phone.

"Hartford," Jesse said. "Lola Hartford, and Antwan's last name is Johnson."

Eastern turned and called the station.

As Eastern spoke on the phone, a conversation with Antwan came back to him. About wanting to retire in the mountains with the woman he loved. In a cabin with an open fireplace and only trees for neighbors. At the time, Lock had thought he was talking about a woman he hadn't met yet. But maybe not. And maybe he already had the cabin…or had access to it.

"A cabin."

Eastern turned, phone still to his ear. "What?"

"Find out if Antwan, his family, or hell, Lola's family, had a cabin somewhere in the mountains."

His brother didn't question him, just nodded and repeated what Lock had said to his deputies.

Lock ran his fingers through his hair, wanting to pull the fucking strands out. Helpless. He felt completely and utterly helpless. He couldn't breathe until he knew she was safe. But he wouldn't have that confirmation until he figured out where the hell she was.

"How didn't I see it?" Lock asked, more to himself than anyone else. "We've seen them together so many times since he got to town. Aspen was around them *twice*, and she saw everything I didn't."

"Because you trusted him, so you weren't looking for this."

"I should have been. For Callie, I should have questioned every damn person in her life." When he got her back—because he *would* get her back—he'd spend the rest of his life making it up to her.

Ten minutes later, Eastern's phone rang.

His brother answered the call, his gaze rising to Lock's, expression unreadable. "Send me the location and meet me there." Eastern hung up, eyes still on him. "Lola's family owns a cabin in the mountains near Asheville, North Carolina."

Lock was moving before his brother had finished speaking. Sprinting out the door and toward the car.

She was there. She had to be.

* * *

257

GOD, her head pounded. She touched her temple and flinched.

That son of a bitch.

She forced her eyes open. She was lying on the couch. She turned her head, groaning at the small movement.

"I didn't want to hurt you, Callie."

She froze at his voice. Then, slowly, she pushed into a sitting position and focused on Antwan. He stood in the kitchen, shirtless, as he dabbed at the stab wound on his stomach with a cloth. A stab wound *she'd* given him.

Fear shuddered down her spine. She'd never hurt another person before, let alone stabbed them.

"You're safe here. But *don't* do that again."

Safe with a lunatic? She absolutely wasn't. "I need you to leave Lock alone."

A muscle clenched in his jaw. He turned toward the sink to rinse out the cloth, and she frowned when she saw something poking out of his back pocket.

Keys. A key to the door, certainly. Maybe the windows too…

Adrenaline spiked her heart rate.

He turned back toward her, cursing as he patted the wound once again.

She straightened. "I'm sorry. When you said you were going to hurt Lock, I freaked out."

"It has to be done," he said, voice unyielding. "For us to be together, he has to die."

Fear for Lock once again crawled around her veins. She had to do something, and she had to do it now. Without a word, she rose to her feet, only to stumble at the sudden dizziness.

Antwan's gaze shot across to her. "Are you okay?"

Really? He was asking her if she was okay after he'd knocked her out? "I'm fine." If you called a blazing headache fine.

She crossed the space between them and stopped in front of him. "Let me."

His brows flickered, but she placed a hand over his and he let go of the cloth. She patted the wound, noticing how Antwan's muscles rippled beneath her touch.

"I really am sorry," she said quietly. "I was scared."

"You don't ever have to be scared with me."

Being this close to him, she wasn't just scared, she was terrified. He was unpredictable and unhinged. Every part of her screamed to step away from the predator. But she didn't have the luxury of doing that right now.

She moved around him and rinsed the cloth before patting the wound once more. "You should get this looked at by a professional."

"No. I'm not seeing anyone."

She swallowed before grabbing the bandage from the counter and placing it over the wound. "Does it hurt?"

"I've had worse." There was a small beat of silence before he asked, "Do you think you could learn to love me?"

She froze. There was almost a desperation in his voice. How had no one realized how unstable Antwan was? How had he hidden this side of himself for so long and so well?

Forcing herself to look him in the eye, she told him what he wanted to hear and made sure it was believable. "Yes, I think I could. I think you would be easy to love."

His chest rose on a deep inhale, eyes heating as he pulled her against him, his face once again dipping into the crook of her neck. "I needed to hear you say that, Cal. I needed it so bad."

Hearing him use her nickname felt wrong. Only people close to her used it. She hugged him back, slipping her arms around his waist and running her hand over his back. As she did, she carefully slipped the keys from his pocket.

When he pulled back, she quickly slipped her hand to her side, half behind her.

"We're going to be okay," he said quietly. "You'll learn to love me. You won't get sick. We'll be happy."

She wouldn't get sick? Why had he said that? Had someone else he loved become sick?

"We'll be okay," she repeated. "I might go lie down, if that's all right?"

Concern tugged his brows together. "Your head—"

"Is fine. I just need some rest."

He was still frowning, but he nodded.

She was careful to turn in a way so that he didn't see what was in her hand. It was hard to walk away slowly when all she wanted to do was run.

Once in the bedroom, she closed the door softly and sat on the bed, making sure the springs made the appropriate sounds before she silently rose again and went to the window.

There were three keys on the ring. She tried the first in the lock. It didn't slide in. She tried the second. It slid in but didn't turn.

One left.

Fear gnawed at her belly. What if this didn't open the window? He'd find out she took the keys and then what? What would he do?

With even breaths, she tried the third key. It slotted in…and turned.

Relief almost caved her knees.

Unlocked. The window was unlocked.

Quietly, she shoved it open. There was the smallest creak, and she cringed, waiting for the bedroom door to bang open and Antwan to be there.

Nothing happened. The room remained silent.

She pushed the window open another few inches and climbed out.

The moment her bare feet hit the ground outside, she started running. Sprinting toward the trees. She had no idea where she was going or if she'd even find help, but she had to try.

A loud shout sounded behind her, and she almost stumbled.

Focus kept her on her feet. Focus to get away. Focus to find help.

CHAPTER 33

*L*ock gripped the Glock firmly in his lap.

Too slow. They were driving too damn slow. But then, any speed would be too slow, even the thirty miles an hour over the speed limit Eastern was driving.

Jesse sat in the back, and deputies were heading to the same location. They had backup, but it didn't stop the fear from crawling around his chest. Fear that they'd be too late. Fear that Antwan would do something to Callie that couldn't be taken back.

"He's not going to hurt her," Eastern said as if reading his mind. "He took her because he's infatuated with her."

"He's unstable," Lock growled. "He's killed two people and tried to kill a third, and that's the people we know about. There could be more. What if Callie doesn't comply? What if she pisses him off and he loses control?"

"He wants her too badly to lose control," Jesse said from the back. "He won't slip up."

Fuck, he hoped Jesse was right.

He leaned his head back. He needed to calm the hell down. He'd done a hundred missions like this before. Successfully extracted hostages and taken down more bad guys than he could count.

But this bad guy was a man he'd trusted. Fought beside. Cared about.

The gun felt heavy in his hand. Would he even be able to shoot Antwan?

Yes. The answer was a shout in his head. *To save Callie, yes.*

Eastern turned right onto a dirt road. "I'm going to park in the mountains, a mile from the house. We move toward it from different directions, and when we find Callie and Antwan, we radio each other."

"Got it," Jesse confirmed.

When Lock didn't answer, his brother glanced at him. "I need to hear you say you're going to call for backup, Lock."

"Getting her out safely is my priority."

"And it should be." Eastern looked at him again. "But if Antwan wants her as badly as we think he does, he won't hesitate to shoot to kill those who threaten him—even you."

Lock's fingers tightened on the weapon. He wanted his brother to be wrong, wanted to believe Antwan would never shoot him, let alone shoot to kill…but Antwan wasn't the man Lock had thought he was.

Eastern pulled off the road and parked the car, nestled it between trees. Once they were all out, Eastern pulled up a map on his phone. "We're here, and the cabin's there. I'll approach from the east. Jesse, you go from south, and Lock, you're west."

Jesse nodded, and Lock was about to move when Eastern grabbed his arm. "Remember, you see them, you call us."

His jaw clicked but he nodded. The second Eastern let go, Lock was running. Sprinting into the forest, feet sinking into the dirt. Callie was all he could think about. Her smile. The way she touched him. Suddenly, the air in his lungs moved with a bit more ease.

He couldn't lose her. He'd been without her for two long years, and they were the hardest of his life.

He sped up, feeling the sting of the air on his face. The snap of branches beneath his feet. When the cabin came into view, he slowed, even though every part of him wanted to speed up. He needed to enter the small house as covertly as possible. Antwan was well trained and could shoot with accuracy from anywhere.

He scanned the windows, not seeing any movement. He kept low as he jogged toward the door, Glock raised and ready to shoot.

He tried the door, not surprised to find it locked.

He was about to pull a pin from his wallet to pick it when the door opened.

He aimed his Glock—only to frown when he saw Jesse. "You got in quickly."

"A back bedroom window was open."

A window was open? What the hell?

"No one's here," Jesse added.

Fuck.

Lock stepped inside, and sure enough, the cabin was quiet.

A shuffling sound behind him had Lock spinning, Glock once again lifting.

Eastern.

"I saw the open front door." His brother lowered his gun. "The place is empty?"

Jesse nodded. "But a bedroom window was open."

Lock's gaze lifted to the hall, his mind working fast to piece it all together. "She got out and he chased after her. Which bedroom had an open window?"

Jesse pointed to the door farthest down the hall, and Lock raced into the room, gaze going straight to the open window. He sprinted toward it and jumped out.

Callie would have taken the shortest route to the trees to use them for cover, and Antwan would have known that.

Lock raced into the forest, praying he found her before Antwan.

* * *

AIR SOARED in and out of Callie's chest as she ran. Her legs ached and felt so heavy, they threatened to cave. And her bare feet, God, they hurt with all the rocks and sticks on the forest floor. But she didn't dare stop, because the second she did, he'd find her. And then he'd drag her back to that cabin.

She'd stabbed him, lied to him and run. What would he do if he caught her?

She pumped her arms faster.

When the distant crunch of leaves beneath feet sounded behind her, her foot caught on a rock and she fell hard to the ground. The air knocked out of her, and she rolled to her side, clutching at her chest.

Breathe, Callie. Get up, run, and breathe.

"Callie!"

Her heart crashed against her ribs at his voice. He was close. Too close.

She forced herself to her feet and took off again, the fear alive and roaring inside her.

Light was almost gone, making it hard to see what was in front of her. When her foot landed on something sharp, she grabbed on to a tree to stop herself from falling forward, barely swallowing the cry.

She started running again and was just nearing a decline when the thumping footsteps got louder. Faster. She turned her head and screamed when a body hit her at full force, tumbling them both down the small hill. At the bottom, she tried to roll to her belly and crawl away, but he snatched her ankle and yanked her back under him.

"Stop...fighting me," he growled, flipping her over.

"Never!"

He gripped a wrist, but before he could grab the other, she pushed her fingers into the bandage on his stomach and dug into his wound.

He howled as he released her wrist to reach for her other one, but she managed to get a foot between them and kick him off. Then she was on her feet and moving again. She had no idea where she was going, whether she was heading back toward the house or away from it. Her head was a hazy mess, the ability to think of anything beyond getting away, gone.

She slipped around trees and jumped over tree roots.

She heard Antwan closing in behind her at the exact moment she saw movement in the distance, in front of her. She squinted. What was that? A person? Oh God, please say it was a person!

She opened her mouth to scream when a band of steel wrapped around her waist, and she was tugged back against a hard chest.

The figure in front of them came into view. Her heart stopped.

Lock.

He was running toward her, a gun in his hand.

He'd found her. Oh God, he'd found her!

Hope slipped through her veins, only to be replaced with cold, hard terror when Antwan lifted his own gun—and pointed it right at Lock.

CHAPTER 34

ock fought for control. One fucking ounce of calm.

Despite all the evidence, a part of him *still* hadn't wanted to believe this was Antwan. A part of him had refused to accept that a man he'd trusted with the woman he loved would take her away from him.

But the evidence was right in front of him. Antwan was aiming a pistol at him while he held Callie in a death grip.

Lock inched another step forward. "Let her go, Antwan. You don't want to do this."

"I *didn't* want to do this. I wanted to come to Misty Peak and have her *choose me*. But that never happened."

"So what?" Lock growled. "The plan changed to *force* her to love you?"

"If you weren't in the way, she would have grown to love me over time."

Fucking delusional. Had he always been like this, and Lock had just missed it?

"She thinks she loves you, but she doesn't," Antwan yelled. "I tried to avoid killing you. That was my mistake. I should have manned up and done it the second I got to Misty Peak."

Another step forward. "She's not Lola."

His muscles visibly tensed, shock widening his eyes.

"She'll never replace what you lost with Lola," Lock continued. "Or Hollie."

Antwan scoffed. "I never cared about Hollie. I tried. But you're right, she wasn't Lola. Probably why it was so easy to kill her."

Lock flinched, the world around him narrowing to pinpoint focus. His next words came out low and slow. "What did you say?"

"*I* killed her. Not Malone—although it was really fucking easy to make everyone think it was him. Leave a note and suddenly everyone's scrambling to find him."

No…if that was true… "What about Winnie and Remi?"

The flicker of regret on Antwan's face almost had Lock falling to his knees.

"*You* killed them?" Lock whispered. "*You* killed Winnie?"

"They saw the blood on my shoe and found my gun. I didn't have a choice."

"There's always a fucking choice." Pain cut through Lock like a knife. The last two years, Winnie's murderer had been right beside him, and he hadn't known. Hadn't even fucking suspected.

If there was any last ounce of care for the man in front of him, it died in that moment. Winnie had been a good person. A good friend. He didn't deserve to die.

Suddenly, Jesse appeared from the right of Antwan, stepping out from a break in the trees, a rage that matched Lock's in his eyes. "You killed a member of our team." It wasn't a question, but there was disbelief in his voice.

"You would have done the same to protect your future," Antwan shouted. "You would have chosen *yourself* in that moment, just like I did!"

"Wrong!" Lock shouted back. "I would have chosen *him*. I

would have chosen to do what was right. You went to his *funeral.* For two years, you mourned his death with us."

"I would have gotten out long ago. But I had to stay close to you. Callie disappeared, and I knew you'd eventually bring her back to me."

Lock's fingers tightened on the gun, a new anger building in his chest. An anger at himself. Because Antwan was right—he'd led the fucker straight to her.

Antwan took a step back, the pistol still pointed at Lock's chest. "Just let us go. Let me have her."

Have her? Like she was a pet or something? "You know I can't do that."

"You're outnumbered, Antwan," Jesse said. "Drop the gun and let's end this."

Antwan laughed, and the sound bordered on hysterical. "You say that like I haven't been waiting for my time with Callie for years. Like I haven't been *patient.*" The last word was a shout, ringing through the trees.

Lock's gaze shifted to Callie. The fear in her eyes gutted him.

He looked back to Antwan. Despite everything, he didn't want to shoot him…but he would if he had to. "Somewhere inside you, there's the man who first joined our team. The man who saved our asses and considered us family. Find that man, Antwan. Put down the gun."

There was a small flicker of his brows. "That man died with Lola. She was…fuck, she was my whole world. And I spent more of my time away, with the *fucking team*, than I did with her. I was saving *other people* when I couldn't even save *her.*"

"She had cancer," Jesse said, stepping forward, weapon still raised.

"She *shouldn't* have! Those scumbags we chased down, *they* deserved to get sick and die. But her? She was good and pure, and I loved her. I fucking loved her!"

"We don't choose who lives and who dies of sickness," Lock said softly.

"It's not fair…"

Jesse dipped his head. "You're right. It's not. But it doesn't give reason to what you're doing."

Antwan's gaze shifted back to Lock, something he couldn't place flickering through the man's eyes. "If I'm not getting out of this with Callie, you'll have to end me."

The gun started to move from Lock to Callie.

"Antwan. *No*," Jesse shouted.

As Antwan's gaze shifted from Lock to Jesse, Callie swung her arm back and punched him between the legs.

Antwan growled, and the second he doubled over, Lock and Jesse took the shots. Kill shots to the head.

Lock sprinted forward, catching Callie before she hit the ground. "Are you okay?"

She buried her head against his chest. "I am now."

* * *

LOCK'S warmth permeated her side as she sat on the edge of the ambulance. People were scattered in front of the cabin. Mostly deputies. But the only person she could focus on was Lock. She barely even paid attention to the paramedic as he checked her over.

Jesse had already left after spending a good chunk of time talking to Eastern and his deputies. Aspen had picked him up. Her best friend had jumped out of the car and tugged Callie into the tightest, longest hug. And God, she'd needed that hug.

She looked up at Lock, but he was focused on the break in the trees. The same break where, just half an hour ago, a stretcher with Antwan's covered body had been carried through.

She hated that he'd lost a friend today. And it wasn't just that he'd lost his friend, it was that he lost the memory of him too. Because every memory involving Antwan was now tainted.

The paramedic stepped back. "Other than a few scrapes and bruises, everything looks okay. No concussion. You said you had no trauma to the abdomen or pain, so your pregnancy should be okay, but I'd encourage you to stop into the hospital and have the baby's heart checked if you're worried."

She touched a hand to her belly. For peace of mind, she'd definitely do that. "Thank you."

Lock helped her off the ambulance just as Eastern stepped out of the cabin. His features were grim, eyes going straight to her and Lock before heading their way.

When he reached them, he looked at Callie. "How are you feeling?"

"As fine as I can be after being kidnapped."

Lock's arm tightened around her.

"Did you find anything in there?" Callie asked.

"He was stocked up with enough supplies to last for months. Possibly up to a year. And we have confirmation from Lola's parents that he had access to this cabin whenever he wanted, since they hadn't stepped foot inside since losing Lola."

She sucked in a sharp breath, still in disbelief that his obsession with her had started because of a resemblance to his ex.

"We also found both the Gamma-Hydroxybutyrate that was used to drug Hamish, and the chloroform that was used on you, Callie." Eastern looked at Lock, his voice lowering. "How are you doing?"

"I'm fine."

His words rang with dishonesty. He wasn't okay.

Eastern gripped his shoulder. "I'm going to wrap things up, then I'll get you guys home."

The second he walked away, Lock turned to her and studied her face. "I'm sorry. I'm so damn sorry about everything."

"It's not your fault."

"I brought him into your world. You were *kidnapped* because of me."

"Because of *him*. You trusted him, and he abused that trust, because he was mentally unwell."

"I should have seen it."

"He hid it well. So well that no one saw, including the rest of your teammates."

Lock lowered his head, touching his temple to hers. "I hated seeing you in his grasp. You looked so damn scared."

"I wasn't scared for me. Antwan had that gun pointed at *you*. I was terrified he'd pull the trigger."

Lock lifted his head. "If I'd lost you today—"

"You didn't. And you won't." Her brows tugged together. "How are you really?" She wanted the truth, and she didn't care if it was hard to hear.

Pain flickered across his features. "It's going to take time to come to terms with everything. And even then, it will always hurt. But I'll get through it because I have you."

She cupped his cheek. "And I'll help you in any way I can."

"Just you being here helps." This time when he lowered his head, he kissed her. The kiss was slow and gentle and healing. "Thank you for loving me."

"I didn't really have a choice. The second we met, I was yours."

"And I was yours right back."

CHAPTER 35

*L*ock's gaze traced Callie's closed eyes as she slept. The slight rise in the corners of her lips. He studied every inch of her, casting it all to memory.

Two weeks had passed since the kidnapping…since Antwan.

It was still fucking hard to think about. To remember what Antwan had done. But every day it got a little easier to accept. What helped was reminding himself of what he had. His brothers. The other guys on his team, who he would always consider family. And Callie and their baby.

He touched a hand to her stomach, and she let out the cutest moan he'd ever heard.

They'd gone to the hospital within twenty-four hours of the kidnapping. Everything was fine.

His family. Callie and this baby were his family, and fuck, he was lucky to have them. Something he was reminded of every day.

His gaze shifted to the crack of light sneaking in between the curtains. He should get up. Jesse was coming over soon to say goodbye before he went back to Amber Ridge. He'd insisted on remaining in town until the investigation was tied up, but he'd stayed with Aspen these last couple weeks to give him and Callie some space. Together, they'd told the other guys on the team about Antwan, and they'd been just as blindsided.

Lock was just about to get up when the fluttering of Callie's eyes had him pausing. One more second passed, then they flicked open, her beautiful green gaze staring up at him.

Damn, she was gorgeous. The kind of gorgeous he could get lost in and stare at all day. "Good morning, beautiful."

Those full lips curved into a smile. "Morning, handsome. Have you been awake long?"

"Long enough to memorize every inch of you." He lowered his head and kissed her bare shoulder, rewarded by a small moan from her lips.

He reached behind him and grabbed some dry crackers from the bedside table, handing them to her. "How do you feel today?"

The morning sickness had come full force this last week, but Callie had barely complained. She sat up, pulling the sheet with her to cover her chest, and nibbled on a cracker. "I feel perfect. How could I not with you taking care of me?"

"I will *always* take care of you."

Her smile softened, and she set the crackers aside before climbing into his lap.

The air in his lungs burned when the sheet dropped, and her naked body pressed against his bare chest.

"You know," she said, breath brushing his neck, "I think there are other ways you could take care of me."

His dick twitched, blood roaring between his ears. Before she could blink, he spun them around and pressed her to the mattress. "How the hell did I get so lucky to have you?"

The fun left her eyes, replaced by something a hell of a lot more serious. "I'm the lucky one, Lock."

His mouth crashed to hers while his hand slipped up her side —just as the ringing of the doorbell sounded.

Goddammit. Jesse.

"I'm not getting that," Lock growled between kisses. "I can say goodbye to the asshole on the phone."

"Lock…he's already here." She pushed at his chest. "We have a lifetime for each other. Go say goodbye to your friend."

Another ring of the doorbell, this time followed by the ringing of Callie's cell.

Jesus Christ, was the world conspiring against them?

Callie giggled. "That will be my dad for his daily check-in." She leaned up and kissed him one more time before sliding out from under him. He hung his head, needing a full minute to calm the hell down.

With a groan, he eventually climbed out of bed and threw on jeans and a T-shirt. Callie was already in a robe, talking to her dad when he left her to step into the hallway.

It wasn't just Jesse at the door when he got there; Aspen stood by his side.

She grinned at him. "Hey. Callie home?"

"She's just talking to her dad."

"Great, I'll make coffee." She walked past him and straight into the kitchen like she owned the damn place.

Jesse grinned as he stepped in after her. "Hey."

"You couldn't have taken the hint when I didn't answer and just called from the airport?"

He was half joking, and his friend's smile told him he knew that. "I thought about it, but then Aspen pressed the doorbell a second time. Don't think she would have gone anywhere."

No, she probably wouldn't have.

"Thanks for staying in town," Lock said once they lowered to the couch.

Jesse leaned back. "It was important that I stay. Although, I'm looking forward to getting home to my family. And did I tell you that Holden's thinking of coming to Amber Ridge?"

Holden was another member of their Ghost Ops team, and he'd always been the closest to Jesse, so that wasn't a surprise. "It will be good for you two to spend time together, after everything."

"It will. You should visit if you get a chance."

"I definitely will."

Jesse paused. "Are you still doing okay?"

"Better than I should be, thanks to Callie and my brothers. You?"

"Yeah. I'm still angry. And the hurt…shit, it's hard to take. But I'm not gonna let his betrayal change me."

"Good. None of us should."

"I was thinking about the mission where we eliminated Malone. It was Antwan who took the kill shot when Malone reached for his weapon."

Lock had been thinking about that too. "So he couldn't talk."

There'd been clues, but no one had seen them.

Aspen stepped back into the room and handed out coffees. "Here you go."

Something glinted in Jesse's eyes when he took the mug from her.

What was going on between those two?

The bedroom door opened, and Lock turned his head to watch Callie step out.

She smiled and said hi to Jesse before heading into the kitchen, where Aspen had returned. The women immediately hugged and started talking.

A phone on the coffee table lit up. The cover was pink and fluffy, definitely not Callie's cell. Aspen must have set it down on her way to the kitchen.

Jesse leaned forward and read whatever was on the screen. Anger immediately darkened his features.

"Everything okay?" Lock asked.

Jesse's gaze shifted to Aspen in the kitchen, then back. He lowered his voice. "It's her ex. He's…a problem."

"What kind of a problem?"

Jesse's jaw clicked. "The kind I want her far away from."

* * *

"IS YOUR DAD STILL FREAKED OUT?"

Callie cringed at Aspen's question as she wrapped her fingers around the hot mug of coffee. "Freaked out is an understatement. He calls every day, and when he's not calling, he's coming over in person. And if he can't reach me, he starts calling *other* people."

"Because he loves you and you were in danger."

"I know. But I'm okay. Better than okay. I'm pregnant with a healthy baby. I'm in love. And I've just reopened my studio after weeks of no classes. I'm doing really well."

Aspen lifted a shoulder. "So remind him of that every time you talk to him."

"I will. A part of me kind of likes that he's calling so often. I get to check in on him at the same time."

"How's he doing?"

"Really well. He's so strong. He never lets anything get to him." And she'd decided that from here on out she was going to be more optimistic about his diagnosis. Her father was a fighter. He'd do everything he could to stay healthy, and she'd do everything she could to help him. She was determined to enjoy every last year she had with him.

"That's where you get it from."

Callie scoffed. "I'm not strong. I cried the other night because I was craving a cola slushie and every place that sold them was closed."

Aspen threw her head back and laughed. "I bet Lock found that tough. He hates it when he can't be your knight in shining armor."

"I got a slushie every day for the next week."

"Man, you guys are cute. And I'm glad you've been able to

open your studio again. I know how much that place means to you."

Callie nibbled her lip. "Hamish came in yesterday."

Aspen paused, mug halfway to her mouth. "Really? Did you talk?"

"I basically cried again. Said I was sorry he was pulled into my mess and almost died because of me. Lock also went around to his place to apologize. It doesn't feel like enough."

"I'm sure he realizes it wasn't your fault."

"He was so sweet. That's why I think I'm going to set him up with Vanessa."

Aspen's brows lifted. "Who's Vanessa?"

"A girl who does my Tuesday morning class. Hamish has a lot of love to give, and I think the two of them would really hit it off."

Aspen's smile softened. "You realize what an awesome person you are, right? Going through all that you've been through and still thinking of others."

"After all the Antwan stuff, this town needs a little happy." She nibbled her bottom lip before adding, "Including you."

Her friend frowned. She looked down at her mug, and when she looked up again, there was resolve in her eyes. And maybe a bit of something else. Regret? She set her mug down. "I've actually been meaning to talk to you about something. It's kind of big."

Something in Aspen's voice had her setting down her own mug and inching closer. "What is it?"

"I'm moving to Amber Ridge."

Callie's jaw dropped. Whatever she'd been expecting her friend to say, it wasn't that. "Amber Ridge? Montana? As in, where Jesse lives?"

"We were talking the other night, and I mentioned how hard it's been to see Dylan all the time...because I do. I see him *all the time.* It's like he finds me even if I'm at the damn grocery store.

And there's also my mom. She's been on a whole new level of crazy lately. She showed up at my house at one in the morning the other night, screaming that I took money from her purse. Jesse saw everything. It was so embarrassing." Aspen shook her head. "He knows I can work from anywhere, so…he offered me the spare room in his house. I said no, because that's crazy, right? I just met the guy, and Misty Peak is my home, and you're pregnant so I need to be here for you, but—"

"Do it."

Aspen stopped. "Really?"

Callie closed the remaining distance between them and took Aspen's hand. "Whatever happened between you and Dylan… it's bad. A man doesn't call and text and follow you everywhere for weeks over a simple breakup. We've always shared everything, Aspen, so I don't know why you don't think you can tell me what happened. I'm just choosing to believe that you'll let me in when you're ready. But I *do* know you haven't been happy."

It wasn't just that her friend hadn't been happy. Aspen hadn't been herself.

Callie tilted her head. "You deserve to be happy. The wild, delirious, can't-help-it kind of happy. And if Misty Peak can't offer you that with Dylan and your mom here, you owe it to yourself to go find it somewhere else."

"I feel bad leaving you."

"Don't. I'll miss you, but I'll be okay. And that's what phones are for, right? And every other modern technology used to keep in touch." Callie smiled. "Trust me, distance is not going to get in the way of our friendship."

Aspen pulled her into a tight hug. "I love you."

"I love you too, Aspen. Just promise me one thing."

Aspen pulled back. "Anything."

"Protect your heart."

Aspen laughed, but there was no humor behind it. "I won't be *risking* my heart, so no protection needed. Dating is off the table for a very long time. Dylan has scared me into a life of celibacy."

"Does Jesse know that?"

"Of course. We've become good friends, but nothing more."

Callie nodded, her gaze slipping behind Aspen to Jesse—to see him looking straight at Aspen. And the look on his face…it wasn't how a friend looked at another friend.

But that was something for the two of them to figure out.

She turned back to Aspen. "Can I visit?"

"I *expect* you to visit. And bring a cute baby after it's born."

"Done. When are you leaving?"

"I've booked a flight for next Friday."

Man, that was soon. But she didn't let her smile slip. "Guess we'll need to make the most of the next week together."

Aspen and Jesse stayed for another hour before it was time for Jesse to get to the airport. After they all hugged and said their goodbyes, Jesse ushered Aspen outside, his hand lingering on the small of her back as he helped her into the car.

Yeah, there was definitely more going on there. But Aspen seemed so against dating. Callie could only hope them living together wouldn't be a recipe for disaster.

Lock's arms slipped around her waist from behind as the car pulled away. "What are you thinking about?"

"Aspen's moving to Amber Ridge."

There was a small pause "Really? Are she and Jesse—"

"No." *Not yet, anyway.*

"What's she hoping to find there?"

"I think the question is more what's she running from." She turned in his arms, immediately getting lost in his blue eyes. "But I'm kind of hoping she finds what we found."

He slipped a lock of hair behind her ear. "And what's that?"

"A life that, a year ago, we could only dream about."

He growled and lifted her up against his chest. "Damn, I love you, Callie Ward."

She set her palm on his cheek, letting his warmth slip inside her. "I love you, Lock Walker. I've always loved you. And I have a feeling I always will."

Follow Jesse and Aspen to Amber Ridge, and order book one, UNAFRAID, now!

ALSO BY NYSSA KATHRYN

PROJECT ARMA SERIES

Uncovering Project Arma

Luca

Eden

Asher

Mason

Wyatt

Bodie

Oliver

Kye

BLUE HALO SERIES

Logan

Jason

Blake

Flynn

Aidan

Tyler

Callum

Liam

MERCY RING

Jackson

Declan

Cole

Ryker

BEAUTIFUL PIECES

Erik's Salvation

Erik's Redemption

Erik's Refuge

SHORT CHRISTMAS STORY

Hidden Shadows

RECKLESS SERIES

Reckless Hope

Reckless Trust

Reckless Fall

Reckless Faith

Reckless Love

AMBER RIDGE SERIES

(Series ongoing)

Unafraid

JOIN my newsletter and be the first to find out about sales and new releases! CLICK HERE

ABOUT THE AUTHOR

Nyssa Kathryn is a romantic suspense author. She lives in South Australia with her daughter and hubby and takes every chance she can to be plotting and writing. Always an avid reader of romance novels, she considers alpha males and happily-ever-afters to be her jam.

Don't forget to follow Nyssa and never miss another release.

Facebook | Instagram | Amazon | Goodreads